ARCTIC AURORA

Canada's Yukon and Northwest Territories

John Holt

Camden, Maine

Portions of this book originally appeared in article format in *Art of Angling Journal, E The Environmental Magazine*, and *Big Sky Journal.*

ISBN 0-89272-557-5

Library of Congress Control Number 2004109065

Interior and cover design by Phil Schirmer

Printed at Versa Press Inc., East Peoria, Illinois

5 4 3 2 1

Countrysport Press
Camden, Maine
A division of Down East Enterprise, Inc.
For orders and catalog information, call 800-685-7962,
or visit www.downeastbooks.com

For Bob one last time . . .

ACKNOWLEDGMENTS

First off, I would like to thank my editor Chris Cornell at Courtysport Press (a division of Down East Enterprise, Inc.). He stayed with this often chaotic project from word one. His patience and understanding will always be appreciated. And I thank Joe Arnette for his solid editing. I would like to thank the following people and companies for advice and for donating gear I needed: Rick Pope at Temple Fork for a fine and durable fly rod; Abel for a new tackle bag; Lowe Pro for their Photo Trekker camera pack, which gave me a fighting chance of finding the lens I was looking for; Nikon for the Travelite Zoom binoculars; Serengeti for a fine world view provided by their glasses while driving; Aquafly for needed fly boxes; Smith Sport Optics for fishing sunglasses; and Bill Liston at Daiwa for excellent spinning rods and his solid advice. Thanks to my daughter Rachel for being a Road Bum extraordinaire on the last trip up to the Territories. Finally, thanks to my family and friends who put up with my talking about this book and the North Country for a lot of years.

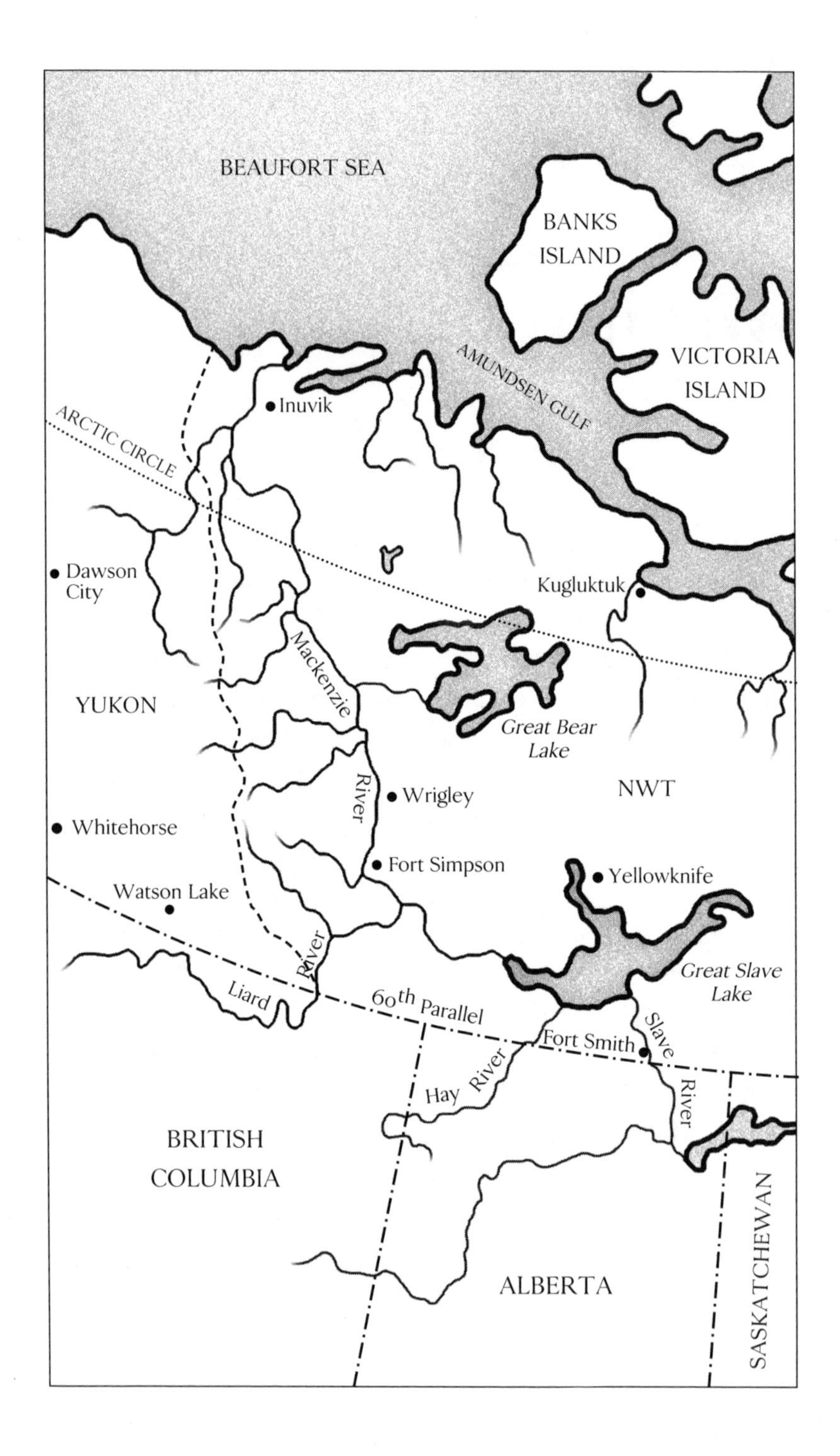
BEAUFORT SEA
BANKS ISLAND
VICTORIA ISLAND
AMUNDSEN GULF
Inuvik
ARCTIC CIRCLE
Dawson City
Kugluktuk
Mackenzie River
Great Bear Lake
YUKON
NWT
Wrigley
Whitehorse
Fort Simpson
Yellowknife
Watson Lake
Liard River
Great Slave Lake
60th Parallel
Fort Smith
Slave River
Hay River
BRITISH COLUMBIA
ALBERTA
SASKATCHEWAN

CONTENTS

INTRODUCTION 11

ONE HAY RIVER COUNTRY 15

TWO MACKENZIE RIVER COUNTRY 29

THREE YELLOWKNIFE 53

FOUR SOUTH SLAVE REGION 81

FIVE RUNNING DOWN THE ROAD UP NORTH 101

COLOR PHOTO SECTION

SIX BRIGHT LIGHTS, BIG CITIES 137

SEVEN PIERCING THE HEART OF THE YUKON 159

EIGHT A NORTH COUNTRY LEGEND 181

NINE WHAT THE HELL'S GOING ON UP HERE? 207

TEN DAYS OF FUTURES PAST 227

EPILOGUE PALE FIRE 241

FURTHER READING 249

And he remembered how on that second expedition of his an Indian woman had caught an excellent pike through a hole in the ice, and none of the Indians would eat of it, saying to him: We are accustomed to starvation, but you are not.

—William T. Vollmann, *The Rifles*

INTRODUCTION /

This book has been an obsession of mine since 1997. Now, nine trips and over fifty thousand miles (or twice around the world) down the road, my impressions of the Far North have reached a point where images of this incredible landscape flash across my mind's vision with disruptive regularity. I'll see them when I'm fishing near home; when I'm writing about something as removed as a trip to the Grand Canyon thirty years ago; when I'm talking with friends. It's hopeless. I'll see the Mackenzie River flowing wide and powerfully with the Canyon Range Mountains in the western distance and the Franklin Mountains running silently north. Or I'll recall a bunch of woodland bison grazing alongside a dirt road near Fort Smith. Or I'll remember an arctic grayling taking my fly on the Blackstone River in the Yukon. I don't fight these images anymore. I know with certainty that once my son and daughter are off to college, I'll be living in a small cabin up near the remote Dene settlement of Wrigley or maybe on a houseboat in a back bay of Yellowknife on Great Slave Lake. The Yukon and Northwest Territories own my imagination, my dreams, and my vision. Montana will always be home in my heart and my base will be there, but the Far North possesses what's left of my soul. The land, animals, weather, and people have me deeply hooked. And I'm more than grateful for this. Fifty years of hard living filled with bad moves, horribly self-centered mistakes, busted romances, venal politicians raping good country for a cheap buck—all of this turned me jaded and cynical. The Far North changed that, and as I said, I'm grateful.

Some of the road-trip research for this book was done with my former companion, photographer Ginny Diers. We split up a couple of years back, though we are now passable acquaintances. The Yukon photographs in this book are hers and they are special. She has the alchemist's gift when it comes to manipulating light onto film. The photos of the Territories are mine and they're okay, but they aren't Ginny's. On my last trip to the Northwest Territories, my daughter Rachel went with me, as I describe in the book's first three chapters. Fifteen at the time, Rachel handled the 6,138 miles of tough road, new places, fierce mosquitoes, and the grind of setting up and breaking camp day after day like a veteran road bum. It must be a curious form of genetics at work here. I'm grateful for the time spent up there with both Ginny and Rachel. They're much of what makes this book what it is.

I saw a good deal of the Far North, but in many respects very little. The land covered in *Arctic Aurora* is many times the size of Montana. And after nearly forty years of living in the state, I am just beginning to understand and appreciate my home. This book is a collection of my impressions, verbal and photographic snapshots in a series of connected vignettes, of what I've seen over the years. I ran out of money or I would have hired a bush pilot to drop me off at various remote mountain valleys for a few weeks or months. And I would have hired a guide to canoe the Thomsen River that flows north on Banks Island into McClure Strait of the Arctic Ocean hundreds of miles above the Arctic Circle, where, possibly, I would have been able to spend some time, at a distance, with polar bears. I'd also like to spend a winter up here, instead of merely experiencing April, May, September, and October blizzards. And I'd like to ride under the northern lights in February with a trucker as he pushes his rig across ice bridges and snow roads north to remote mining camps above the Arctic Circle. And there are other books about this seemingly unreal land that are running around in my head—a novel about the diamond mines, and a factual account of the Royal Northwest Mounted Police infamous Lost Patrol of 1911. With luck, I'll get to some of the country I missed and write those other books and maybe a few more about the North. All in good time. There are children to finish raising, good Montana country to enjoy, and on and on.

That being said, *Arctic Aurora* is a heartfelt recounting and examination of all that I did see and feel, which was quite a bit. As I did with an earlier book, *Coyote Nowhere,* I've written the chapters of this one as the individual subjects appealed to me. I did this for a couple of reasons. As I move through a project like this, along with the seasons and my life, my outlook and attitude changes and varies. This has a direct impact on my work. By writing the chapters out of sequence, I largely avoid the problem of all of them running into each other, merging into a one-pace, one-dimensional narrative. Each of the chapters is a short story in its own right, with its own personality. A couple of reviewers accused *Coyote Nowhere* of being inconsistent because of this. I can live with that complaint, knowing that this approach brings more energy and life to my writing. The book has lived inside me for years, as now does the country up there. I made it above the Arctic Circle four times, spent countless hours exploring the backcountry and fishing for grayling, northern pike, arctic char, walleye (known as pickerel up this way), and inconnu (they resemble whitefish to some extent). And I met many wonderful people who are blessed with the good fortune to have made this country their home. Almost all that I saw is in the following words, but still is only a taste of this way-out-there, special place. A damn good taste, though.

AUTHOR PHOTO

LOUISE FALLS ON THE MACKENZIE HIGHWAY IN THE NORTHWEST TERRITORIES.

ONE /

HAY RIVER COUNTRY

Nothing ever prepares me for the power and immensity of the North Country. I think that I remember what this place really looks like and, more importantly, what it feels like in my gut. But even a few months away, the brief span of time between trips up this way, fades images, sensations, emotions. So, even after all of my trips over the past half-dozen years, the power and the immensity of the Northwest Territories (NWT) overwhelms me, disorients me, literally makes me a little dizzy.

Standing near the edge of the watery precipice that is Alexandra Falls, I watch as the tannin stained brown water hurtles out into misty space before its momentum gives in to gravity and everything tumbles a couple of hundred feet down through the sandstone canyon. The Hay River crashes, breaks up, then explodes back upward, covering the lost altitude in the form of thick mist that whirls and spins, forming miniature tornados that whip across the surface downstream, kicking up large chunks of beige foam and sending it flying, like crazed Styrofoam, into the sky or against the rock walls. The sun breaks out. After all, it's only 10 P.M. in mid-June. The hot yellow orange rays slant through the mist, creating rainbows that arc all over the place—they bend through damp pines, shimmer across the river above the falls, and downriver light up small, rocky islands. The prismatic curves turn the landscape into a kaleidoscope of brilliant, moist color. The sound of all of this liquid motion is deafening, a constant roar of the potential energy contained in the current not only being released but also being amplified by the lengthy plunge. Puffs of cold spray bump into me and curl around where I'm standing. The current foams and boils as far as I can see until the river disappears around a wide bend as it rushes toward Great Slave Lake thirty miles distant. A trio of enormous, shiny-black ravens works the turbulent air above the canyon walls. The birds squawk and grouse at each other, sounding like longtime drunks who've chain smoked too many Sailor navy cut cigarettes over the years. Maybe they have.

A couple of hours earlier, my daughter, Rachel, and I were barely forty miles across the southern border dividing the Northwest Territories and Alberta, not far above that province's small settlements of Steen River and Indian Cabins, places that sometimes offer gasoline along with food and drink and rough lodging for the curious traveler. This was Rachel's first trip on the road with me so far from home in Montana, but any concerns I had about how well she would adapt to the routine had disappeared. She approached each day and each new experience with an open mind along with an inquisitive and cheerful attitude.

When we finally reached the NWT at the 60th parallel after many hours of driving up from our home in Livingston, we pulled into the visitor center parking lot and entered the pleasant building that is heated with a woodstove. Our steps made the varnished pine flooring creak as we moved about selecting brochures and looking at the various artifacts and archival photographs on display. I've done this each time I've come up this way, and the activity now has the trappings of a minor ritual. I said "Hello" to the woman behind the counter, made myself a cup of coffee, said "Have a nice day," then Rachel and I walked outside.

Even this far north, for mid-June it was cool. Maybe thirty-five degrees, but that didn't bother the mosquitoes that buzzed around us and attempted to bite as we walked to the Suburban. Once inside I started the engine and drove to Alexandra Falls, where I'm now standing. In a little while we'll drive up the road another mile, pull over and be knocked out by Alexandra's sister, Louise Falls. We'll watch as the brown water pours over a rectangular shelf the size of several football fields before it continues on to Great Slave Lake in another excited combination of roaring water, mist, and foam, all viewed from a wooden overlook hundreds of feet above the river.

The people up this way consider those of us not fortunate enough to live in the Northwest Territories or the Yukon to be outsiders. I understand and accept this. I feel the same way about those who come to Montana with out-of-state license plates or those who have vacation homes that they occupy for a month of each year. All the same, whenever I travel to either of these places—both are termed territories, not provinces, and they definitely are not a part of Alaska as many American tourists mistakenly think—I feel like I'm coming home to a special place of magic, surreal wonder, and infinite possibility.

•

There is a misperception held by many from outside this remote region—including me at one time—that any camping this far north will be dangerous, difficult, and unpleasant. Lots of bugs, mean bears, the only amenities being those packed or flown in by the happy camper; those were my thoughts on the subject years ago. And in most instances this is true. Whether back in the mountains, deep in the boreal forest, or far north on the barren grounds, this country is no place for the inexperienced or poorly prepared. Along most of the highways (this is largely a relative term given that most of these roads have little pavement and can be impassable in a decent rain) like the Mackenzie, Liard, and the road to Wood Buffalo National Park, there are a number of campgrounds that vary from nice to North Country opulent. Sambaa Deh Falls Park at Alexandra Falls is a good example.

The drill is simple: enter the park, ask the attendant which loop or loops are open, cruise around and pick the spot you like best, return and pay the guy, then set up shop. Sambaa Deh offers heated showers, plenty of cut firewood, and clean locations with tables and a fire pit. Normally, I avoid these places, but in this country, especially after a lot of driving, anything that makes life easier is fine with me. They cost less than ten dollars American, and other campers are few and far between, particularly on weekdays.

The site Rachel and I choose is in the open pine forest. We set up the tent, arrange the cooking stuff, build a fire, and spray on bug dope. (I've tried all of the bug sprays and none of them work. The mosquitoes, black flies, and moose flies—deer flies times ten—seem to be drawn to the stuff or bite right through it. The only real value is psychological.) The bugs are around, but not in significant numbers and the cool temperatures do slow them down. Smoke from our fire also helps. The worst of times seems to be on warm days the hour or so preceding a thunderstorm when the charged atmosphere drives mosquitoes wild with bloodthirsty hunger. Following the storm's passage they calm down somewhat.

We are settled in the heart of the boreal forest, a densely wooded region that stretches six hundred miles north and south above the temperate forest—the type common to the Lower-48—beginning a little more than halfway up Alberta before fading out in latitudes north of Great Slave Lake. The region sprawls well over one thousand miles from the mountain ranges that run into the Yukon far east to Hudson's Bay. This forest, also called taiga, makes up one-third of Canada's land mass. The area is remarkably similar to Siberia. One-half of the plant species are identical between the two regions. Major tree species include trembling aspen, white and black spruce, tamarack, and jack pine.

There are three major ecological zones in the boreal forest—northern taiga, middle taiga, and southern taiga. The northern zone borders the tree line far to the north. Above this, the permafrost is too

AUTHOR PHOTO

THE HAY RIVER.

close to the surface for trees to subsist. The northern taiga forms a transition between the forest and the tundra. Trees are well-spaced, forming an open canopy over a deep carpet of lichen. Tree heights seldom reach thirty feet. The middle taiga forms the classic boreal forest where trees are mainly coniferous with a coniferous-deciduous mixture in more favorable sites, meaning less moisture and deeper soil. Trees are more closely spaced and the shaded forest floor is normally thick with brushy undergrowth. The southern taiga is also a transition zone, this time between forest and prairie, in which deciduous trees predominant. It is often referred to as aspen parkland because of the millions of trembling aspen that thrive here. Because of prairie fire suppression by man, this zone is constantly expanding southward.

Much of the boreal forest is an immense sponge-like plateau that absorbs rain and snowmelt, then slowly releases this abundance in the forms of dark ponds and nearly motionless streams that move through the bush at imperceptible speeds. This country is impassable in the warm months, and a person could easily become lost within fifty yards of the Mackenzie Highway. Northern pike, walleyes, moose, woodland bison, fur bearers, and hordes of insects live in this place that has driven Dene (the native "people"), white trappers, and animals mad with its impenetrability and sometimes malevolent nature. Eventually, this water gains speed and forms black-water creeks that funnel into larger streams that all combine to make majestic rivers like the Hay, Trout, and Slave which, in turn, are merely tributaries of the Mackenzie. When I first drove into this forest, coming up through the town of High Level, Alberta, I was blown away. I'd never experienced such an immense, uncut forest. The few high points in the road gave vantage to mile after mile of virgin forest rolling off thickly in all directions. A lush, green carpet that seemed to be endless. As I said, I was blown away.

The time is closing in on midnight, so Rachel and I begin dinner—grilled steaks, foil-wrapped potatoes and onions, salad, and tea. Once in the Territories we never see darkness since it is the middle of June and the longest days of the year stretch before us. After eating and cleaning up, we take the one-mile hike to Alexandra Falls for another look at this powerful sight.

They are visible in the near-dusk light conditions, looming as an ominous presence that both my daughter and I feel. Gone are the earlier sparkling rainbow splashes of color and the wild energy of falling water. We'd passed a bear trap along the way. This was a large culvert-like container baited with a chunk of rotting meat in hopes of snaring a black bear that, earlier in the week, had raided some motor-home travelers from Edmonton, Alberta. Apparently the animal had run off the quartet of visitors, torn off the vehicle's screen door, then laid waste to the expensively appointed interior while devouring all the food stuffs—steaks, roasts, twenty pounds of frozen halibut, several large jars of pickled herring, along with most of the booze, and apparently some furniture stuffing. That black bear is probably lying dead somewhere in the woods clutching its egregiously bloated belly. The story was humorous when we first heard the campground attendant tell it, but in the dusky light we hurry back to the illusion of protection our tent offers, looking over our shoulders as we go. We build up the fire, pack the food into sealed containers that we store in the Suburban that I then drive to an empty campsite. When I return, Rachel has made hot cocoa, which we sip around the blaze before finally turning in at the crack of 2:30 A.M. A new day is already dawning and small birds are singing reveille. Time truly has no meaning up here in the summer or, for that matter, in a reverse way during the near-perpetual darkness of winter.

After breakfast around midmorning, we decide to go fishing. I'd noticed a rough trail leading down to the Hay River last night as we returned from the falls. The water here is too large for fly rods, so I rig a couple of lightweight spinning rods with yellow lead-head jigs, which have always produced walleyes for me in northern Wisconsin and the rivers of Ontario such as in the Kenora region. The trail is steep, rocky, and a little slippery from the light snow that is falling even though the sun is making a sporadic appearance between the thinning layers of cloud. The air is scented heavily with pine, churning water, and snow.

The bank is mainly a shelf of ancient gray purple sedimentary rock. Mollusk-like fossils are embedded in the stone. We separate several yards and begin casting. I love launching high, arcing casts that send the lure far out in the water, quartering upstream. I let the jig sink to the bottom and begin a slow, halting retrieve. Both of us do this dozens of times with no results. Where are the walleye? But fish don't really matter as I drift off into the timelessness of the moving water that rushes and swirls in large whirlpools up and down the canyon. Ravens constantly soar overhead. Squirrels chatter in the pines behind us. This place seems as wild and undisturbed as it must have to the First Nations Dene a thousand years ago or to the adventuresome (and I'm being conservative here) white voyagers of three centuries past. I wonder how many of those early residents shot over one or both of these falls with screams of obscenities, backed by fast prayers to seldom worshipped deities, that still resonant, if ever-so-softly, within this canyon. The temperature is climbing. The day is brightening, bringing along our friends the rainbows. A dozen more casts and then midway through another one, a few yards below an eddy, I feel a bump and set the hook. There is some head shaking and a few slow, strong runs—classic walleye acrobatics if you can call them that—and the fish is at my feet. Five or six pounds and fat, dark green with a hint of the brown water, and a milky belly. Filleted, this fish will make a superb dinner tonight. One more and we'd be set. As I'm thinking this Rachel walks up to me with a nearly identical walleye and a smile that shames the sun-generated rainbows.

"Not bad Rache babe," I say. "We have dinner. Let's clean them here and I'll show you the fine art of filleting."

"You already did that on the Little Fork of the Powder with the catfish this spring," she says.

"I forgot."

"You're getting old, Dad." We set to our task. Gut, slice along the rib cage, rinse in the water, then store in large zip-lock bags that will soon be buried in our coolers' ice. Not a bad beginning to the day and this run through the Territories.

We strike off up the now-drying trail to break camp and head out, with the town of Hay River firmly in our sights.

As we begin to close in on Hay River, population slightly less than three thousand, we pass a sign for Paradise Garden Campground. A gravel road leads down to a peninsula protruding into the Hay River. There are tended gardens, lush lawns, and thick, leafy trees everywhere. This is something of an Eden in the middle of the wilderness. All of the homes are older. There are cabins and well-tended wood-frame structures painted white.

When Ginny Diers, my past traveling companion, and I first came up this way we stayed at Paradise Garden, arranging for a spot in a grassy field beneath an orchard and next to a field of Saskatoon berries that owner Ben Greenfield raises each season. We were the only campers and had the peaceful place to ourselves. Ben is an older gentleman, stooped with age but full of energy, as is his wife. His eyes are filled with light. In addition to the Saskatoons, they also grow about every vegetable imaginable, along with raspberries and strawberries and currants, in the rich soil under long, bright days. Enormous bright-orange carrots, large, firm white onions, and huge heads of leaf lettuce were arranged on a wooden stand by the office entrance. They have also constructed a large stone medicine wheel. And life rolls on in the Territories.

When Ginny and I got out of our rig it was nearly midnight, but the couple was still busy pruning branches in the berry patch. We checked in amid smiles, several black cats, and some mosquitoes—always mosquitoes. We then drove down a grassy two-track to our spot, which featured a fire pit, a raised grill, and a picnic table. We set up our tent, built a fire, grilled vegetables and boiled pasta, ate like wolves, then retired to bed at around 2 A.M. When we woke at 10 A.M.,

I could see through the mosquito netting that Ben and his wife were out in the fields already (or were they still in them?). We walked down to the rustic shower-house by the river, cleaned up, and thought about breakfast. While Ginny took care of this task, I went down to an exposed point along the river to cast for walleye with my ubiquitous yellow jig. In no time I'd caught four, which I cleaned on the spot and shoved into a plastic bag, then the cooler. Breakfast was pancakes, eggs, bacon, and juice. We finished, packed, and rolled out around noon, waving to the industrious pair as we went. A peaceful place, indeed.

I think about all this as Rachel and I cruise past the Paradise Garden sign, about how nice things had been on the road when life was good between Ginny and me in what seemed like a distant period, but was only four years past. Some pain takes a long time to go away or at least dissipate. I doubt that I'll ever go down to, let alone stay at, Ben's serene gardens. Life does roll on, though often with relentless honesty.

Nearing Hay River, I turn to the east on the highway that leads to Fort Resolution and the Wood Buffalo National Park. Eventually, Rachel and I will aim with purpose in that direction, but for now I hang a left on a rough dirt and sand road that leads down past a narrow bay of Great Slave Lake to the Dene cultural center. There is an excellent store with a fine collection of books. I'd like to pick up a few and also buy Rachel something crafted by the tribe. The center was built several years ago, and its main meeting room is wallpapered in the thinnest of aspen bark. The gift shop is located in a rustic cabin heated with a smoky woodstove. We bounce and lurch past the modern alcoholic treatment center. Booze is a serious problem not only with the Dene but all First Nation People, more so than with whites because of a genetic predilection that makes the effects of alcohol immediate and extreme. This facility has gone a long way toward eliminating the tragic sight of Indians drunk and staggering along the streets of Hay River or passed out in parking lots, streets, or store entranceways. Finally we reach the center, but nothing is really the same after an absence of only two years. The gift shop is boarded up. The parking lot is rutted and unkempt. I walk inside and formerly friendly people answer my questions in surly fashion saying that they are too busy to give us a tour, the gift shop has been closed for a "long time," and so on. We leave on this depressing note and head for Hay River. I later learn that much government funding has been eliminated causing these problems.

Coming into town we pass the busy airport with its steady traffic of float planes, DC-3s—the acme of cargo hauling up here—and an occasional commercial jet bringing sportsmen north to stay at some of the world-famous lodges scattered about the territory. World record lake trout, many over one hundred twenty-five years old, are caught in Great Slave and Great Bear Lakes to the north. As we come into the town center, we cross the Hay River. Barges, ore boats, and smaller craft are tied up at docks along the way. Motels, restaurants, and other structures look, as always, weathered and not all that well maintained. The tallest building in the NWT, at thirteen stories, towers above the forest. It too needs a fresh coat of paint. The town is set along about six blocks, with banks and sporting goods, grocery, and hardware stores evenly spaced. There is a good bookstore and an even better bakery where we pull in and make spectacles of ourselves. We stop at the hardware store to buy a new rain jacket for Rachel. After stocking up on groceries, we drive past the new and well-appointed winter sports center for figure skating and hockey. I gas up at a Shell station before heading for the old town.

This is where the fishermen live; men who work the deep and often deadly waters of Great Slave Lake hauling in catches of walleye, lake trout, and inconnu. The homes are modest, again weathered, but kept in repair. Yards are mostly sand with tufts of brave grass buffeting in the wind. Dogs are chained in most yards, quiet, resting in the patches of sun. Children too young for school play in the sand or on rusting swing sets. Women are hanging or retrieving laundry from stout lines. Most of the vehicles are either old pickup trucks or smaller American cars. Television antennas or dishes sprout from every roof or high wall. This used to be the original townsite, but one year during ice breakup a storm slammed the ice hundreds of yards inland destroying many buildings. Hay River was rebuilt farther inland at a slightly higher, more secure site. All businesses moved away from the ice. Despite the houses, this section of Hay River feels forsaken, forlorn. It has felt the same every time I've been here, as though the memory of life remains but without any of the enthusiasm. Melancholy—there is no escaping the emotion this day. As we angle down a paved road filled with chuckholes, we come upon an old man, maybe in his eighties, walking slowly in the sand that has accumulated from the nearby beach. He leans in through the passenger window. His face is covered in gray whiskers and stained deep brown from the sun and the wind of many decades out on this inland sea. I ask if he needs a ride somewhere.

"Oh no. No thanks," he says, his eyes clear and hard blue. "You wouldn't happen to have smoke you could spare, would ya? Government check doesn't arrive until tomorrow."

I hand him a couple of packs of Marlboro Lights from a carton I have along with ten dollars in Canadian money, saying, "Here, smoke these and buy yourself some ale."

The guy lights up, his eyes sparkle, and he says, "God bless you two on your journey." He shakes hands with both of us, then turns around and begins retracing his steps toward a distant territorial liquor store.

Small kindnesses sometimes brings much joy for all involved. Rachel and I smile at each other as I turn down a sandy lane leading to Great Slave Lake. When we reach the end of the road, we get out. Rachel runs up and over a dune down to the shore. I walk slowly, thinking of the last time I was here, one of the last road trips with Ginny. Before starting this current adventure I was curious and a little concerned about the degree of melancholy that would surface without her on the road. I do not miss our relationship, I am very glad it's over. I no longer love her (I never thought I'd get to the point where I could say that with honesty), but mixed in with the hellish episodes were some damn good moments, like the first time we came to this spot. She hurried to the beach and suddenly sank knee-deep in the wet sand yelling, "John, the lake wants me. I'm stuck," and she laughed at the absurdity of all of it as I went down to extricate her. We then walked along the beach, climbing and scrambling over immense logs washed in from distant forests by forgotten storms. A number of old, ruined boats were lying in the aspen forest at the end of the beach. Some of the trees were growing through the rotting wood, testaments to the age of the disasters. The water glowed sapphire, then beyond a series of ragged reefs the sea was a dark blue that stretched to the horizon. I remember staring off to the west where the lake gives way to the Mackenzie River, several miles wide at the outlet, as it begins the long and isolated journey to the high arctic. I recall wondering what was out in that direction.

Today the wind is brisk, almost cold. The sky is a mixture of robin's egg blue and puffy bands of clouds coming down from the north-northwest. I remember all the years with Ginny and what might have been, though never really had a chance of being. So far from home and so very sad.

"God, make this all go away," I whisper.

"Dad. Look at these small shells," yells Rachel as she huffs and puffs her way to me through the dry sand, her cheeks flushed from exertion and the cool air. She holds them out in her hands. Three of them, with striations of brown, black, gray, olive. "We'll put them on the dash board," she says, full of life and the joy of living.

I look over west across many miles of water one more time and wonder again "What's over there?"

This trip I'll find out, and I will have fun doing so with my daughter.

Life does indeed roll along.

AUTHOR PHOTO

THE CATHOLIC CHURCH IN WRIGLEY, NORTHWEST TERRITORIES.

TWO /

MACKENZIE RIVER COUNTRY

First, there were lots of people living in the mountains.
Then, in the far distant past, something like little pieces
Of meat fell from the sky and the Dene lived on this.
Lots of people went to collect it for they lived on it.
The meat had something small inside it and enough fell
For each person. There was nothing before that and
It was difficult to survive. Then the meat fell from the
sky with something contained inside it and they put it
into containers. This is all I know, I remember my father
told me that.

The Meat Falling From Above, *The Book of Dene*

Driving along the road to Wrigley, the Dene tale of falling meat makes sense from my outsider perspective. The country up here is so large, powerful, and devoid of nearly everything human that anything seems possible. Apparitions in the form of albino moose, three-foot grayling, and even hunks of meat falling from the sky seem quite likely. Everywhere Rachel and I drive in this land something new, something awesome (as in "causing respect combined with fear or wonder" and not the meaningless contemporary "That's awesome, dude" nonsense), something that feels like natural magic appears. On my left the Mackenzie River flows powerfully toward the Arctic Ocean. I notice a large boat pushing a barge upstream toward Great Slave Lake and probably the port of Hay River. The craft looks like a toy from my vantage point hundreds of feet above the river. And this effect is exaggerated even more by the towering Canyon Ranges and the Mackenzie Mountains beyond them in the west. The river at this point is nearly two miles wide and many feet deep. More water is flowing north here than in all of the rivers, streams, and creeks of Montana combined. The scale of everything in the Territories is enormous, immense to the point where size, space, and distance are meaningless to me. Despite a number of trips to this land, I still have not spent enough time in-country to gain any sort of reference points or sense of perspective. Everything I do or see appears new and alien. I feel as if I'm in another dimension whose boundaries far exceed any drug I've ever done or read about. The power I feel from this unfamiliarity is immense. It's as if all the bullshit of down south, all my past screwups and disappointments, no longer exist, perhaps never existed. I'm free and to hell with past nonsense.

It is past 7 P.M., but the sun is far above the horizon on this mid-June day. Rafts of white, silky clouds drift to the southeast powered by a gentle wind that formed far above the Arctic Circle, up in the ice-clear sky that soars in a transparent silver blue dome above the ice cap of the North Pole. The bright green leaves of small birch flutter in the breeze. Downsized fir, darker green but still radiant, tilt at odd angles on this plateau of small rock hills, glowing marsh grass, and bright moss. A large moose, not white but dark brown, shows itself as it glides out of birch-tree cover, then disappears with speed and silence into a copse of taller trees. An enormous raven slides across the road just a few feet ahead of me. The bird squawks twice, its black head and beak angled down toward the truck.

Rachel and I are rolling along at about forty-five miles an hour, leaving a large salmon-colored stream of dust in our wake. To the north and east we see the Ebbets Hills, a rounded collection of rocks covered with pines that gives way to eroded cliffs of gray rock. They're called hills, but they look like aging mountains, worn and stooped from hard living and rough weather. Ahead, beyond where I perceive Wrigley to be, is the McConnell Range and then the Franklin Mountains. These mountains are also smooth, but they front large reefs of broken cliffs that cascade down the ranges' western faces in a still-life rock fall. Leafy trees mark the softer portions of the slopes in patches of light green, while the conifers stretch in dark, ragged bands that run north and out of view. There are no clouds floating over these peaks, which seem to be generating their own updrafts and whirlwinds that keep the air clear. Sunlight sparkles off distant waterfalls, and I imagine lakes hidden in ancient, eroded cirques filled with never-fished-for northern pike or perhaps isolated populations of grayling. Moose, grizzly, wolves, caribou, and wolverines wander the surrounding forest.

The view, this country, overwhelms me. This is the stuff of dreams for a person who loves wild, unspoiled landscape.

A few hours farther on, I think that this may continue forever and that I've seen it all before. Maybe it does, and maybe I have. The reddish dirt and gravel road still drifts its dusty way through subalpine fir and stunted poplar growing with apparent stubbornness here above the 62nd parallel. The trees are leaning at odd angles, tilting and listing like hapless drunks making a last attempt at decorum as closing time approaches in some unknown bar. Black bears wander across the road and silently vanish in the cover. Small bands of woodland caribou ghost through the trees. A bald eagle cruises the thermals nearly out of sight. To the west the Mackenzie River still flows deep, wide, and immense toward the Beaufort Sea far above the Arctic Circle. Beyond the mile-wide and more river, mountains rise up and tear at a sky that is the essence of purity. The clarity of the blue above me drops on the land as wisps of white cloud float through this sweep of sapphire on a wind that moves easily from the north along the front of the Canyon Range. The breeze swirls and eddies, pushing aspen leaves like foam on a mountain stream, before moving on. Wild peaks and ridges many miles away shimmer purple, salmon, rock-hard gray, all of this shaded azure with distance. Beyond those peaks, and rising higher, are the Mackenzie Mountains that eventually give way to the Selwyns in the Yukon Territory. Hundreds of miles of seldom seen or even explored mountains running as far as Montana, two thousand miles to the south, stretch east to west.

Much of this country wasn't even mapped twenty-five years ago. There are canyons thousands of feet deep and high plateaus of rock, snow, and ice that have never seen a human. Spending a couple of months in these places for each of several summers and falls is a goal of mine. I want to see Dolly Varden and grayling measured in pounds and not inches; moose, grizzlies, and wolves that have never heard the sound of a rifle shot; and a piece of the earth with no adventure or ecotourist bullshit. In three years both Rachel and my son will be in college. After that, at the youthful age of fifty-six, I'm gone. Perhaps to wander the country of burning coal seams below the Great Bear River, a site described by Sir John Franklin with ". . . a few miles above the Bear Lake River . . . the banks of the Mackenzie contain much wood coal, which was on fire at the time we passed, as it had been observed by Mackenzie (1789). Its smell was very disagreeable." Well, maybe not.

The road to Wrigley is a very long way from home—all the way north through Alberta, itself one and one-half times the size of my Montana, then northwest for hundreds of miles on a paved road that gives way to packed dirt and ferry crossings over both the Liard and Mackenzie Rivers. These gigantic watersheds make the Yellowstone River running through the town I live in take on creek-like dimensions. The Dene, who've lived on this land for thousands of years, call the Mackenzie Deh Cho, meaning "big river." This road I'm on keeps rolling, climbing, twisting, and dropping as though it means to pierce the heart of pristine eternity like a long-lost, halcyon acid trip.

Wrigley has been on my mind for years, ever since I looked at a map of the Territories and saw that the place of less than two hundred inhabitants was at the end of the road, as far as a person can drive unless he waited for winter and was up for traveling the snow road with its creaking and crackling ice bridges over the big rivers. Then it is possible to advance for hundreds of miles to places like Tilita, Norman, and Fort Good Hope in near constant night with the billions of stars and the aurora borealis flaming overhead. Some year I'll make that surreal journey. And the name Wrigley appeals to me because of my lifelong affliction known as being a Chicago Cubs' fan. Genetic birthrights can cause terrible woe.

The Dene, who still practice the old ways of hunting and trapping to exist, refer to Wrigley as Pehdzah Ki, "clay place." I find myself preferring the sound of their language and its natural life meanings for their world. The town was originally known to traders as Old Fort Island when in 1870 the Dene settled at what was then a trading post operated by the Hudson Bay Company. The first few years of the twentieth century were mean ones for the Dene. One-third of their people died from tuberculosis and famine. The remaining forty-eight families moved about thirty miles away to a landform called Roche-qui-trempe-a-l'eau, or "the rock that plunges into the water." The site, now called Old Fort Wrigley, remains in the form of a few decaying log cabins along the riverbank. Thirty-five years ago the town moved to higher, drier ground in a clearing surrounded by poplar and spruce. Drier ground translates into fewer mosquitoes, which drive caribou mad and can suck a weak animal dry in minutes. Nothing can prepare an individual for the numbers and ferocity of the insects. They are a presence, an all-pervasive presence.

When the people moved, they brought with them by barge the Roman Catholic church, the Hudson Bay store and warehouse, the one-room school, and the teacher's residence. All of this—the end of the road, the hard times, the relocation of important structures—set in the middle of some of the most fantastic landscape anywhere, appeals to my romantic nature.

Nearly everyone we meet up here is friendly and, unlike in the United States where a firm handshake is a curious indication of inner strength and honesty, greets us with a soft, warm grip and a polite probing with their eyes along the lines of "Why are you here from Montana?" "What do you think of our land?" "Where have you been?" I experience this style of greeting everywhere I travel up here, from the crews on the river ferries, to the Dene in Fort Providence, to a well-read campground operator in Fort Smith. Territorial residents all live hard, determined lives, but they also impress one with their friendliness and enthusiasm for just about everything.

Diamond, tungsten, copper, emeralds, and timber fuel the economy, as does a burgeoning sport-fishing industry where float planes taking off in a steady buzz whisk the sports far north to the above-tree-line barren grounds to fish for large Arctic char, lake trout, Arctic grayling, and northern pike. Ecotourism is coming on, too. An ambitious, industrious place racing into the new world. Yet the always tough, remote land and the extreme weather with brutally cold winters and long nights doesn't appeal to many of us outsiders. Those that live in the North are a special breed of human that is focused and hardworking, yet tempered by the fire of the enormity of the untamed wilderness.

Wherever a road leads in this country, powerful and unchecked waterfalls blast, tumble, and cascade over towering rock shelves or boulder jumbles as rivers carve and gouge their way deeply through bedrock. The energy of the Northwest Territories is palpable, sizzling, and crackling through the country, charging the air with what seems to be a perceptible platinum glow.

Wrigley appears abruptly out of the forest with its combination of new and old—some modern homes next to teepees, dirt streets and new pickups, a hotel holding forth within a recent assemblage of trailers like the ones used for oil-rig crews in west Texas. Entering town, we see a barricade to the winter road that in a few months will carry people and supplies to towns farther north. The track through the forest is thickly overgrown with tall emerald grass studded with wild flowers—indigo, crimson, orange, white. The McConnell Range can be seen in a narrow slice of open sky between the tall poplars. At the north end of town, we stop in front of the Catholic church. Rachel leaves for a short walk, while I stay to take pictures. The church is a perfectly maintained structure of white with green trim, numerous windows, and a tall steeple of silver metal. The cross at the crown flickers in a sunlight perfectly chilled by the cool wind moving down from the polar ice cap many miles above.

"A peaceful town isn't it," says a voice behind me. I turn and a Dene man with sun- and genetically-darkened skin in his forties is smiling and offering his hand. The soft, warm grip once again. We introduce ourselves. He's Albert. We talk about his country. He offers to take me far into the mountains whenever I have time on return visits—"I can see that you will return here"—where grizzlies, wolves, and "many fish" can be found, as can lakes and crystalline streams.

Albert tells me that generators provide his town with electricity for lights, water pumps, satellite television, and even computers. He says his son "chats" with people from all over the world on the internet. He smiles, shakes his head, and says, "This is beyond me. It doesn't make sense. Perhaps it's good. I don't know. Many of us prefer the old ways, yet we hunt with snowmobiles and high-powered rifles. Life is changing for all of us. We have a small hotel for tourists. How we adapt is what matters these days." Albert smiles and lights a nonfilter Players cigarette. He draws deeply and exhales, the smooth cloud of bluish smoke dispersing a few mosquitoes that buzz in the evening air with no apparent intent.

AUTHOR PHOTO

THE BOREAL FOREST LOOKING NORTH TOWARD THE MACKENZIE RIVER ON THE LIARD HIGHWAY.

We talk some about the fishing, and he says that there are many fish in the river. That the Mackenzie is a reliable source of food—grayling, northerns, Dolly Varden, and much farther downstream toward the sea, arctic char in late summer. Moose, the ever present black bear, caribou, even sheep in the high country provide meat, and the hides are used for clothing. Furbearers like beaver and fox are plentiful.

"Everything we need is given us, including herbs that help with wounds and sickness," he says. "Alcohol is not the problem here," he adds, and looks around his peaceful village. The sound of children playing drifts across space. "Not like it is for the People in Fort Simpson and Fort Smith, very bad there, and down in Hay River. Of all the things that have harmed us, of those things brought by whites, alcohol is the worst, more so than disease and government and its laws and regulations. We are fighting those things, but alcohol kills our spirit." He stops, lights another smoke (they're around ten dollars a pack up here), looks at me, and laughs with a resignation borne of experience. "I see you know what I'm speaking of," and we both nod and laugh a little.

Albert and I finish our conversation just as Rachel returns from her walk. We say our goodbyes. I promise that I'll return. I don't want to leave but must, a victim of my own planning and obsession with being somewhere else by tomorrow. Plain foolishness. We climb into the Suburban and drive away. I feel that I'm leaving a place where I should be staying. Next year. Hell, always next year.

This and more, the energy and spirit of good country, are the source of Dene life, Albert had told me. He wants to share this. And he's right—I'll return to this peacefully strong place. We drive south out of town to camp along a river not named on my map, one I saw coming in that is flowing clear down from the Ebbets Hills through the forest to join the nearby Mackenzie.

Despite the time's being after 9 P.M., the sun is still well above the northwestern horizon where it will dip briefly out of view after midnight before rising a little after one o'clock to begin another June day. The birds will rest in this short span before resuming their singing and free-form chatter. As I top a rise, we see the river and its islands and Nahanni Butte many miles away. I stop the Suburban, step out and take all of this in with my eyes, then capture it on film. I turn to look behind me and see an off-white wolf standing in the middle of the road forty feet away staring at me with dark eyes. His fur would be pure white were it not for the slight dusting of coal black hairs through his coat. We hold each other's gaze for a long time until I shift my view to Nahanni Butte. When I glance back I see the wolf moving silently through the small trees. Then he is gone. I get into the car and continue driving.

About twenty miles down the road, a small two-track cuts off toward the Mackenzie River as the narrow path winds through a tunnel made by overhanging birch leaves. The Suburban splashes through puddles left from last night's rain as the course twists, turns, and doubles back on itself before fading completely as it leaves the trees and enters a sandy, grassy open area that looks like downs along the Atlantic Ocean near Kiawah Island in South Carolina. The Mackenzie is about one-quarter mile to the west, its surface sparkling and flashing in sheets of quicksilver interspersed with ripples of pewter with an internally soft glow of cerulean fired by the Mackenzie's powerful current. Just ahead, a river about the size of the Madison in Montana flows clear, though tinted brown from the tannin of pine needles. The water rushes and boils over a gravel and large-rock streambed. Boulders block the swift current up and down the river that heads up in the McConnell Range. It is unnamed on our maps, as are many streams up this way. To earn recognition on all but the most detailed of maps a river must be enormous or ferocious like the Mackenzie, the Liard, the Slave, or the Hay. A minor stream such as this plies its course in relative anonymity.

I park the Suburban on a level spot overlooking both rivers and we set up camp. Rachel does the tent, then gathers firewood while I unload the rig—cooking crate, food containers, water jugs, chairs, sleeping gear. As I move around the spot I see plenty of moose sign—large tracks in the sandy soil and large oval-shaped dark-brown droppings. They are all at least a few days old judging from the worn edges of the prints. I also see weathered bear tracks in damp areas. Because of their smaller size, I judge the tracks to be from a black bear and more than a week old. A bit of big-game caution is required here as anywhere else in the Territories. I spot a northern shrike, distinctive with its hooked carnivore's beak, perched on a nearby limb with what looks like a vole or possibly a lemming.

I walk down to the bluff overlooking the Mackenzie. Large trees floating toward the arctic look like matchsticks. Several Sabine's gulls ride easily upriver on the breeze coming down from the north. The birds are recognizable by their forked tails and ink-black wingtips. Swallows by the hundreds swoop and plummet in downdrafts along the banks. (Seeing all of these birds conjures the self-righteously mad John J. Audubon, who killed thousands of birds, then tacked them to his studio walls so he had real-life models to paint from. His approach to wildlife art and ornithology has always bothered me to the point of anger. I supposed all of us should be grateful that he wasn't drawing the human form in all its many shapes and colors.) I positively identify the northern shrike and the Sabine's gull—the first sighting of either for me—later while sitting around the cooking fire.

Next is the setup of a pair of nine-foot fly rods for us. Nine-foot leaders tapered to a 1X (a slight hedge against the murderous rows of razor teeth of the northerns) and a red-and-white woolhead tied on a bendback hook for me and a #2 long-shank olive Woolly Bugger for Rachel. The water is fast and several feet deep, so I add a split shot to each outfit—there is less than delicate casting here in the North Country.

The river is too fast and deep to wade, but large, relatively flat rocks help us work out into the current and allow us plenty of room away from pines, birch, alder, and willow. The birch are a subarctic hardwood known commonly as paper birch (*Betula papyrifera*) and have cream-colored rather than white bark. They are also called Alaska birch, and some botanists consider them a separate species. The pines are mainly black spruce (*Picea mariana*). The black spruce, along with the white variety, are the two most important trees up here because of their numbers, which provide shelter from the weather, wood for fires, and lumber for building cabins. Black spruce can thrive in soils of less than ten inches that consist of heavy clay or in the acidic peat bogs.

While Rachel begins fishing, I pause to puff on a Honduran cigar and read about these tree species in E. C. Pielou's *A Naturalist's Guide to the Arctic*. I clearly drive my daughter nuts with all of this information, but she manages as best she can. And reading these guides allows me the illusion of acquiring serious educator-type knowledge about where I roam. "You bet, buddy. Those *Picea mar-*

iana are some kind of trees. Shallow soil, widespread roots and such, you know." Right. You bet.

After finishing my cigar and reading, I look up and see that Rachel is moving away from the shore with her arced rod held high. A large fish is thrashing in the water near shore. I hustle down and scoop the northern onto the moss and grass. It's between thirty and thirty-three inches and fat, perhaps eight or ten pounds. I have a stringer in my hip pocket. I run the metal point through the pike's left gill and out its mouth, staking the other end in the ground with a large stick.

Rachel and I both say "Dinner!" at the same time, and head off to catch more pike for the hell of it. I work about one hundred yards upstream from my daughter, making sure she is in clear view. Animals and current concern me, though she is cautious. My first cast quarters upstream about sixty feet above a midstream boulder. I let the heavy pattern swing and sink in the current, but the line quickly grows taut and I reach back, setting the hook. A northern shakes its head, then hunkers down behind another boulder. I pull as hard as I can and get nowhere for a minute, but the fish gradually gives ground before releasing its hold in the icy water and racing downstream. I check the fish, move down even with it, and repeat the process, gaining half my line. I do the dance one more time and soon have a northern nearly as big as my daughter's at my feet.

I'm not wearing waders, so I manage to get wet as soon as possible much as a Labrador retriever will find a puddle in the middle of the Gobi Desert. I release the fish. It rockets out of sight in a long flash of bluish olive green, creamy white, and reddish brown streaked on the edges of its fins. For the next few hours I catch fish—all about the same size—on nearly every cast. I watch as Rachel does the same. I walk down to her and see a larger northern casually follow her Woolly Bugger as she drags it to her and out of the water. No way in hell would we go meatless in this drainage. (I've also seen a number of spruce grouse along the road. They appear as intelligent as their Montana cousins. They stand dead still in the middle of the road, oblivious to the motorized potential carnage bearing down on their feathered bodies.) I clean and scale the pike on the stringer, then cut it into two-inch steaks, similar to salmon, and place them in a plastic grocery bag. We walk back to camp.

I start some charcoal in an old fire pit while Rachel slices a brace of large Yukon baking potatoes. She wedges onion slices in the cuts, adds lots of butter, salt, and pepper, then triple-wraps them in aluminum foil. I place these in the coals, then arrange a grill on three flat rocks over the fire. I sip some iced tea and look across the wide Mackenzie River into the distant mountains, scanning the ice and snow fields and the deep-cut canyons with a pair of Nikon zoom binoculars. I can't observe much detail in the dusk-like light of midnight, but I have fun anyway. Easily amused. The mind of a child. Rachel reads a novel in the dim light, a feat beyond the capabilities of my eyes. The air is around 65 degrees, with a slight breeze, and only a couple of stars or planets showing in the light night sky. In the distance, toward the east and the Ebbets Hills, the sound of a wolf, then another, slides to us like an ancient ghostly call to wild arms. The wolves keep this up for a long time and when they've finished I feel as though I'm as far from home as I've ever been. The territories are magic every second of every long, bright summer day.

After about an hour, I place the pike, now seasoned with more black pepper and sea salt after being brushed with olive oil, over the gray coals. The potatoes finish in the few minutes it takes to brown and cook the northern. Thick paper plates, Chinette of course! placed on metal camp plates, hold the potatoes, fish, and sourdough bread. We eat in silence enjoying the sunset-sunrise of 2 A.M. The sun is just visible above the northern horizon. The entire half of the sky downriver glows orange, blood red, pink, golden against a background of indigo and deepest purple. Thin rafts of clouds play with this light, shooting it in subtle shade variations down into the river and through the sky toward the invisible stars. Shafts of new-day sunlight arc above the clouds and fan out like searchlights at a Hollywood premiere. The magic of this place continues, never ends, varies, flickers, alters shape among the seconds that string together in their own concept of time.

We finish eating. I smoke a couple of cigarettes with a cup of the tea Rachel has made, then take a long look through the entire 360 degrees of our campsite before reluctantly going inside the tent to sleep. The wolves howl again across this eternal space. That's all I can remember.

The next morning we drive back down the road to the ferry landing for our recrossing of the Mackenzie River. The same crew as before is working, and they spot the rig with its Montana license plate. All of them wave, and the captain blasts his horn. It's early and we're the only car for this crossing. The deckhand, Darrell, is a Dene—a big, husky man in his midtwenties with short-cropped black hair and a mustache. He wears orange coveralls. He guides us to the far end of the ferry, begins to hand us a plastic-covered sheet of safety instructions, then abruptly pulls it back saying, "You already know the drill."

I get out of the Suburban and look upriver toward the Canyon Range shining lavender blue far in the distance. A few clouds are already forming on what will be a warm day in this country. Perhaps 75 degrees. The ferry's engines power up with a deep, in-your-gut rumble, and we head into the river. The current is fast and powerful, and the boat crabs upstream to reach the far shore a little above the landing, where the captain will then slip the boat, steering it with the engines, onto the dirt embankment.

Darrell points out the grease soaking the skids and dirt on the near shore and says that it is "rank" cooking grease that has been dumped and attracts bears from all over. He aims a thick forefinger at a nearby clump of trees and I see a couple of black bears, their thick coats glistening in the morning sun.

When I ask him how things are going for his people up here he says, "Big business, mining companies and the like, want what we have in the ground, but we won't let them in. We say 'No!' " He mentions emeralds, tungsten, copper, gold, diamonds, rubies—minerals that would make the Deh Cho Dene wealthy by anyone's standards. But Darrell adds that his people value the land in its unspoiled state more than money and that they are winning the fight against tribal members who would like to see sudden and great change.

"We've seen what happens when we let the companies from down south onto the land," he says. "Look at Alberta or British Columbia. We don't want that. We've learned that our old ways of living have values far beyond 'civilized'," and he laughs both at the concept the word implies and at the brief show of anger he has betrayed.

We talk some more and Darrell mentions his home, wife, and two children in Fort Simpson; the changes he's seen, ranging from computers, to satellite television; and the programs designed to deal with the alcohol problems rampant among his people. I tell him that the Dene aren't alone. All of us are bombarded with commercials and social pressure to drink.

"That's right. That's right," he says. "I turn on the television at eight in the morning and there are commercials for Budweiser and Miller Genuine Draft. I don't drink, but after looking at those ice-cold bottles, sometimes I start to wonder." He laughs again, then moves forward to deal with our approach.

The captain reverses the engines and deftly guides the ferry into the bank with a firm but smooth bump. Darrell kicks a lever that drops a heavy metal ramp onto the brown gray, hard-packed dirt. I start up my rig, wave to my friend, and drive off the craft and up the steep cut between the tall ramparts of the river and on into the dense pine forest.

Rachel and I stop and fish many rivers that are similar to the one we camped at last night. We catch northerns and grayling. The pike weigh from three to ten pounds. The grayling average a little over two pounds, though Rachel quietly hooks and lands a fish that is well over three pounds. Where I would be shaking with excitement, she goes about this angling business with surety and quiet pleasure. My daughter amazes me with her intense examination and delight in the world that is, only slightly, tempered by her pragmatic approach to the act of moving through one's life. So much like me in many ways, but so very different in this aspect.

By the time we reach Fort Simpson, less than fifty-five miles from the ferry, the sun is low on the horizon and it is 11 P.M. The days are indeed long up here, but they sweep past my daughter and me in a rapid rush of time that I am not yet used to, despite this being my ninth trip up to the NWT and the Yukon. Maybe a person never grows accustomed to this form of linear motion of the days, weeks, months. I don't know, but perhaps I'll have a chance to find out some year.

To reach Fort Simpson heading south out of Wrigley, you cross a bridge that connects the narrow island the town is built on with the mainland, then hang a left off a gravel road and roll along through more forest, past the airport, and down a steep, twisting hill and a potholed road into town. Fort Simpson is not large by Lower-48 standards—twelve hundred residents—but along with Hay River and Fort Smith, it is one of the larger towns in the NWT, though all three are dwarfed by Yellowknife. Of the approximately 41,000 people living in the NWT more than 21,000 are First Nation People like the Dene and Inuit. The main street runs about a mile past two gas stations, a couple of churches, modest motels, liquor store, grocery store, library, back-country flight services like Wolverine Air, which is little more than a small metal building near a landing strip and a number of airplanes including Beavers and Otters. We see many Dene walking along the streets, working in the grocery store, or sitting around talking and smoking cigarettes. The Mackenzie flows along the northern edge of Fort Simpson and the Liard comes in from the south and west just east of the town. The natives' name for

Fort Simpson is Liidlii Kue, "the place where the rivers come together."

I stop to get gas at a Shell station owned by a surly Chinese man. The place is little more than a crumbling cinder block building apparently supported by mounds of discarded and quite greasy carburetors, generators, engine blocks, burned out manifolds, rotten exhaust pipes, and holey radiators. A thoroughly shot blue Buick Riviera sits on blocks in front of a work bay that is filled with old tires and radiator hoses. The poor car's windows are shattered and its leather upholstery is ripped to pieces; its body is dinged, banged, and hammered; and rust is growing everywhere. A Chevy Corvair is sinking into the ground nearby.

The owner sits on a stool in the office staring at me through grimy windows. I begin to pump gas. He comes rushing out screaming a torrent of Chinese, grabs the nozzle from me, and finishes the job in a flurry of indignation. It comes to about $200 Canadian. When I hand him some bills, he quickly disappears into his office, parks his ass on the stool, and begins reading a book. I go in and demand my change, about $10 Canadian. He pleads Chinese ignorance, but I notice that the book he is reading is an English version of Livingston, Montana, resident Max Crawford's *Waltz Across Texas.* Not the brightest bulb on the planet, but this weird taste of synchronicity convinces me that $10 Canadian (about $7 American at the time) isn't worth the struggle. I shrug, point to his book, and say, "The guy who wrote that lives in my home town. Adios Sport." He grunts, not looking up. I stroll back to the Suburban. Rachel is hunched down in the front seat. She didn't like the vibes of the station from the start and was worried that I might make a scene about the change.

"I'm proud of you, Dad," she says as we drive away, leaving the mad Chinaman to his literary pursuits. "Maybe we'll get you married off yet," and she laughs. I don't. The merest thought of another marriage scares the hell out of me. So much for being a tough-guy writer.

Because of the late hour we turn down toward the river and into the trees looking for the entrance to Fort Simpson Park. We find a small log cabin at the entrance. The smell of wood smoke permeates the air. A sign says to find a campsite, then return and register. We cruise the place and find a quiet spot on the edge of the trees about one-quarter mile from the Mackenzie River. Returning to register, a man with gray hair and a mustache, perhaps in his late-forties, walks out smoking a cigarette and holding a book. I notice the title: *Mosquitoes* by William Faulkner. I laugh and say, "Appropriate," as I point at the book. He nods, introduces himself as Mike, then says he'll keep the showers open past midnight for us and deliver some wood in a few minutes. We smile at each other and return to begin our camp-setup routine that Rachel and I have down to an art that takes less than fifteen minutes. While she puts up the tent, I start the cooking fire in our miniature Weber known as a Little Smokey. (This trusted mealtime friend was to later die a wicked death when a vicious storm blew it over a one-thousand-foot cliff in Wyoming's Middle Fork of the Powder River high country. I still remember that horrible next morning as I looked down toward the river through binoculars and saw the battered and crushed Weber lying on a narrow ledge. The memory haunts me to this day. Perhaps time will heal this most grievous of emotional wounds.) Rachel has the potatoes ready in moments and goes about preparing a fruit salad to go with the large porterhouse steaks I will grill shortly. The meat on this trip has been excellent. The beef all comes from Alberta or even the Yukon, where some cleared forest is now home to, of all things, Texas longhorns. As Darrell said, life is about change, bringing slightly incongruous shifts in the Far North's economic base. Our meals on the trip are basic and always include meat of some form. Lots of it. This type of protein is needed to keep us going. No vegetarian jive for this crew. While our meal is cooking, we walk down the road to the shower house. Luxury in the Territories.

The mosquitoes would be considered intolerable down in the States but are just part of the routine in the Territories. Serious bug-gage will come later. We've been taking B-complex vitamins, which produce some chemicals that deter the mosquitoes and the few black flies we encounter. Coupled with Deep Woods Off and the smoke from our fires, we sit in the open talking, reading, or merely taking in the midnight dusk or morning daylight with little notice of the insects.

Rachel retires to the tent in what passes for night up here, but I can't get to sleep, so I stoke the fire with more of the wood that our friend Mike dropped off a little while ago. I think about the chapter in R. M. Patterson's book *Far Pastures* that details some of the history of this spot and recounts his time spent here in the 1920s.

There has been a fort at the confluence of the Liard and Mackenzie—"La Grande Riviere en Bas" of the voyageurs—since the North West Company arrived in 1805. The fort burned down and was rebuilt in 1820. In 1821 it passed into the hands of the Hudson Bay Company and the name was changed from Mackenzie Forks to Fort Simpson. There were other forts in the region including Liard, Norman, and Good Hope. All of them traded in furs brought in by the First Nation People who lived in the mountains and carried with them stories of rivers that ran "toward the setting sun."

Explorers and trappers were obsessed with finding a path through the Rocky Mountains via the Liard River. Many met their deaths on this dangerous waterway. One positive report came from Chief Factor Edward Smith, who wrote in 1831,"You will be joyed to hear that success has attended our undertakings in the West Branch Liard River. Mr. McLeod junior returned the 9th September and followed its Waters 500 miles to its source in the Icy Mountains. His route was through a fine country abounding in Fur-bearing animals . . . inhabited by Indians friendly and hospitable. From this voyage five new tribes is in a manner introduced to our acquaintance. The navigation is dangerous. With smart canoe men, care and caution, it may be navigated without the loss of life. . . . There is no success without some loss. On the return of the expedition and when far advanced on their way home, in running a rapid the canoe filled, broke in three pieces, two men drowned. . . ."

The years had passed, but the life seemed to have changed little, as exemplified by R. M. Patterson's comments about an evening in 1929: "That night Gordon and I were asked to supper with Inspector and Mrs. Moorhead of the RCMP (Royal Canadian Mounted Police) at their house. On the way up there from Andy's, Gordon besought me to remember that this was a civilized house we were going to: we would be sitting on chairs, he explained, and not on rocks or up-turned canoes. It was most considerate of him. 'None of your camp habits tonight,' he said. 'Don't gnaw the meat off the bones and chuck them over your shoulder like you do in the bush, and if you don't like the coffee, don't say Perfect Muck and pour it out on the floor. Remember . . .' However, we rallied our table manners and spent a most enjoyable evening with these two kind people who were to be our hosts again in the spring. It was pretty late when we left them and walked back to Andy's. Gordon took a look at the thermometer by the hotel door. 'Sixty-seven below, and dropping,' he said as we went in."

Change did come. Steamboats like *The Wrigley* (1886), *The Mackenzie* (1908), and *The Distributor* (1920-1947) brought supplies for the town and the Hudson Bay Company. The construction of a winter road from Fort Providence, two hundred miles to the east along the north side of the Mackenzie on the way to Yellowknife, plus the new airport built during World War II by the United States Army dramatically changed how supplies arrived in town. In 1972 the Mackenzie Highway was completed with the causeway that links the island with the mainland.

Hordes of black flies and mosquitoes, wicked rivers, unknown country, brutal cold, never-before-fished streams, never-hunted mountains and honest, generous, tough people. I am certain that I was born at least fifty years too late.

While I work on both a cigar and the problem of my birth date,

I notice a Fort Simpson cop car making the rounds. There is only one other campsite in use, by a large motor home with Alberta plates, but a number of teenagers have been roaring along the park's one-lane roads at upward of sixty miles an hours (about one hundred kilometers an hour for those of a foreign twist) in a couple of old beaters—a rusted out Oldsmobile Cutlass sans muffler and a vintage Datsun pickup. Both rigs are loud and easy to track by the trails of largely black exhaust they spew. The cops patrol easily with the confidence that living in a small town with the ferries shut down for the night brings. They both wave and nod as they pass me. A few minutes later I see the red-and-blue flickerings of their lights through the trees and two sets of headlights in front of the squad car. The situation is under control, and without the use of a siren. I am impressed.

It is now about 2 A.M. Mike walks by and I invite him to the fire. He sits down, lights a smoke, and offers me one. The currency of conversational exchange up here. He proves to be well-read with a fondness for Ernest Hemingway and even William T. Vollmann. When I tell him I am a writer, he is visibly impressed. (He doesn't know me all that well.) I dig out a copy of my novel *Hunted* and inscribe it for him.

"Would you by any chance have another copy?" Mike asks. "I'd like to give it to my friend, who's the librarian in town. Books are hard to come by up here."

I go back to the Suburban and my book box and find another *Hunted* along with copies of *Coyote Nowhere, Waist Deep in Montana's Rivers,* and an oldy but a favorite *Knee Deep in Montana's Trout Streams.* I sign them all and hand them to my new friend.

"Here you are, Mike," I say. "More Holtian bullshit than a nice town like Fort Simpson deserves."

I always carry copies of my books on the road. They sometimes legitimize my strange and arcane behavior with local authorities and seem to be good for a few drinks at most taverns. On this trip I donated about seventy books to libraries around the Northwest

Territories. I feel good about having my books on shelves in the Far North.

Mike is extremely grateful for the books, so much so that he tells me that every river from here to the crossing at Fort Providence is experiencing a run of walleyes. He says, "When the cotton from the trees falls, those pickerel (the NWT's term for walleye) are on the move." He suggests I use any large nymph in bright yellow or orange and weighted down. "Just drift the damn thing slowly along the bottom on the soft edges of runs. Little creeks, the rivers, all of them have fish. Grayling and northerns, too."

We talk until around 3:30 A.M., then he leaves. The sun is up above the horizon turning everything crimson and blaze orange. I make the walk through the trees, then across a pair of baseball fields (every town in Canada seems to have a field) to the edge of the river. To my left I watch the Liard's muddy, tree- and limb-choked flow slide into the clear Mackenzie. The two rivers move north side-by-side and without mingling as far as I can see. The white rock and soil escarpments that mark the far banks of both rivers glow in the new day's light. Below me along the shore, chunks of ice as big as cars lie in crazed jumbles. Enormous slabs the size of small skating rinks are piled on top of the chunks—the remains of ice-out five or six weeks ago. All of the ice is coated with dark mud and small gravel. When the morning breeze puffs warmly downriver, it washes me with cold air when it curls over the ice. All is silence. The town is asleep. The sun is bloody gold on the northeast horizon. I am alone with the sound of the surging rivers, large whirlpools spinning and sucking the snags and ridges and layers of nearly silent standing waves pulsing far from shore. I continue to absorb the scene, the wildness unlike anything back home. When I return to camp, Rachel is already up cooking bacon and eggs. I'd spaced away the night. It is nearly 7 A.M.

AUTHOR PHOTO

CAMERON FALLS OUTSIDE OF YELLOWKNIFE, NORTHWEST TERRITORIES.

THREE /

YELLOWKNIFE

The Liard Highway is anything but smooth sailing. From Fort Simpson to the ferry crossing of the Mackenzie below the outlet of Great Slave Lake at Fort Providence, the road runs about two hundred miles through thick boreal forest, across marshy tundra, and over rushing rivers like the Trout and the Red Knife. With few smooth exceptions, the word "highway" is a polite euphemism for hardpacked, and often muddy, dirt roads. Repaired stretches of soft gravel come upon us suddenly, and the Suburban sinks in and wallows briefly, even at fifty miles an hour. Ruts, potholes, and just plain rock-hard surfaces are the norm. Our average speed is about forty miles an hour. But considering the harsh and remote nature of this land, the road is a blessing, allowing us to access country that until a few decades ago could only be traveled by foot in the winter or by canoe, motorboat, or bush plane equipped with floats. Much of the travel throughout the Northwest Territories still takes place in these time-tested ways.

As Rachel and I bounce along, we see dozens of black bears, a few isolated woodland caribou, singles and groups of three to five woodland bison alongside the road or walking through the dense forest and brush. The caribou are skittish and vanish as we pass nearby. The bison don't give a damn. The older bulls look up at our unnatural approach, then saunter across the road on what appear to be dainty hooves supporting enormous bodies that expand at the shoulders to distinctive humps of muscle holding up massive heads with furry manes, ratty black goatees, and curved horns. A couple of times the animals break into a run and my speedometer indicates that they are moving at over twenty-five miles an hour. They're surly, like ranch bulls, and have gored and killed a number of unwary tourists over the years. We also spot a couple of gray wolves loping across the road and into the trees. Wildlife is everywhere. Ravens abound: on the road, perched in trees, flying overhead. The birds are as big as small spaniels with beaks that could jackhammer concrete, though they seem more interested in roadside attractions that include well-dead small mammals and birds. A few pickup trucks and a rogue semi or two hauling fuel or supplies are about it for vehicular traffic.

This country is truly "the bush." I can't imagine hacking my way through this stuff, map or no map, with clouds of biting insects eating me literally alive as I fight my way through thick stands of choking pine trees and ripping tangles of wild raspberry or sink chest deep into a mucky, miasmic muskeg swamp. The old-time voyageurs who moved through this land with speed and confidence, when it wasn't frozen solid like an immense sheet of granite, were tough. Not Hollywood movie lala-land tough like the overpaid phonies in *Jeremiah Johnson* or the silly *Dances With Wolves.* These long-ago guys were hard, determined, at least slightly crazy, and tough. Factor in the Northwest Territories' 780,500 square miles—an area larger than Alaska and Montana combined—and the enormity of trying to trap, haul goods, or just survive is overwhelming. This doesn't consider the fact that some of the native people up this way were a bit on the aggressive side a couple of centuries back, but more on that in a later chapter.

We stop at the Red Knife River, then scout the water and

decide to camp, taking a steep, rocky two-track down to the stream. The setting-up-camp dance is quickly dispensed with, and Rachel and I begin fishing. The roar of the water shooting through two ten-foot-diameter culverts is muted by its quarter-mile distance from where we camped. Much of the water in these rivers has Montana-like runs, pools, and riffles, but rarely do the northerns or grayling hold here. We take these fish on the edges of deep, fierce white-water or in the middle of boiling, effervescent cauldrons of the cold, clear flow at the base of falls or within deadly chutes that roar between gaps in midstream boulders. How any fish holds, let alone survives, in this type of aquatic mayhem confounds me. I watch Rachel and suddenly her rod bends double and vibrates up and down. She determinedly hauls in the largest grayling I've seen since fishing the Blackstone River along the Dempster Highway in the Yukon a couple of years ago. She marks it against her rod and yells that it is nearly twenty-two inches and close to four pounds. The state record in Montana is a little over three pounds, and my daughter just blew that away on her first cast in this NWT stream. I wave and walk downriver.

Looking for water that reminds me of walleye habitat in the Ontario rivers I fished as a kid, I find a deep, dark run at the edge of a slowly swirling eddy. I put on a large yellow stonefly nymph that is heavily weighted. I add a split shot to drop the mess down through six, eight, ten feet of water. Casting upstream and allowing the delightful setup to dredge the bottom produces immediate results. The line stops, moves forward a few inches and I set the hook, feel something living on the other end, then nothing. Lost it. I repeat the process with similar results, except the fish, whatever it is, stays on. A firm take, a few short runs, and a four- to five-pound walleye is at my feet. This fish is more bronze than the olive green ones of Ontario and is wider and thinner in shape.

Walleye don't fight much and fishing for them is not all that thrilling to me, but they are one of the best freshwater table fish around. Firm, white flesh that tastes of chicken, the water they live in, and a hint of channel catfish. I work this run for another hour and take several more fish of the same size. I keep three that I fillet. I return to camp with about six pounds of walleye that will taste great dredged in cornmeal, sea salt, and freshly ground black pepper, then fried in hot corn oil. A little squeeze of lemon, sourdough French bread and unsalted butter, and a side dish of the premixed salad we bought in Fort Simpson and we'll be living. Bernstein's garlic and cheese dressing helps, too.

While we prepare the meal, the sky darkens with thick boiling clouds. *Mammatus* they're called, and they always mean rough weather. Lightning and thunder rip the air, the reports crashing and echoing up and down the canyon of the river. The dense, charged air compacts the mosquitoes into a black cloud of frenzied feeding. We throw the food on plates, grab a jug of orange juice, and retreat to the tent at the unheard-of early dining hour of 8 P.M. Rachel annihilates the few mosquitoes that come in with us, and we eat in comfort and luxury as a wild thunderstorm washes over. Gusts of wind rock the trees and whip water off the surface of the Red Knife. The lightning whites out the landscape in electric brilliance. The thunder makes talk pointless, blasting with such intensity that when it rips the charged atmosphere the walls of the tent push in quickly then reexpand. We stuff ourselves on bread, salad, and walleye and luxuriate in the perceived safety and very real comfort of the tent. The storm lasts for a couple of hours, far longer than they do down home. A quick riff of hail about the size of gumdrops splatters down, pinging with metallic tones off the Suburban. Then the surly storm moves on east, pushing the thunder and lightning ahead, the sound and light intensity quickly fading. When we step out of the tent the air temperature has dropped from the midseventies to the upper forties and a steady drizzle has set in. We pack up as much gear as we can for an early departure tomorrow, then secure the rest with tarps before retiring to the tent to read and go to sleep before midnight.

Mosquitoes bombard the netting at both entrances, but we laugh at such danger, enjoying the warmth of our sleeping bags, a lazy evening reading, then several hours of sleeping oblivion.

The next morning, around half-past seven, is clear and heading for warm and breezy. We eat a quick breakfast and drive up the two-track and back on the Liard Highway. The road is still damp from last night's storm. Mist swirls above the road and drifts through the forest. Fresh bear droppings litter the road and several of them casually graze on roadside grasses. Bison look out from the trees or just munch away on the thick grass without raising their heads.

We fish more rivers, catch more walleye and grayling and northerns, and let all of them go. We have a lunch of bread, sausage, brie, grapes, and iced tea and arrive at the southern shore of the Mackenzie crossing in early evening. The ferry, HMS *Merv Hardie,* is in midstream loaded with semis and a couple of pickups. In minutes it lands, unloads, reloads, and heads back across river. We plan to stay at the Territorial Park at Fort Providence, have a lazy meal, then wing a few spoons on spinning tackle into the river. We sign in, pay for a nice spot on the edge of the trees above the river, and start to set up camp. Before I have one crate out or even think about building a fire, I am covered with large black mosquitoes. The things eat my exposed flesh, bore through my shirt, fly into my eyes and up my nose.

"Screw this," I yell.

Rachel doesn't say a thing. She's frantically assembling the tent. I help. We're being devoured. We throw the sleeping gear, some books, a light, a can of Planters Mixed Nuts, some Almond Joys and Butternut candy bars, a half-gallon of orange juice, and ourselves into the tent. This takes less than thirty seconds but there are already hundreds of insects inside. We kill them with savagery and vengeance. Later in July, while camping along the Musselshell River in Montana, I find the dead things when I set up the tent. Fond memories of northern wildlife. A week or so later, during a conversation with a woman at a gas station along the Liard Highway, I learn that a woman traveler was killed by mosquitoes at the Blackwater River that comes out of the McConnell Range. Apparently, she wandered off alone on a trail along a stream through a boggy forest. The insects descended on her; she panicked, fell, and was swarmed. The mosquitoes took a good deal of her blood, and the toxic overload from thousands of bites finished the job. Reports of caribou being stampeded and some animals sucked down to leather husks are anything but far-fetched up this way.

A room at a bed-and-breakfast in Yellowknife takes on paradise overtones. A warm shower, a restaurant meal where people wait on us, maybe a movie, and then a real bed sounds damn good to both of us.

A new pickup pulls up and a Dene in a park ranger uniform steps out. He is about six feet tall and husky. He wears a ball cap and a shortsleeve shirt. The bugs don't bite his dark, walnut-toned skin. They don't even land or swarm him. I get out and show him our camping permit, swatting mosquitoes all the while. He checks the permit, makes a note on a clipboard, and hands the paper back with a smile.

"Mosquitoes don't bother us," he says. "Get bitten so much as kids we're immune. Feel free to fill a few garbage bags with them to take home to your friends. We've got plenty." He introduces himself as Albert. Another Albert. Both of them friendly, happy. He takes out the ritual pack of smokes, offers me one, and lights up both of us. The smoke holds back the mosquitoes a little,

"Any fishing here?" I ask.

"Oh my, yes, plenty of pike. Pickerel [walleye to Americans] and a few grayling, too. Just throw any old lure in and you'll catch pike. Five pounds. Ten. Twenty," Albert says with a laugh and a cloud of smoke. "Bunch of Mennonites drove up here from Alberta to catch fish for their freezers. Looked like a fish cannery around here last weekend. They must have caught a couple of tons. They'll be tired

AUTHOR PHOTO

THE ENTRANCE SIGN FOR BULLOCKS' BISTRO IN YELLOWKNIFE.

of eating them by January is my guess. This river is full of fish." As if to punctuate Albert's point, a couple of barges, heading in opposite directions, hoot their horns at each other out in the middle of the river—two longs, a short, then a long just like a diesel train on the Hi-Line railroad tracks in Montana.

We finish our cigarettes. (I've since quit the things—no booze, no drugs, no Marlboros, no girlfriend these days. I'm starting to bore the hell out of myself. Maybe I'll go back to robbing small-town liquor stores. I have a dandy little place in mind in Camp Crook just over the Montana line in South Dakota—a little thrill and some quick cash.) Albert and I shake hands, and he climbs into his truck bound for other campers, though there are none in sight. I zip back in the tent. Rachel murders my trailing exhaust of mosquitoes. We munch down our haphazard, gourmandish dinner. I swipe all of the Brazil nuts. We read in the late evening sunlight, then go to sleep in the later evening sunlight. The lowering sun turns the landscape outside soft orange. A warm breeze riffles the birch leaves that rustle musically. The fecund smell of the river mixes with the green scents of the forest.

In the morning the mosquitoes are, if anything, worse. Late June is near the end of the peak season for these bugs. By mid-July they will cease to be a problem of any note. But the insects of the past dozen hours are as bad as any I've encountered up here, in the Yukon, the North Woods of Minnesota, or the forests of Ontario. I can see how they drive men and animals insane before sucking them dry. Bug spray is nothing more than a human affectation to the mosquitoes. It has absolutely no effect. We toss everything in the back of the Suburban and blow out of the park.

The highway north to Yellowknife is wide, paved, and in fine shape. We cruise at seventy miles an hour but are passed by trucks, semis, and passenger cars. After about fifty miles we come to an empty place by a sly blue lake called Chan. We pull over and get out. There's a nice breeze and no mosquitoes. We take a couple of hours to eat breakfast, clean up, and completely repack the car so that we'll be in fighting trim for Yellowknife. Across the road a group of maybe fifty bison leisurely grazes on the rich and abundant roadside grasses. We've seen hundreds of the animals already today and will see many more on the way to the city.

We have about two hours to go before we reach Yellowknife. The highway's quality holds until about forty miles south of town, then construction turns it into a lurching muddy or dusty narrow death trap. Dynamite explodes all around us, blasting the Shields bedrock. We are amply warned and carefully shepherded through these blasting zones, but I still feel like I'm tripping through some unnamed war with an enemy of nobody. To our right, or east, Great Slave Lake sparkles in the sunlight. Far out in the water I can just make out the ghostly shapes of large ships probably hauling ore from distant northern mines and supplies for the north country. Or perhaps they are fishing vessels taking in walleye, inconnu (similar to whitefish though larger), and lake trout for Yellowknife restaurants. Tanker rigs, pickups, and passenger cars lurch and careen by in the opposite direction, all of us staggering along in a veil of dust shot through with sounds of exploding dynamite. Raucous civilization here in the Far North. Can Yellowknife be far away?

No it isn't. The airport is on our left. Commercial jets, the distinctive green-and-white Buffalo Air Express prop-planes, and private de Havilland Beavers and Otters, Cessna Caravans, and Beech King Airs fill the air in a Far North traffic jam with some planes landing or taking off and others coming and going from the surrounding bays and lakes. A modern terminal and control tower shine like monuments to western progress. A parking lot is jammed with newer sport-utility vehicles, pickups, and luxury cars made by Cadillac, BMW, Mercedes, GMC, Acura, Jaguar, and a British racing Aston Martin. An Aston Martin! Maybe they are filming a James Bond movie. Perhaps "Musk Ox Are Forever." And there is a less-than-healthy selection of beaters that I am more comfortable with. The skyline of modern downtown Yellowknife, squared or rectangular glassed structures a dozen or more stories tall, is clearly visible in the distance. While not impressive by Calgary or New York standards, after so many days in the wilderness, seeing all of these eight-story skyscrapers makes me feel like I am cruising along Michigan Avenue in Chicago. We turn right on Old Airport Road, passing modern fast-food joints, discount stores, gas stations, and insurance agencies. We then angle left onto the main drag called Franklin Avenue, which takes us through the heart of the bustling city. It is noon, sunny and warm. People are out all over the place heading for lunch or just enjoying the summer day.

Yellowknife is largely a modern city on the northern shore of Great Slave Lake. Perhaps the number of people here doesn't translate to a city in the Lower-48, but the entire population of the Territories, a land larger than California, Montana, and Wyoming combined (I love these comparisons), is less than forty-two thousand. Great Falls, Montana, is considered small by American standards and it has over seventy thousand residents. Downtown Yellowknife is modern, bustling, and filled with new high-rise structures. Boston Pizza, A&W, and McDonalds have invaded. The citizens are mostly successful, with the exception of the displaced Dene that sit on benches and wander back streets probably wondering what all of this modern chaos is about. There are Germans, French, expatriate Yanks, South Africans, Austrians, Swedes, Vietnamese, Chinese, Japanese, and Australians. White, black, yellow, red. And so many different languages that you'd think you were in Orly Airport in Paris. Yellowknife is nothing if not cosmopolitan in its own compressed manner.

Rachel and I spent time in this new part of the city when we shopped for books and gifts and went to a movie one night Jim Carey in *Bruce Almighty*. A weird experience. The kids were dressed like American youngsters, the amenities were the same, the Surround Sound blasted and shook the walls. Twenty-four hours earlier we had been fending off bugs, catching fish, and hanging out with bears, bison, and wolves. Now we could have been at a triplex in Bozeman, Montana.

The part of Yellowknife we like best is Old Town, a hodgepodge collection of old and somewhat newer structures arranged in a haphazard pattern along the shores, hills, and cliffs of a narrow peninsula and an equally narrow island called N'Dilo that is connected to the mainland by a short bridge. Houses rise in eccentric patterns that reflect owners' whims, personalities, and private madnesses. Decks hang at odd angles from third-story bedrooms. Windows wrap around corners. Small gardens grow out of thin air, hanging far above the streets. The place is a miniature amalgamation of a Seattle, Hong Kong, and Nantucket peyote get-together. Free-form, out-to-lunch styles mix casually with funky local businesses and a few sedate items that appear to be dedicated to ripping off the tourista mooches, though the latter seem to swim in infrequent and small schools way up here not far from the Arctic Circle and just a healthy plane ride from that ice cap of the really-high-no-peyote-here-silliness Arctic. North Pole stuff and all that.

Earlier, Rachel had scoured brochures for the city, searching for the ultimate bed-and-breakfast and firmly decided on Back Bay Boat Bed and Breakfast. I'm not a big fan of B and B's; that is, of sleeping in a stranger's home and eating breakfast with even more strangers who pry ever deeper into my shallow life.

"What do you do, John?" they ask with insidiously wicked, and sometimes smarmy, smiles.

"Well, not a hell of a lot of anything, really," I tell them. Write a bit now and then. Occasionally wander off into the middle of nowhere out on the high plains and drink way the hell too much, shoot guns, and pray for a rich relative to die and leave me lots of money."

"Oh, how lovely. Anything else?"

"I've considered shooting heroin, but I'm frightfully afraid of needles, so I settled on following the Cubs again this summer," I say. "Would you pass that yogurt and some of those bagels and the pitcher of orange juice please." I crack open a pair of Smirnoff miniatures I've been clutching in my left hand beneath the lace tablecloth, build a screwdriver, say "Cheers!" then bolt my food and head down the road.

But Rachel's been a trooper on a fairly severe road trip so far, so I acquiesce to the bed-and-breakfast. We find Back Bay Boat after cruising around the narrow one-way roads for several laps. By our sixth circuit, people on the decks above are laughing and waving small Canadian flags. "What has this charming U.S. couple won today, Jay?" And then on a hunch we jerk left and climb up a gravel alley to the entrance to our digs for the next few nights. A woman in her midforties is working in a garden next to a house that is modern in a European or Icelandic way—bright yellows, blues, whites, large rectangular windows, and an immaculate yard. We'd called ahead, so when she sees the Montana plates, she recognizes us.

Standing, she removes her sunglasses and says, "Hi, John and Rachel. Beautiful weather, yes? With all that camping you must be road weary. I'll show you your room and where everything is, then be out of your way."

She acts like my parole officer, but I'm in love anyway, until I notice a diamond ring on her left hand and a large Germanic-looking fellow, who appears from within the home and that she's apparently married to or living with. We do the formal introduction gig, then talk briefly as we get a functional and succinct tour. From their accents it's clear that they are from Germany. Lothar Ebke and Regina Pfeiffer. "Wir sprechen Deutsch" their brochure says. The house is European modern—uncluttered, open, high-tech appliances, futuristic furniture and decorations. I like it and its contrast to Wrigley, the boreal forest, camping. Our room, named Quiet Court, and the adjoining bathroom are more than adequate. After telling us about a great local fish house nearby and saying that breakfast will be at 7 A.M., if that's okay, the couple leaves us to shower, nap, and regroup. We strike off downhill for a place called Reflections, where we both have pasta, iced tea, and carrot cake. This is a tourist place, but we're being lazy and having someone cook our food and wait on us is luxury of the finest kind and worth the inflated prices. Nothing is cheap up here, even with the favorable exchange rate. This modest lunch comes to about $35 American with tip.

Time passes and we decide to eat dinner around nine o'clock. Just down the hill from our new home is yet another of the tourista mooch joints I mentioned. This one's called The Prospector and, judging by the fancy menu, it caters to well-heeled travelers and erudite sports—happy voyagers in diamonds, dinner jackets, tortoise-shell shades, and $200 hand-painted ties. We say "The hell with it," again too lazy to find a real place tonight, and grab a table in the sun on a porch overlooking the bay and its dancing blue gold water. I order rack of caribou. Rachel has musk ox steak. We're into the tourist jazz full-tilt. I go for local berry tea, wild onions, and Yukon potatoes. All I need now is a pink felt hat that says "Yellowknife—Love It Or Leave It" replete with a long chartreuse feather in a red band. The food arrives and is quite good. The caribou tastes like antelope; the musk ox a bit like properly aged beef. This meal comes in at about $110 American, but when I'm on the road eating is one of the true pleasures of traveling. I learn more about a place by watching the clientele and staff at a restaurant than almost anywhere else. A tourist place, yes, but friendly, and the young workers are open, energetic, and laid back. Good signs. We head back to our room. I read John Steinbeck's *The Log From the Sea of Cortez.* Rachel plays cards. The sound of float planes taking off and landing goes on throughout the night. Pleasant and uncommon background noise when coupled with the light wind and the sound of small waves washing against wooden docks. I love the mind-twist that I get wandering through days that never grow truly dark. A child of the 1960s at heart. We both sleep in real beds.

Not bad. Not bad at all. Yellowknife feels OK for a city.

In the morning, during breakfast, Lothar and Regina ask what I do. I play it straight and say I'm a writer, leaving the gunplay and other stuff alone. I give them a couple of my books—*Hunted* and *Coyote Nowhere*— and explain about this one you're reading now. They say that they think the best time to observe the northern lights is during late September because there is no snow on the ground to reflect the star- and moonlight. The added darkness really "sets up" the lights. They offer to take us out for the show in their canoe any year we get up there again. We finish our breakfast of home-baked breads, cold cuts, cheeses, yogurts, strong coffee, juice, and fruit. My opinion of bed-and-breakfasts mellows some.

In the morning, Rachel and I head out and play sightseers. On our way back we stop at the Wild Cat Café for lunch. The establishment, a ramshackle log cabin, is the oldest café in town. Built in 1937 by Willy Wiley and Smokey Stout (and probably a previous incarnation of Keith Richards), the place reminds me of Wisconsin northwoods restaurants of the late 1960s around Presque Isle and Rice Lake. I feel like ordering a Point beer and a shot of Kessler's. Our waiter is John, who seems a happy young man of Asian lineage. Youthful locals—men bearded, women in jeans or long dresses, all with bandanas or ball caps—come in and greet each other, wander into the kitchen and back out again with cups of coffee and/or soup. The stereo is playing the Talking Heads, then Humble Pie, then the Grateful Dead. Rachel orders caribou chili, and I opt for the caribou "Boo" burger. We both have home fries. While waiting, I wander around looking at the old, framed black-and-white photos of Old Town (back then probably new town), winter, float planes, the Wild Cat Café, and dogsled teams.

The history of the region is an old one, but a brief tour of the relatively recent past includes the Northwest Territories becoming part of Canada in 1870. The area encompassed what is now the NWT, Nunavut (the eastern half of the Territories stretching to

Hudson Bay, until a few years ago), Yukon, Alberta, Saskatchewan, Manitoba, northern Ontario, and northern Quebec. In 1896 prospectors on their way to the Klondike discovered gold in Yellowknife Bay. Pitchblende (uranium-bearing ore) was discovered on Great Bear Lake in the north, leading to air travel and the use of float planes. Visible gold was found on the shores of Yellowknife Bay in 1934, setting off a gold rush two years later that saw the corporate sinking of mine shafts on the Con, Negus, and Giant claims. In 1938 commercial gold production began, and Yellowknife, with a population of one thousand, becomes an administrative district. During World War II, gold production shut down, but a new rush began at the end of the war, leading to the overcrowding of Old Town in 1947, in turn causing surveying for the construction of New Town. In 1953 Yellowknife became a municipal district and elected its first mayor, John McNiven. In the 1960s snowmobiles replaced the dogsleds used by most trappers, miners, and prospectors. The seat of government moved from Ottawa to Yellowknife in 1967, and in 1970 it became the first city in the Northwest Territories.

The Royal Family visited Yellowknife in 1975 (oh boy!), and the residents held a beach party for that fop, Prince Charles. In 1982 Pope John II made an unscheduled visit and blessed the place. Scientists discovered the oldest known rock in the world in 1988 north of Great Slave Lake. It is 3.8 billion years old. Diamonds were discovered in 1991, sparking an insane claim-staking rush, and the first mine opened in 1998. In 1992 nine men were killed in an underground explosion during a strike at Giant Mine. It was one of the largest mass "murders" in Canadian history. In 1999 the NWT divided creating Nunavut, Canada's Inuit Territory in the eastern Arctic. Yellowknife became the territorial capital. The legislative building as well as the Northern Heritage Center and the Northern Frontier Visitor Center are striking examples of modern architecture set among the trees and running out along the water. Old and new.

Traditional and hip. Compressed, fast-moving history. That's the Territories these days.

Also, and this is bonus information here of an entirely useless nature, there is a street called Lois Lane that may be named after actress Margot Kidder, who was born here and played the part next to Superman in the movie, but now lives in Livingston, Montana, two blocks from my home. There is also a street called Ragged Ass Lane, which appears to have no connection to Lois Lane or Ms. Kidder or Livingston.

A few natural facts. The Aurora borealis is visible an average of 243 days a year. Average sunrise in June is 3:39 A.M. and sunset is 11:40 p.m. (We're here on June 20 and the times are more like 3:30 and midnight). In December it is 10:07 A.M. and 3:04 P.M. The average July high temperature is seventy degrees F. The average low in January is minus thirty-one degrees F. There are at least 237 documented bird species within 35 miles of Great Slave Lake, nearly one for every day you can see the northern lights. Yellowknife is about 1,000 miles from Edmonton and 3,000 miles from Chicago.

I bore the hell out of Rachel with all this while we eat our meal. We chat some more with our waiter, John, wander out the low doorway, and climb up Pilot's Monument on top of The Rock, which honors bush pilots of the North. The view takes in the bays and lakes that surround the city. I can see the skyline of New Town along the southern horizon and the delightful chaos of Old Town at my feet.

The day's itinerary has been chosen by my daughter, who seems determined to kill me off. Next up is a drive out into the forested lake country along the Ingraham Trail, which is a dirt road that winds and bends through blasted cuts of Precambrian rock. We motor along digesting our caribou for about thirty-five miles, leaving behind the largely abandoned mining district that lies just outside of the city limits and features ochre, rust, and dirty orange slag heaps, rusting mills, trammels, trucks, tractors, conveyor belts, and the like. Gold mining is an ugly business, and the waste area shimmers toxically in the noon heat. A country torn apart so that we can shine with gold; an amazing madness that would make Montezuma smile.

We pull over at the trailhead leading to Cameron Falls, spray on bug dope, load water bottles, and bring a couple of ultralight spinning rods. Rachel marches off on the trail that drifts through thick stands of birch, then climbs up rounded hills of exposed rock covered with open stands of pine. Mosquitoes go after us with lame intent. The way climbs higher still before switchbacking steeply down to a marshy area, then climbing severely to the ridge of more rounded rock. The sound of Cameron Falls greets us before we spot the snowy-white water cascading a hundred feet or more down from Hidden Lake. We sit on a ledge and enjoy the solitude. Less than an hour from Yellowknife and we're back in the wilderness. A moose grazes on aquatic plants in a wide bay below the falls. Ravens glide among the trees making strange calls. The water roars. We head off down the trail to the base of the falls before climbing along the edge of the water that glides across bright green moss-covered rock at the head or plummets five, ten, twenty feet over rock shelves scattered across this shallow stretch of river.

We cross a sturdy footbridge to the other side and follow a game trail back down to the base of the falls. The river is more than two hundred yards wide here. We both fling small spoons out to the edge of the fast current created by the cascade. Before either of us can start to reel in the lures, northerns attack. The fights are spirited but brief, and we soon have a matching pair of eight-pound pike at our feet. We twist the hooks free and the fish glide away. We repeat this twice, then look at each other, laugh, and call it an angling day. We climb back up and sit in the sun, soaking up the river and the falls. The hike back a couple of hours later is serene, the only word for this natural stroll.

The drive back to our room is more of the same. We both shower and nap before heading down the alley to delightful madness that is Bullocks' Bistro at dinner hour.

Bullocks' Bistro is one of those places that I'm convinced is born out of a half-empty Jim Beam bottle, tempered by unrestrained sex on a table, and sanctified with a bar fight. The elongated wooden structure was part of a supply business decades ago. Now the old girl has her walls covered with thousands of snapshots of patrons having decidedly good times. Names and comments are scrawled on the ceiling in ink, crayon, or pencil dry mark. Weird animals hang from the walls. Bumper stickers and mottos are plastered here and there. Music fights to be heard above the dining racket. The place is packed with tourists, locals, assorted lunatics, and two crazed women in their forties who own the place, fry the fish, serve the food, collect the money. And they collect lots of it, with wild energy, smiles, humor, and truly crazy hair that seems determined to always point north no matter what direction they're headed. The place is infused with the aroma of deep-fried fish and potatoes. We grab a table that says "Reserved for Johnson Party—8 P.M." One of the owners snatches the card and throws it on the weathered wood floor. I ask for a menu.

She laughs in my face and says, "We have deep-fried fish and potatoes. Or just fish. Walleye caught this morning." She pats the expanding bald spot on my head and says, "You're all right. You're wearing Converse cutters [meaning my tennis shoes]." We place our order.

Rachel goes to a cooler and snares a pair of iced teas, then muscles her way through the yelling, cheering crowd. (Cheering for what I don't know; maybe someone was sacrificed with a filet knife on the front porch.) While she is gone—the sixty-foot trek takes nearly ten minutes—the other woman comes by and says, "We're having a party next door later. Come on over. We'll be having some fun."

I say, "Thanks, next year. My daughter's with me." The woman grins, hits me on the shoulder, and says, "Good man. We'll be looking for the likes of you come next summer." I plan on making that one.

The fish-and-chips arrive in baskets lined with newspaper, along with large cups of homemade tartar sauce, slices of lemon, large salt and pepper shakers, and some catsup in a bottle. It's all hot, burning-fingertip hot, and just-right greasy. I splash some lemon and salt on a large piece of walleye, swipe it through the tartar sauce, and take a steaming bite. This is the best damned fish I've ever had. I finish the piece and then another and then a handful of fries. Looking up, I see one of the women staring at me and nodding as if to say, "We got this act covered. Imagine the parties we throw." I nod back. We both know that come hell, high water, bankruptcy, or broken legs, I'll be back for the fish and the good times.

By the time we finish eating, the noise level is off the charts, on par with a Boeing 747 during take off. We pay with good, colorful Canadian folding money and a couple of two-dollar "Loonies"—silver coins with brass centers stamped with loons or beavers or polar bears—leave a tip, and step outside. The crowd's roar follows us. It's a beautiful evening—sunshine, cool breeze, warm temperature. We walk along the waterfront. The happy sounds of Bullocks' Bistro ricochet through alleys, between homes, and across the water like stoned-happy gunshots.

Here and there across the small bays we see houseboats and floating cabins painted all colors of the rainbow and sporting wild flags from forgotten nations, kites, wind chimes, rags flapping in the wind; moose racks, caribou racks, deer horns, bison horns, and god knows what else are hammered to walls, roofs, windowsills; petunias, daffodils, marigolds, roses, oregano, asparagus, tomatoes, serano peppers, lemon basil grows from window boxes and planters rocking on dilapidated wooden docks; ancient, leaking boats with prewar Johnson outboards, canoes recovered from the old Ed Ames television series about Mohawks, derelict wooden catboats with cotton sails, 1947 Dodge pickups, Edsels, float planes from another time zone; television antennas cocked at bizarre angles to receive long-ago signals. It's all here and a whole lot more if you're cognizant of the seeing-without-looking shuffle. What a hell of a place Old Town is. I could live among all of this oddball joy. Easy. Nothing to it. I'd have no trouble looking past the slight tourist-business jive and disappearing into the routine. This little part of the world is way out there.

One portion of the world up here that is anything but way out there or part of the old northern way of life is the diamond industry. From a zero-percent share of the world market a few years ago to projections of 12 to 15 percent by 2007, the industry in the NWT is exploding. Fueled by a private find from two determined diamond geologists, gem fever is raging across the mindscape of the Territories. Pipes, or geologic structures that run more or less vertically through the earth's surface and contain the precious stones, are turning up all over the place. The South African diamond giant De Beers, the world's largest producer hands down, has formed De Beers Exploration, which is spending more than $40 million yearly—more than half of its exploration budget worldwide—in Canada. Diamondex Resources is drilling 135 miles northeast of Yellowknife. GGL Diamond Corporation has acquired 16,000 acres (known as the Zip claims) in the NWT. An indicator mineral vein with G-10 garnet values, higher than world-class diamond producing pipes located at operations like Diavik, has been found in the area. BHP Billiton's Ekati mine and the Rio Tinto-Aber Diamond Corporation Diavik Project are in production. A recently completed mine cost more than $1 billion. In 1996 over $220 million was spent on exploration by all companies in the region. De Beers is in the environmental review process for another mine at Snap Lake, and on and on.

And in Yellowknife proper, a new and growing industry of cutting and polishing diamonds, the hardest of all gemstones, is flourishing. Tiffany's and Rosy Blue, the largest diamond trading company in the world, are among the investors in the area. Retail businesses featuring jewelry made with diamonds are increasing in number. I notice that a lot of city residents are wearing the sparkling stones in rings, bracelets, necklaces, watchbands, ear- and nose-rings, and places I probably shouldn't think about too much. Many of these are set in gold and accented with emeralds and garnets that were more than likely unearthed in the NWT.

The magazine *Canadian Diamonds* is published in the city and features interviews with industry scions, profiles of operations around the world, glossy stock, and high-quality photography. Another item I found, this time on a chair at a laundromat, is called *Mining: Our Northern Legacy*. This is a real slick piece of propaganda published by the NWT Chamber of Mines. The title reminds me of a photo caption in a gold mining company puff piece about Montana, where beneath a photo of a terrified white-tailed deer standing shakily next to an enormous earth-hauling rig were the words "Mining—We all need it." Damn straight. I'm with you there, buddy. Page after page of this NWT publication details the wonders and benefits of mining in all forms—oil, gas, gem stones, gold. Smiling employees, happy dogs, peacefully grazing caribou next to a runway with a company jet taking off somewhere out on the Barren Grounds. Sort of like the brain-dead mind set of the Cleaver family in *Leave It To Beaver* comes north. Read this baby a few times and you begin to believe that there are no problems associated with mining. The slogan on the publication's back cover is the clincher: "Industry and Government—Working to Build a Strong Future." I'm sold. Where do I sign up?

All of this means an influx of money, a whole bunch of it, to Yellowknife and the NWT in general. Even the common man has the very real chance to be modestly wealthy up here. But there are problems. The mining takes place in sensitive areas, often on tundra far above the Arctic Circle. Footsteps in this fragile environment do damage. Dynamite, road construction, heavy earthmoving and earth-hauling machinery, hundreds of miners, and related facilities. I can't imagine what horrors this will lead to. Damage here lasts for centuries. Wildlife is often displaced or their numbers are decreased dramatically or even reduced to zero. The way of life in nearby native settlements is disrupted or destroyed. Most of the jobs go to career industry workers from other countries, though both the industry and the Territorial government are making efforts to hire and train native people. And the life of a mine is finite, measured in a few decades. When the pipes are exhausted, when all of the sparkling little stones are gathered, companies pull up stakes and head somewhere else, leaving behind large open-pit carnage—wide, deep holes sunk into the bedrock; delicate grasses and mosses now a distant memory growing still dimmer.

While the diamond industry is somewhat more stable in terms of the boom-and-bust disasters associated with the oil, gas, and coal industries, there is still a tremendous drop in the level of money flowing through a given community when a diamond operation shuts down. When the faucet of cash is closed, homes, trucks, campers, ATVs, maybe even firstborn sons are repossessed by the banks, who have been doing this since their inception. They play this greedy game like financial maestros, and they'll make out like the bandits they are.

I can see it now. "Hey kid, want a deal on a dandy three-quarter-ton GMC pickup? Just grabbed the sucker from a busted family up Yellowknife way. They don't need it, son. Hell, they don't even have a pot to piss in anymore—we sold that last week right out from under the poor, dumb bastards," says a smooth-talking, well-dressed resale wizard from one of the bank's branch offices in, say, Grande Cache, Alberta, just a short run down south. "Only three years old. Less than twenty thousand miles on her. Mint condition. Make me an offer." And the vicious, venal dance continues.

Nearly every brochure and magazine I read in Yellowknife extols the virtues, benefits, and wonders of this new industry that has descended on the Territories. Not one of these publications adequately explores the downside, the problems both while the mines are in operation and after the industry blows the scene. All of this reminds me of similar disastrous cycles in the American West with gold, oil, gas, coal, silver, and copper. Hopefully, the citizens up here that care will look south for cautionary tales and hard-learned advice from those of us still standing. One can dream.

This is turning grim. Time to trundle on to other business.

Of all of the man-made, or man-contrived, aspects of the modern world as it spins about in the Far North, nothing intrigues me more than the ice roads. While there are many miles of roads to run in the warm months, many more exist in the winter, usually beginning in January when the wet, often swampy terrain and the rivers freeze. These ice roads run for hundreds of miles along wild mountain ranges, across vast stretches of Barren Ground tundra, over muskeg swamps, lakes, rivers, and through summertime-impassable forests.

One road runs from Yellowknife for hundreds of miles northeast to the previously mentioned diamond mines. It crosses enormous lakes like de Gras and Contwoyto and ends well above tree line at a gold mine. Still another courses due north to the remote settlements of Wha Ti and Rae Lakes, passing over the middle of Faber Lake. And the one that really grabs me goes north along the Mackenzie River to Tulita, Norman Wells, and Fort Good Hope with a jog east for sixty-five miles to Deline on the shore of Great Slave Lake at the historical site of Old Fort Franklin. I'd love to cruise along with a veteran driver as we haul enormous fuel tanks the size of garages or in a tanker carrying thousands of gallons of fuel all the while crunching over expanding and contracting river and lake ice floating above hundreds of feet of frigid, dark water or moving along beneath the forbidding slopes of the Franklin Mountains towering dimly in the brief dusk-like days and eternal star- and aurora-filled nights of winter with the snow and ice of the way ahead flashing the green, blue, violet, and crimson of those Northern Lights—oh yeah, that appeals to me. Or maybe striking out from Inuvik on the vast Mackenzie

Delta bound for the Inuit settlement of Aklavik or farther north still to another native village called Tuktoyaktuk and the edge of the ice-bound Beaufort Sea and the Arctic Ocean. Temperatures hovering around minus fifty degrees. Wind blowing near whiteout. Or dead calm under the brief sun with air so cold ice cracks and trees explode like cannon shots.

The company that is largely responsible for making and maintaining these eccentric roads is Robinson Enterprises Ltd. With more than thirty years of experience, Robinson Enterprises Ltd. is considered the elite in winter ice-road route selection, construction, and maintenance. For example, in 1997 the company hauled approximately 107.5 million litters (nearly 30 million gallons) of fuel across the winter roads and 20.5 million kilograms (22,000 tons) of dry freight in the one season.

Planning for winter roads can start as early as July. The company uses float planes and helicopters to study terrain, underwater reefs, and currents—ice over shallow and/or fast-moving water is often thin and fragile. This information is mapped, then used to select winter road routings and to determine construction methods. Robinson Enterprises uses helicopters to survey the area with Ground Penetrating Radar to determine ice thickness. When it is safe to venture out on the ice, a light track-vehicle scouts the area with the use of a GPR revalidating ice thickness. Depending on the amount of ice, plows with balloon tires may follow, or regular graders, cats, and plow trucks may be used to clear the road and accelerate ice buildup. Snow acts as an insulator, so removing it exposes the ice to greater cold, which allows it to freeze faster and to a greater thickness. Heading into the isolated areas of the Northwest Territories in subzero temperatures, the radio equipped winter road crews are accompanied by fully equipped, self-contained camp units, portable workshops with generators and welders, and their own fuel and oil supply. The crews are self-supporting for up to thirty days. Communication is vital for ice-road construction crews and for the drivers who haul loads once construction is complete.

During the construction period, communication is maintained with the head office via VHF and HF radios, satellite phones, and radios. Drivers, who always travel in groups of two or more for safety reasons, also keep in radio contact with each other. With satellite dispatch radios in the head office, branch offices, and in over a quarter of the company highway vehicles and supervisor pickups, all three dispatch offices are able to communicate not only between themselves but with the highway units at the same time, twenty-four hours a day regardless of where the units are located. Aircraft are an integral part of the winter road operation by maintaining radio contact with construction crews, scouting alternate routes, checking ice thickness, resupplying camps, and conducting crew changes. They are on emergency standby from the time road construction starts in midwinter until the ice roads are closed. Once the road has been opened, six-wheel-drive and eight-wheel-drive trucks, with custom-designed plows, maintain the lake crossings while hauling freight and leading convoys of trucks over the route.

Maintenance of winter roads is a continuous process of constant adaptation to unpredictable situations. In addition to the hazards of extreme cold and severe winter storms with visibility whiteouts, dangers such as ice blowouts, overflow, washouts, pressure ridges, cracks, worn portages, and so on must be considered. The monitoring of ice to determine how freight can be moved safely is becoming more of a scientific process with each passing season. There is a close relationship between the thickness of ice, proximity to reefs and shore, the weight of the loads, the speed of the vehicles, and the distance between vehicles. Miscalculations may result in wave action strong enough to break through the ice blowouts. When these occur, making the transition from ice to solid ground becomes impossible until refreezing or by the use of specially designed tracks to span the open space. During the winter of 1987, a program of ice testing was initiated and carried out by Robinson Enterprises Ltd.. These tests were conducted under various conditions to establish ice deflection and water movement when moving loads are applied to ice. They are used to determine how fast vehicles can travel and what distance they must maintain from each other on any given part of the road. Traffic is also regulated to avoid storm conditions and to prevent excessive wearing of the roads. At times blizzards force the temporary closure of ice roads. To get the maximum use of the short hauling season, operation continues twenty-four hours a day whenever possible. Near the end of the winter hauling season, when warm weather threatens the road surface, monitoring the portages becomes increasingly important. Robinson Enterprises checks the portages to prevent environmental damage and risk to personnel and equipment. Ice and weather conditions are the major factors in decisions to close the roads.

So that's pretty much all there is to this ice-road stuff. Hop in your rig and head out into some of the coldest, most remote territory on the planet during the coldest and snowiest part of the year or maybe push the season and creep across the melting and rotting ice.

Eventually, Rachel and I decide that it's time to leave Yellowknife and all of its free-form, crazy luxury, good food, nice beds, and wonderful people. We buy a few modest gifts—stone carvings, canned musk ox, caribou, and arctic char—and, of course, a bunch of books. It's time to head down the road and check out some more of the NWT. We negotiate the rough stretch of ripped-up highway outside of Yellowknife, the road blasting eerily absent, stop at a likely looking spot on a small swampy river, cast a few times and fail to turn a fish (the only time in the Territories this happened to us). We move on and cruise at seventy-five miles an hour past feeding bison and ravens and marauding packs of mosquitoes to the ferry crossing at Fort Providence.

A couple of Royal Northwest Mounted Police squad cars are parked at the entrance, lights flashing. Whatever it is, we didn't do it.

The officers work their way up to us and ask where we're from, how long we stayed in Yellowknife, and where we are headed. Satisfied with our answers, they wait for another car. I ask one of the officers what's the deal and he replies, "Found a girl's murdered body in a park at Yellowknife yesterday. Right downtown. We're trying to stop any suspects from escaping this way." The officer, a tall, fit black man in an immaculate uniform is not phased by the swarming mosquitoes that seem to be this area's chief attraction. He leans close and says in a voice shaded with the slightest of British accents, "Don't pick anyone up from alongside the highway. No one. We've a pretty good idea who this chap is, and he's a bad one, but he may have an accomplice. Don't worry. We have the situation in hand. He won't be crossing this river."

The HMS *Merv Hardie* docks in a rumble of reversing engines and swirling prop wash. We drive on board and cross the river to safety. The sun is shining. It's warm. A beautiful day.

AUTHOR PHOTO

SINKHOLE IN THE LIMESTONE WEST OF FORT SMITH.

FOUR /

SOUTH SLAVE REGION

I am traveling alone on this trip to the Northwest Territories, something I like to do. Running east, then southeast beneath a lowering, dark, surly sky from Hay River on the southern shore of Great Slave Lake and the road to Wood Buffalo National Park, I encounter some of the finest pavement north of the 60th parallel. After many hundreds of miles of being kicked around, bounced and lurched skyward, slipped and shoved across greasy, muddy roads during thunderstorms with forest, ditches, and severe drop-offs racing toward the windshield in an ongoing *mélange* of fear, this wide-open, smooth stretch of highway is like a long-ago good dream barely remembered, with perhaps a pinch of *déjà vu* thrown in for seasoning. With the exception of the teaser stretch south of Yellowknife and an even briefer tease on the Liard Highway near the Hay River turnoff, the roads up here, while good, even by American back-road standards, are rough affairs that require a good deal of concentration. Mack trucks blowing by in elongated clouds of blinding road dust, soft spots, moose, bears, bison, and wolves wandering across the road on blind curves—all of this makes for, at the least, marginal, roadwork entertainment. So whenever pavement drifts into my driving life, like now, I throw caution and the ninety-kilometers-an hour-speed limit (around fifty-four miles an hour) out the window, ratcheting up the Suburban to one hundred thirty (about eighty miles an hour). I feel like a North Woods version of a NASCAR driver as the Suburban roars down the road, intense guitar licks by Jimi Hendrix trailing tortured notes in the exhaust. I ignore the sign for Highway 6 and Fort Resolution along the southern shore of the Great Slave Lake. I've been there before and now want to see the bison at Wood Buffalo National Park, so I swing right onto Highway 5.

I fly by a breeding pair of motor homes with Alberta plates, zip around a fuel tank-truck, and scream by an old Volkswagen bug driven by a now-terrified soul with tie-dyed polo shirt and dreadlocks. Hendrix rips chords from "Voodoo Child" on my overtaxed sound system. Away I soar toward lots of buffalo, historic Fort Smith, and the Slave River. An orange rectangular sign saying something about "pavement" and "abrupt" whips past me, then "whoosh," a skid and a 360-degree two-step as I plummet off the edge of modern highway construction onto the familiar hard knocks turf of broken road. The Suburban slips into, then sideways through, a quicksand of soft fill in a deep chuckhole that might well pass for a dry lake bed. The rig lurches and tilts at previously unexplored angles. I gain brief but close examination of tan packed dirt. The forest and a herd of distant bison spin around me in a green, dark brown, beige, and now blue sky kaleidoscope, everything taking place in very slow motion. I see a pair of ravens hanging out on a tree limb. They just stare, motionless, as I twirl by. Then they're gone, replaced by bison and now trees of birch or poplar or aspen and lots of conifers, possibly black spruce. Yes, definitely black spruce. I recognize them. And on my next whirlwind rotation, I spot a large truck with bright lights. The beast is pulling tandem fuel tanks behind it. I decide to see if I can recover from this revolving North Country carousel. The big truck seems closer now as I tap the brakes, steer slightly into the direction of my rotation, and tap the brakes again. Now I am going in only one direction. Backward and pretty much in my lane. The truck looms monstrous in the rearview mirror, now by the driver's side windows, then ahead of me. A storm of reddish tan dust, pebbles, and small boulders accompanied by a continuous blast of air horns trails in the wake of the tanker.

I come to a stop. The dust and roadside detritus begin to settle. The truck's roar fades. The forest is silent. The only sounds are the cooling engine ticking and sporadic gurgling from the radiator. I open my door, get out, light a smoke, and look behind me in the direction I was initially going. Forty, fifty, perhaps seventy bison stare at me from twenty paces. Several bulls are standing in the middle of the road. They have enormous dark brown humps; furry jet-black mangy manes, fuzzy heads, and short, mean-looking horns; dark eyes that gleam in the afternoon light; and black, roughed hooves at the end of dainty forelegs. The bulls are very large, bigger than their Lower-48 relatives. They snort, kick at the dirt surface of the road, and flick their tails. Some bees, mosquitoes, and even a few black flies buzz around all of us. The rest of the herd munches away at roadside grasses, now tall and luxuriant with the June rain and sun. The bulls try to stare me down. They win easily. I climb back in the Suburban. Looking at the map, I see that the park boundary is still a number of miles distant. These bison are outlaws on the run, no doubt, from park authorities. What have they done? Trampled a Prowler motor home? Run roughshod over an outhouse? I turn, back up, pull forward, turn some more, then repeat the process. Now aimed in my original easterly direction, I creep past the four bulls who grudgingly move just enough to allow me safe passage. I hope. One of them glares at me through my window. The bison's head is much larger than the opening, as big as the door. I can smell warm, grass-tinged, slightly fetid breath. The animal's hide is dusty and splattered with mud—no, make that manure. The aroma is a give away. Small bugs work along the thick hair. The tail is ropey, like a quirt. Then I'm past the buffalo (actually they're bison, but buffalo sounds better to my inner ear right now). The adrenaline rush from the merry-go-round adventure has subsided. I gain speed. I reach forty miles an hour and stay there. No more NASCAR escapades for me on this stretch or for the remainder of the trip in the Northwest Territories. I'll try and put "the mind of a child" motif away in the glove box for a few more weeks.

On another trip to Yellowknife, I observed more bison along the road and in the trees than I have anywhere else. The so-called herds of Yellowstone and other parts of the American West pale compared to what's running loose in the Territories. And forget about the concept of a "Buffalo Commons" on the high plains, where ranchers, conservationists, and business interests somehow get together and agree to tear down fences, quit ranching and farming, and file environmental litigation at the drop of a Junco feather so the land can return to the way it was two hundred years ago. Talk about pipe dreams. Besides, they've already got a preserve system going up this way that's bigger than New England and a bit of the Midwest thrown in for flatland measure.

Along the road to Fort Smith, single animals, small bands, and large groups are scattered throughout the forest, along the road, or grazing in treeless areas that remind me of open range in Montana. There are so many bison that after the first few hundred the excitement wears off; that is, except for the wild realization that this land is still so completely intact that enormous wild animals roam the countryside much as they used to in the American West during the early nineteenth century.

In addition to Wood Buffalo National Park, there is the Alberta Bison Management Area and the Bison Control Area west of the park. Both of these are larger than the park. The Mackenzie herd area is of similar size and has two thousand animals. There are also the Slave River Lowlands and the Nahani herds.

Ahead, looming above the forest canopy, I spot what looks like a futuristic red telephone booth suspended atop a flimsy framework of iron girders. I don't care how bad things get, how dire a mess I get myself into, I'm not going up there to call 911. Fortunately, a few hundred yards farther on a sign says something about the Angus Tower fire lookout. There's also something about a sinkhole, and for some odd reason the vision of my sending countless manuscripts and book proposals to publishers and agents in New York erupts in front of me. I pull in, get out, unlock the back doors, open the cooler, grab a Molson Ale, and down the sucker. Feeling better, images of a dinosaur industry blinking confusedly in the bright sun of a new era now fading from mind view, I walk over to a large, somewhat circular fenced area. Peering over and down, I look upon the largest sinkhole I've ever seen—several hundred feet across and more than one hundred feet deep. Small pines and aspen cling to eroding limestone walls that are covered with moss and lichen in shades of green I don't think the artist boys have named yet. At the bottom is a small pond of water that fades from blue to black. Leaves, limbs, twigs, and a small dead animal that could have once been a muskrat float on the water's surface.

I read the other day, in one of my reference books, that sinkholes are formed by the action of seeping and percolating water from rain and snowmelt that erodes large caves, then eventually washes away enough of the porous stone to cause a collapse, leading to the geologic feature before my eyes. I walk around the hole, even going inside the fence despite warnings that this is a bad thing to do, for better photographic angles. Something about this place creeps me out, feels of death. I turn my back on the sinkhole, look up at the fire lookout—man, anyone going up in that baby is nuts, but I imagine there is one hell of a view of the muskeg and boreal forest from that thing—then walk back to the truck. I grab one more icy Molson's, a large chunk of summer sausage, some French bread, and a wedge of brie. Lunch, while sitting on the engine hood, is excellent. I lean back against the windshield and take a nap in the early summer sun, the earlier bad weather now moved east. Time to burn. It's not like it will be dark anytime soon.

An hour later I wake up with visions of a windshield wiper impressed in my back. Like all good naps as I grow older, I come to with a delightfully familiar sense of disorientation. For some reason, I think I'm in northeastern Montana parked next to a little stream filled with northerns and that I'm up this way camping with my long-lost high-school sweetie, Karen. The shambles that is my recognizable reality returns, looking like the rail hoboes I see beneath a viaduct along the tracks between Big Timber and Reedspoint in Montana. No woman of my youth. No youth period, but at least there are northern pike around.

The day is in the seventies, with blue sky and white cumulous clouds and, thousands of feet higher, bands of wispy cirrus. The bison are fewer now, having dispersed into the boreal forest to escape the sun. Within a couple of miles I reach the Nyarling River pull off. I'm in my humble, play-it-by-the-road-sign tourist format now, so I stop. There really isn't much of a pull off, more like a wide spot in the road. And I sure don't see a river. I've never been down this way, so I earlier thought that when I did reach this destination, I'd rig up a fly rod and try for northern pike and walleye. But there isn't even a dry stream course, just a gradual depression, like a wide, grassy canal, that quickly vanishes in the trees. I spot a large sign, and the mystery is soon explained. The Nyarling is right here, running beneath me in a subterranean limestone corridor. The river resurfaces some miles downstream from where I am standing. The entire region is a porous, spongelike layer of ancient ocean bedrock. Not only is there the immense amount of water visible in the lakes, ponds, rivers, and swamps, but there is also a vast underground reservoir that one geologist I ran into later, down in Toad River, British Columbia, told me probably contains more water than the surface and rivals the Oglala aquifer of the central United States. An entire world beneath my feet, and yes, in answer to my question, he said there are fish in these waters; some normal, some blind and albino. I haven't been able to find any mention of these unique pop-

AUTHOR PHOTO

WOODLAND BISON ALONG A ROAD SOUTH OF YELLOWKNIFE.

ulations either in libraries or on the Internet, so maybe the geologist was having a bit of sport at my expense.

Still, whenever I return to Wood Buffalo National Park and stop at the Nyarling River, I will let my imagination run its usual riot: enormous northerns with white eyes and scales of bleached greens hunting down four-pound albino walleyes; giant all-white beavers building dams with whatever debris washes down in the dank darkness; stonefly nymphs that never hatch; lake trout spawning runs up from Great Slave Lake. Crazy. Ludicrous. Possible?

As I roll to the east and Fort Smith another sign greets me. Whooping crane nesting areas are off to my right, to the south in some boggy wetlands. I stop, walk a trail to the top of a sandy bluff, and look out on an expanse of flat, wet brush marked here and there by islands of black spruce. I remember watching a nature show on whoopers many years ago and vividly recall a stretch of film showing the great white birds winging their way to these nesting grounds, the shadow of the photographer's plane rippling up and down slightly with the minor variations in elevation of this very location. Only a few dozen birds were left way back then. Now there are many more, but they are still hanging on precariously. Avian cholera or any number of climatic disasters and goodbye whooping cranes. I scan the marsh, the small blue-water channels, the bays, and the pines with binoculars but fail to sight any of the rare birds. I do see mallards, Canada geese, grebes, and a ragtag flight of white pelicans squawking away as they aim for nesting grounds at the rapids of Slave River below Fort Smith.

As has become my method of operation on the road when I have nowhere to be, I stop and fish every likely looking piece of water I spy along the road. The weather is still sunny, but a cold blast off Great Slave Lake drops the temperature twenty-five degrees. I turn some small northerns here and there, but that's all. Nearing 7 P.M., a gray-and-blue sign announcing Little Buffalo River Falls Campground appears as if ordered. The narrow gravel road I'm on drops down off a bench and into aspen and pine forest. The wind has died to a hint of breeze that rustles the silvery green leaves in evening's light.

I cruise the loop of the camping area. The place is clean, deserted, and primitive, sporting a pair of outhouses. The campground does not appear to have had any campers for months. Perfect. I set out the gear, build a fire, and arrange my sleeping stuff—pad, bag, pillow, quilt (I've softened from the days of passing out under my truck wearing only a waxed-cotton coat and a stocking cap). I throw a foil-wrapped potato in the coals, then make a cool beverage that tastes great in the changing temperatures. High clouds, blue skies, warm wind. Weather unlike Montana. I can hear the falls. A short walk brings me to an overlook where I see copper-colored water pour through a narrow cut in the bedrock, maybe forty feet below. The spill crashes into a plunge pool and onto large cracked slabs of rock one hundred feet down. Looks like northern pike and walleye water.

I have an hour or so before dinner, so I grab my light spinning rod, a small plastic box of spoons, and clamber down a game trail that is steep and maybe eighteen inches wide. A fall here would hurt, so I drop down and slide ever-so-gracefully on my ass to the bottom. Regrouping, I quickly attach a Johnson Silver Minnow, launch the thing into the cascade, let it sink and roil around, then begin the retrieve. A strike immediately, and I haul in a two-pound northern. Several more casts and several more pike of identical size and shape. Either that or the first fish is an enthusiastic moron. A couple of dozen casts result in a dozen or so pike that are all alike. Is this pool and river a rearing water for the northerns before they drop back down to the Slave River to play hardball with the big boys? Beats me. I climb-crawl back up the path, grabbing at thorny rose hips, exposed roots, small tree trunks to reach the top of the downsized canyon. I'm sweating, out of breath, and jazzed from my fear of heights. Die here and no one would know what happened until my ragged corpse turned up in Great Slave Lake. A pleasant thought that appeals to me a good deal more than dying from a coronary while walking along Callender Street in Livingston.

Back at camp, the potato is done and some Italian sausages cook in minutes. I slice an apple and pour orange juice. By the time I finish eating and playing with the fire it's nearing midnight. Even the sun is low, just above the tree line at this lower latitude. Looking around, I see a full moon rising. I scope out the sky with zoom binoculars, moving closer, then back out, where I can just make out a few stars struggling to be seen in what passes for night up this way during summer. An hour of this and my little brain tires. I climb into my bag in the back of the Suburban, doors and windows wide open. A few small birds chirp and chatter briefly, so I know that either sunset or dawn is approaching. Regardless, it's light enough to read at 1 A.M. Sleep comes quickly at this peaceful, out-of-the-way place.

By midmorning I'm at the South Loop of the Salt River Trail that starts out by following a grassy meadow, the northernmost grasslands of its kind in interior Canada. These dryland grasses, which normally flourish much farther south, thrive in this well-drained, south-facing, nutrient-rich soil. Historic evidence suggests that these small grasslands scattered throughout the park were once significantly larger. Climate change and wildfire suppression are possible causes for their shrinkage. Park officials are now lighting controlled burns to prevent shrubs and aspen from encroaching any further. Sunlight reflects off the thin crust of salt on the mudflats as I near Grosbeak Lake. Macabre-shaped shadows that stretch across the barren surface are cast by hundreds of granite, gneiss, and sandstone boulders scattered about this moonscape. The boulders were left behind by the retreating ice of a glacier ten thousand years ago. I rub my hand through some of the rough soil and lick the residue. There is a slight taste of salt and, more pronounced, other minerals I can't identify. I'll probably be dead shortly.

"How'd Holt die this time," friends ask.

"He ate a bunch of dirt up in the Northwest Territories and it made him sick," another responds.

"Oh," and the two acquaintances return to their quarter-table pool game and shots of bar whiskey.

After this easy five-and-a-half-mile stroll, I return to the Suburban for a lunchtime redux of yesterday. I pass on the nap and set my sights on the North Loop, this circuit only about four and one-half miles. The forested trail winds through aspen, white and black spruce, and jackpine (lodgepole pine relations up here). I can still see charred wood fragments and blackened scars on some of the remaining big trees on the hike, signs of the 1953 wildfire that raced through this country driven by high winds. On the crest of the escarpment at the south end of the trail there is a good view of Salt Pan Lake. Fossils of warmwater sea organisms are eroding out of the unstable pillars of bedrock along the escarpment edge. The layers of limestone and dolostone are from 350 to 400 million years old, a legacy of inland seas that once covered a large part of the area that is now Alberta, Saskatchewan, Manitoba, and the Northwest Territories. The limestone-gypsum sinkholes that I described earlier are a part of this process and are unique in the world.

The nearby Karstland Trail features jumbled blocks of gray limestone. Numerous small holes and cracks in the rock lead to underground dens, or hibernacula, below the frost line. Thousands of red-sided garter snakes, at their northernmost limit, hibernate in these places. The well-developed gypsum-karst is one of the reasons that Wood Buffalo National Park is designated a World Heritage site.

On the Salt Plains Trail in the same area, a sign tells me to remove my shoes and socks to avoid damaging the fragile salt-tolerant vegetation. Many of the plants are common only to marine environments, making their growth here unique. Behind an island of vegetation, there is an enormous mound of salt with a saltwater spring slicing its way toward a small creek. In the early morning hours it is not uncommon to spot bison, sandhill cranes, black bears, and semi-palmated plovers. Even the whooping cranes come here for the salt.

Back at the Suburban I work on another ale, LaBatts this time, while looking at a map of the park. One year I'm bringing my sixteen-foot expedition canoe up this way to spend a couple of weeks making the 224-kilometer trip down the Peace and Slave Rivers that glide and rush through this untouched part of the boreal forest all the way from Peace Point to Hay Camp. Late August or early September would be best—after the mosquitoes and black flies have been slapped around by frost—with all the insanely brilliant colors of autumn flashing against the green of the trees and blues of the sky. Fishing for northerns and walleye would be fun, too. My next goal is to find a woman who likes canoes, especially the paddle work up front while I steer and fly-fish from the stern, but my mind is drifting again. I realize that this small corner of the NWT and northern Alberta could occupy me for several lifetimes. Along with the unspoiled, raging wildness of the North Country, there are the overwhelming impressions, feelings, sensations that wash over me whenever I journey up this way; almost a sense of manic frustration at wanting, but not being able, to experience the whole place all at once. I must force myself to slow down, to step back, to learn patience and submission to this great land all over again, as I did in Montana so many years ago.

When I pull into Fort Smith, to say that what I find is a disappointment would be an understatement. And the cause of this dissatisfaction is mainly the result of my expectations. In my mind's eye, I had visualized a rustic settlement of a few thousand rugged souls, a mixture of South Slave Dene and modern-day trappers and voyageurs. I know this is a childish, bordering on imbecilic, visualization. The twenty-first century, the new-millenium jive con, reaches its complicated, perverse, and often obscene skeletal fingers into all but a few corners of the planet. But what I see is awful to my eyes. Housing developments, hustler tourist operations, fast-food joints, plastic motels, bad drivers, the works. I may as well be stuck at a traffic light during lunch hour in Bozeman, Montana. And the Dene themselves seem overwhelmed and outmuscled by this industrialized garbage. I see black-haired, brown-skinned youths with striking, handsome Mongol facial structures sucking down cigarettes, exchanging folding money for small foil-wrapped bindles (crack cocaine? hash? heroin?), withering inevitably towards chemically-ruined human husks, native people of all ages staggering about in various stages of intoxication or passed out on benches or on the pavement leaning against walls, eyes rolling unfocused or glazed over from too much booze, hands palsied even in unconsciousness. Maybe I caught the town and the people at an awkward moment. I don't know. Fort Simpson had modern stuff and problems, but they seem minor compared to the scope of what is happening here.

Fort Smith, or Thebacha meaning "at the foot of the rapids," is situated on a large sand and rock bluff above the Slave River rapids. The river is big here, over a mile wide. I look out upon this watery vastness as I trudge through thick, loose sand at a park on the south end of town. Native youths sit in a ragged circle on a patch of grass passing joints and bottles of wine—me, thirty-five years ago. They look at my road-bum dishevelment and laugh. Hell, I get this down in Mobridge, North Dakota. No big deal from these northland stiffs. I smile and shuffle on. I selectively filter out everything new and man-made, trying to visualize the river, these sand dunes, the warm wind, as though this were the seventeenth century. Even in a twenty-foot-long voyager canoe, the Slave River below the rapids would be fearsome, deadly with its brown water, white-flecked haystacks, standing waves, and whirlpools that cruise about the channel with the vagaries of an unseen current. I can image Dene and trappers alike coming to this stretch of fierce, broken water two hundred years ago, and approaching the next stretch of their journey with trepidation. Many died on this river over the centuries. The river here broadcasts danger and death. For hundreds of years every piece of freight, every fur bound for the north, had to be portaged fifteen-plus miles around this obstacle.

Back at the rig, I look at a brochure on the area and find a description of Fort Smith: "Today's friendly small town offers hotels, lodges, B&Bs and restaurants, a museum [museum of what? drug paraphernalia?] and a historic park." Maybe I was experiencing the town on a bad day.

Today's South Slave population is a blend of aboriginal groups—Dene, Chipewyan, Cree, and Metis. Evidence indicates that the South Slave Region has been inhabited for more than eight thousand years. The Talthheilei people, ancestors of the Slavey Dene, came here from the west on the far side of the Mackenzie Mountains, beyond the Backbone Ranges, more than twenty-five hundred years ago.

Wherever all of this originally came from, our fast-paced society has trampled it to death here in Fort Smith. I decide to blow town and spend the night at Little Buffalo River Falls again. Redux, and redux once again. That's been my mode these past two days. I don't like the modern monster that's devouring all of us. These native people dying with imagined purpose from booze and drugs remind me of me some years past, when a death of spirit was king. The loss of vision, dreams, even righteous anger, eats away at all of us. An insidious, greedy beast. That's why I'm drawn to this North Country. I can run and I can hide. I do it down south in Montana, way out on my hot, seemingly dead-dry and dusty high plains, and even in Livingston when I play invisible, which is easy if you know how to be obvious. No one fucks with you when they can see that you don't care, really don't care. But up here in the Yukon and Northwest Territories running—not facing the real truth that good country is history sooner or, hopefully, a little later—is easy and natural. So much so that I almost believe there's a bit of hope in the future for us. Just like the taste of those last drops of whiskey in a pint bottle found under the front seat of a truck. Not much, but enough to fire up the memory of something larger and temporarily better. So I run from the awful pictures I see in Fort Smith. They're still with me or I wouldn't be writing this, but for that day and the rest of the trip I was able to put that man-made misery behind me, out of sight.

As I drive past the last of the cookie-cutter structures in the last housing development, I'm reminded of a pair of statements I read in a book called *Denedah: A Dene Celebration.* The first by George Erasmus says the following: "Development has to be something that is transferring control to the people. If you look at either pipelines, or sawmills, or dams, or new mines, we are not against any of those kinds of things. What we are saying is that development should be orderly, it should be planned, it should be at the pace of the local people, it should benefit the local people."

If only these words had been heard in Fort Smith twenty years ago. The second group of words is anonymous Dene and says so much to me and all of us: "As a child, I understood how to give. I have forgotten this grace since I became civilized."

Forty minutes later, as I'm driving down the dirt road past the salt-encrusted mud flats, I realize that Fort Smith is a cautionary tale in constant motion, a distilled photograph of everything diseased in the modern age, the image all the more stark with its juxtaposition with the surrounding fierce wilderness beauty of the boreal forest.

I also recall the Declaration of Rights by the Dene of the De Cho, which states:

> "We the Dene of the De Cho have lived on our homeland according to our own laws and systems of government since time immemorial. Our homeland is comprised of the ancestral territories and waters of the De Cho Dene. We were put here by the Creator as keepers of our water and land. The Peace Treaties of 1889 and 1921 with the non-Dene recognized the inherent political rights and powers of the Deh Cho First Nation. Only sovereign peoples can make treaties with each other. Therefore our aboriginal rights and titles and oral treaties cannot be extinguished by a Euro-Canadian government. Our laws from the Creator do not allow us to cede, release, surrender or extinguish our inherent rights. The leadership of the Deh Cho upholds the teaching of the Elders as the guiding principles of Dene government now and in the future. Today we reaffirm, assert and exercise our inherent rights and powers to govern ourselves as a nation. We, the Dene Deh Cho, stand firm behind our First Nation government."

All that I have read and all that I have learned from my conversations with the Dene is that they believe, justly so, in their right to self-determination and that they will not waver from this position. They also recognize the rights of nonDene to travel and live in this land. Perhaps the Dene are the future's light for the Northwest Territories.

By the time I arrive back at last night's campsite above Little Buffalo River Falls, it is well past 10 P.M. Starting a fire in the small Weber, arranging camp, and building a modest drink doesn't take long. After a pot of water boils, I add a few potatoes to grate and fry as hash browns to complement sliced zucchini that, basted in olive oil and laid across the grill, will go quite nicely with a rib-eye steak I purchased at a grocery store in Fort Smith. The town is looney tunes, but the stores have excellent beef. I bought three of the rib eyes and some thick-sliced bacon for breakfast. The sun, blazing bloody orange, is still a few inches above the northwestern horizon. The sky in the southeast is lavender with hints of purple near the horizon. No stars are visible, but the beginnings of the leftovers from last evening's full moon are shooting up above the trees in a hurry. I can see the white disk climbing steadily. Hopefully, I'll never become used to this nearly perpetual daylight of the Far North. During each of my trips to this country, after a few days I've all but put the lack of darkness out of my mind. I enjoy the slightly psychotic freedom of moving through twenty-four hour segments as though any hour of the day could be any other.

When I begin to move back down south, heading reluctantly home, by the time I reach Grimshaw in the northern middle of Alberta night will be present for about four hours. I can make the run from the NWT that far south in one day's driving, so the shift to days and nights is abrupt, startling, and almost frightening in minor ways. Several weeks of no real darkness and the body clock and other senses become used to a routine with no parameters. I can only imagine the change to perpetual night up here, say in Yellowknife, in December and January, when sunlight is a weak afterthought that hangs limply in the sky from maybe 10:30 A.M. until about 3 P.M. Above the Arctic Circle it is just plain dark. One morning back in Livingston in late December, I checked on the weather for Inuvik with a program I have on my computer. For sunrise and sunset the word *none* appeared. Only moonrise and moonset times were given.

The swing back to rapidly growing daylight hours in late spring must wash over residents up here in a joyful, energetic, near epiphanic wave. Come winter, hundreds of miles above where I'm now sitting and watching the coals while nursing some whiskey and ice, the only real light in this dark season comes from planets, the moon, billions of stars and galaxies, and the aurora borealis.

I'll miss the show this time around, but come September on my trip to the Yukon in a few months, the lights will be in full-tilt glory. (Note: The northern lights were spectacular that trip, but as I mention in Chapter 10, I was up in the Yukon for the first time just to play, so I left my laptop and camera gear at home. No shots of the finest displays I've ever experienced. I'll not make that moronic mistake again.) Yellowknife in the NWT and Whitehorse in the Yukon are considered prime viewing areas because of a combination of latitude and cold, clear air. Both cities can observe the spectacle well over two hundred nights each year.

In Montana there are a number of evenings when I can see a green glow and even the swirling curtains of light while walking through my neighborhood, despite the ambient light. And when I've camped in the Tongue River country in southeastern Montana in late April, there have been four nights where the lights began as a green boiling cloud along the northern horizon, then ignited in sheets and curtains far over my head to the south and Wyoming. The lights would silently die down, only to repeat the orgasmic light show again and again. The only problem with these lights, which were bright enough to read by, was that they always foretold of a vicious spring snowstorm that began before first light the next morning. Bitter cold wind, rain, then slight snow, followed by a thick whiteout. The first two times, I was stranded at my camp for a few days. No problem. I had plenty of food, water, wood, and warm gear. The next two times, I piled everything in the Suburban and made for the main road and a high spot to camp before my morning evacuation. A pain in the ass, but snowbound in camp when it's cold and wet wears thin in a hurry.

I've seen the aurora borealis a number of times in the Far North beginning as early as late August on the Dempster Highway near the Arctic Circle or camped down along the Olgilvie River below Eagle Plains. The lights begin as ghostly flickerings of green sheets that curl and circle well above the horizon. By mid-September they are intense and shot through with orange, white, and a few times the most pure shade of blue or, even rarer, crimson.

Generally, the best time for viewing the aurora is around midnight. If there is a brilliant show one night you can expect others the next few evenings because prime conditions run for several days and recur on twenty-seven-day intervals. Riotous outbursts of intense, colorful displays are most common around the spring and fall equinoxes. Although the northern lights are always present, they experience a regular increase and decrease in vibrance. Over a period of five or six years, the lights build in magnitude and spill over into nontraditional auroral zones, then ebb for the same length of time. The next peak is expected in 2013 and then in 2024.

The lights are between roughly sixty and six hundred fifty miles above the earth, or about ten times the altitude of the highest jet flight. As much as 99.9 percent of the matter in the universe is in a plasma state, which is more diffuse than ordinary gases and present in man-made devices such as mercury-vapor lamps and neon lights. In the earth's outer atmosphere, magnetic field, solar atmosphere—the environment of the aurora—most matter is in a plasma state. The aurora is a glimpse into the workings of this matter. The solar wind—energy and matter blasted from our sun—traveling at up to two million miles an hour encounters our planet's magnetic field, and electrons of various elements like oxygen and nitrogen produce, respectively, green and pink and faint blue violet light. The best explanation for the phenomenon is described in Candace Savage's excellent book *Aurora.*

Many individuals, including myself, claim to hear a faint tinkling or vibrating hum when the lights are present. The only problem with this is that northern lights are not associated with any movements or vibrations that humans could hear. And since sound travels much slower than light, the aurora's visuals would not coincide with their audio displays, if there were any. So what is the source of these sounds? Possibly, radio waves produced in the upper atmosphere of auroras may trigger vibrations in piezoelectric materials within soil and rock. These naturally occurring crystals expand and contract when subjected to electromagnetic radiation. Those with sensitive hearing may be picking up on this. Or it could be a buildup of static electricity, or even a direct sensation within the ear, explaining why the sound has never been recorded.

So that's what little I know about the aurora, the namesake of this book. The northern lights are unique and magical, and I am always awed, transported somewhere unknown, by their bright presence.

For now I content myself with making one more drink before sleep, lighting a Cuban cigar I bought in Calgary—I always miss the turn for the bypass and wind up in the inner city, usually surfacing in Chinatown not far from a marvelous tobacconist—and enjoying the soft glow of the sun as it begins to disappear below the distant trees. A few birds begin singing. I throw some small pieces of pine on the coals in the grill. They smoke briefly, then ignite into bright, dancing flames. A soft breeze mixes the smoke from my cigar with that of the little fire. Serenity is a rare commodity, but I feel it drifting all through this pleasant camp. Through me.

GINNY DIERS PHOTO

FISHING THE RANCHERIA RIVER IN NORTHERN BRITISH COLUMBIA ON THE WAY TO THE YUKON.

FIVE /

RUNNING DOWN THE ROAD UP NORTH

If I keep shoving through the brush, bush, and low limbs of fir and jack pine the mosquitoes are bearable. Movement makes it difficult for the little bastards to zero in on my tender, well-seasoned-with-sweat flesh. The temperature is about seventy degrees, maybe a little warmer, and it's muggy. The evening—it's around 9 P.M—is overcast with a dense mat of slowly moving clouds stacked in ratty layers of varying densities of gray. The forest is overpowering, depressing, and eerily primeval in the gloom. The ground, even on ridges far above the clearly disturbed, brown currents of the Trout River, is damp; the moss and mud squish beneath my boots, black water oozing around each footstep. The bright greens of sunshine are muted in a charcoal twilight haze. Nothing seems friendly about the boreal forest here about two miles south of the Liard Highway. There is no rain now, but small drops of moisture drip from every edge and pointed surface of needle, leaf, stick, rough piece of bark. A billion reminders of the shower just past and the downpour coming in the next few minutes. White light slashes through the trees followed a number of seconds later by the muffled roars of thunder tearing the atmosphere to pieces a few miles west.

I stop for a drink from a plastic jug, and to wipe the sweat from my forehead and eyes. Mosquitoes descend in a biting, madly humming crowd. A quick drink, a wipe of my hand, and twenty of the things are dead. I swat at them. I flap my arms like a lunatic to drive away the mosquitoes and the few precocious blackflies moving silently around me. I move on swiftly.

"This is bullshit. Screw this!" I mutter, as the narrow game trail works higher above the river toward the falls. An instant of wind. No more. Then dead calm. Even working rapidly through the growth, breaking limbs and crashing through clinging brush, even with all this noise I'm making, the hum of insects dominates. A steady background droning.

When I am able to calmly consider the life of a mosquito, and this isn't often, I realize that the ability of this fragile creature to flourish is amazing. I've watched the buggers up close as they probed, then drilled into my skin, the rear sack swelling to the shape of a tiny red Christmas tree bulb with my blood (there have been times in the somewhat dim past when the insects must have been courting DUIs after feeding on me). The mosquitoes' legs are thin, their bodies slim and elongated, and the slightest pressure from my finger mashes them. Strong winds make flying impossible at times. During this turbulence the insects crawl along the ground, often to flowers for nectar, a chief source of food, and often the only source for males.

Short northern summers allow little time for breeding and laying eggs that produce a biomass that must be in the hundreds of pounds for each person on the planet. The female lays her eggs in the summer in a location that allows for the hatching as early as possible the next season. Immature mosquitoes—larvae then pupae—live in water, so the eggs are laid on the edges of ponds or marshy regions just above summer water levels. Snowmelt the following year raises the water to cover the eggs. The larvae take about a month to mature and can grow in temperatures barely above freezing. The females often have trouble finding vertebrate animals as a source of blood to nourish their eggs; typically, they must have a blood meal before they can lay eggs. This can be from amphibians, birds, reptiles, and mammals, including me. Arctic species have adapted to the point where they can lay at least a few eggs to preserve the species autogenously, meaning they rely on food reserves stored as larvae. But blood ensures more and usually healthier eggs. The young, after emerging from water, head for nearby flowers, such as the arctic dryad, for food, shelter, and a place to dry themselves in the sun. Some other flowers they like are the purple cress (which seems more pink to my eyes), the light-blue alpine forget-me-nots, and the brilliantly yellow golden draba that brightens the ground in oval-shaped, ground-hugging bunches.

Mosquitoes are one of the key plant pollinators in the north. Masses of pollen grains, like those accumulated from bog orchids in the low arctic, are carried from flower to flower on the mosquitoes' heads. Without the mosquito, many plants would cease to exist. They are prey for yellowjackets that pounce on them, then crush the bodies for easy carrying back to their underground nests to feed their own young.

Below the 70th parallel, blackflies rival mosquitoes in terms of numbers. In temperate latitudes females must have a blood meal before developing eggs that they attach to rocks in running water. But as you move farther north the insects need no nourishment at all after their larval stage. Their mouth parts have become useless through evolution. In the high arctic, this streamlined process has advanced to the point where there are no males and the females reproduce parthenogenetically, frequently laying their eggs as soon as they emerge from the water. In some cases the adult insect never emerges from the pupa. Instead the eggs develop inside the pupa and are liberated into the water when the pupa dies and disintegrates.

Although mosquitoes and blackflies are nuisances in the north country, their straightforward bloodsucking attacks seem quite civilized when compared with two parasites that caribou must deal with.

Caribou warble flies resemble bumblebees with their dense fur of black, orange, and yellow stripes, but warbles are disgusting creatures. They lay their eggs in the caribou's fur, normally on the belly or legs. When the larvae hatch, they burrow into the animal, tunneling inside until they are just under the skin, fairly near the spine. In early fall, the maggots cut breathing holes through the skin of the caribou's back and remain until they develop. A single animal may be infested with two thousand maggots that seriously weaken the caribou by feeding off its flesh. The breathing holes become infected and abscessed. Late the next spring, when they are about one centimeter long, they emerge through the breathing holes, drop to the ground, and begin the process all over again.

Bad as these things are, the caribou nose bot is worse. It is a large, hairy fly that deposits its young in the caribou's nostrils. The young are live, active maggots that migrate through the animal's nasal passages and collect at the opening of its throat, where they grow all winter. Come spring, the dense mass of maggots forms a lump in the caribou's throat, often obstructing its breathing. But enough of this insect frivolity.

I had decided on this hike upriver to the falls after dinner because I didn't feel like fighting the bugs around the fire or crawling defeated into my tent, and I wanted some exercise after a number of hours behind the wheel. So I opted for this walk and perhaps some fishing below the falls. A fly rod, some streamers, a cigar, and a small flask of Canadian whiskey sounded like a pleasant alternative to hanging around camp at Samba Deh Falls Park—a very well run and maintained operation in the heart of the forest just off the Liard Highway. I've camped here a number of times. Hot showers, split wood, clean sites, few people, and the Slavey Dene who manage the place are friendly and helpful. Generous with their time, energy, and spirit. An older woman, the one with walnut-colored skin wrinkled by years of real living, thinks I'm funny or nuts or both. She laughs and smiles, showing teeth yellowed from years of smoking cigarettes, at everything I say.

"Not many people on the road these days," I offer.

Laughter.

"Is there wood at the campsite?"

"My husband will bring you some soon," and I thought she was going to collapse from the humor of it all. "Enjoy your stay here with us. See you in the morning," and she went out through the door of the log frame office. I could hear her chuckling all the way across the gravel lot to her home. I started laughing myself, at what, I had no idea. It felt good to be back here. The more I get to know these people, the more I like their honesty, their straightforward approach to living, their humor and warmth that seems only mildly tempered by the need for the harsh pragmatism needed to survive in the Northwest Territories. I like it here, but a couple of weeks each summer are hell on wheels with the mosquitoes. And with exquisite timing I nailed the peak activity this time around. As for the fishing, maybe there would be some moving air generated by the falling water and I could cast my large streamers in some semblance of peace, at least before I was forced back into the trees to shelter from the short-lived thunderstorms that have been cruising over this country for the past few days, beginning in early evening and dying away around 2 A.M They'd breeze in from the west, rock the trees, shatter the silence, light up the woods, then move on, leaving everything dripping and peaceful for an hour, before another squall line hammered through on its way east.

This chapter is about doing the road from my camp here at Trout River all the way west and north to Dawson City, Yukon, about fourteen hundred miles, which may not seem like much when cruising along in South Dakota or Montana, but things are different up here.

The Liard Highway begins about twenty miles south of Hay River at Enterprise and runs pretty much due west until Nahanni

Butte, then south to Highway 97 and Fort Nelson, about a four-hundred-fifty-mile spin through some wild, thick forest—the bush. My former companion, Ginny Diers, hated this part of the north. She became claustrophobic and muttered over and over, "Nothing but damn trees. I can't see anything." But I love this forest—the fact that these thousands and thousands of square miles are uncut and sparsely (this is a generous assessment) inhabited. The closeness, the woodland bison, black bears, woodland caribou, eagles, the fish in the streams, the rivers that flow darkly through the ancient woods and disappear in a flash around an overgrown bend, the Dene—this is all good stuff for me. I feel free, alive in this country. These rivers that run mysteriously every few miles remind me of images from Joseph Conrad's *Heart of Darkness.* The Liard Highway is like all of the land I wander through up here—immense, filled with unimagined, insane possibilities. Like the Dempster Highway in the Yukon or the country around Wrigley or over by Dawson City, I say, "I could spend a bunch of lifetimes here." And when I finish my stay at Samba Deh early tomorrow morning, I'll head down the road toward Nahanni Butte, then Fort Liard, and finally Fort Nelson and a motel room before spinning west over countless ridges of ripped up mountains and into the Yukon. The road. I live for the road. Up north the road is like no other—beautiful, wild, crazy, dangerous, frightening in places—an adventure the first time on any given stretch. And just as fresh and mysterious on the fifth run.

Finally, my hike takes me down a series of switchbacks worn into the sandstone that lead to about one hundred feet below the base of the thirty-foot falls. The river is a couple hundred yards wide here. The sound of the crashing, boiling water is deafening. Spray whips over me propelled by whirling wind generated by the tumultuous creamy brown water which is worked into a froth that resembles a gigantic root-beer float with white foam of waves and whirlpools washing up on the rocky banks. My friends the mosquitoes are still around, but in slightly lesser, sodden numbers.

A large yellow stonefly nymph, on a sink-tip line with a couple of split shot at its head, is sidearm catapulted up into the maelstrom, allowed to spin and sink, then drag along the bottom, the line bellying out ahead of it in the faster surface currents. I strip the slack and begin to haul in line for another delightful, fun-filled cast that I'm convinced will be as futile as this one, but the nymph is snagged. Probably on rocks. I reef back for the hell of it and the entire mess begins to scissor through the water downstream. The bank is mainly a smooth shelf of stone sloping into the Trout River, so following whatever is on the other end of the line is simple. After clattering across the shelf, kicking broken pieces of stone along the way, I'd gathered in about half of the line. The fish stops, then swings back and forth before giving up and coming to shore with steady pressure. A northern pike. Maybe ten pounds. What could this fish have found of interest in a #6 nymph. The fact that the pike even saw the pattern is amazing. I twist the hook free, carefully, from its niche in the upper jaw near rows of mean teeth that curve slightly backward. The northern slides backward into the current, drifts sideways for a few yards, then swishes its tail and vanishes. The stonefly is shredded, as is what's left of the leader. It's amazing that the fish took the nymph, and equally amazing that the leader held.

Then all hell breaks loose again, this time from above, as lightning, thunder, riotous gusts of wind, and thick sheets of rain blast down. The other side of the river is lost from view. The forest provides scant relief, though, at least psychologically, crouching down like a turtle in a narrow creek bed seems safer than remaining exposed to the weather alongside the river while waving nine feet of graphite. Lightning crackles directly above as everything darkens with the lowering, rolling clouds that spin past just overhead like an airborne steamroller. The rain becomes a cloudburst. Tops of trees snap and crash to the ground. Scared to death but high on the charge of the storm and still cruising on the surprise of the northern, I uncork my water bottle and take a hit and wait things out.

The weather moves on as suddenly as it approached unnoticed, while I was playing the pike. Thunder rattles and fades quickly to the east as it does in these flurries. I step from the perceived shelter of the woods, along with my buddies the mosquitoes, cast some more without success, retrace my steps up the bank to the trail, dogtrot back downhill through the swarming bugs, while stumbling over exposed rocks and roots, reach camp, wing everything into the back of the Suburban, and disappear into the tent. I'm through. Done. Finished until morning. My watch says midnight under the scrutiny of my flashlight's beam in the overcast dimness of dusk. Lightning, then thunder herald another storm. I climb into my sleeping bag and enjoy the show before fading into oblivion.

At 6 A.M, the morning is bright, clear, and cool in the low forties. A high pressure ridge has arrived. I have yogurt, orange juice, a banana, summer sausage, cups of black coffee, and a few smokes. I love my cigarettes, and they've loved me to death all these mad years. Even from the distance of several months without a cigarette, I miss the morning Marlboros with the coffee. So many things in life that I crave at times—booze, cigs, women, weird drugs, lawlessness—they all seem to have my ill health in their collective mind. Breaking camp takes a few minutes, then I'm off around the camp loop waving goodbye to the old Dene woman. Hanging a left on the Liard Highway, I set sight for Nahanni Butte (or *Tthenaago*, meaning "strong rock") turnoff about two hundred forty kilometers to the west. The day just keeps growing clearer and brighter. The sky is without clouds and is a shade of pure blue that is without peer. Looking into the blueness makes my eyes feel pleasantly like they do when sunlight reflects off a trout stream on a July afternoon in Montana.

The time passes quickly, and I'm at the Liard River after coursing along a road that gradually narrows and grows rougher. Nahanni Butte has been playing hide-and-seek across the river for over an hour, large mounds of purple and lavender and gray rock holding forth against the blue sky in the hot sunlight. The Dene community offers an inn and a general store and water taxis to Blackstone Territorial Park. I won't be crossing the Liard River this time around to wander up into South Nahanni River country. This is something I plan to do when both my kids are in college. Several months on my own and, hopefully, mostly away from the too many tourist float day-trips to the falls of the South Nahanni and back. I became hooked on this place reading R. M. Patterson's *Dangerous River* a couple of years back and I want to see the beginnings of this fabulous country from the banks of the Liard River. Patterson was not above exaggerating his experiences or writing them in a way that fit his image of himself, but we all do this to some extent during the course of our confused lives. The following is a small sample of what Patterson has to say about the South Nahanni country:

> *I climbed quickly up the creek in the sunshine, mist and rain, and at 3,000 feet above the Nahanni I came to the last of the trees. . . . The creek valley ran on up into the bald hills and the blue sky, walled in by gray screes and grassy, rock-strewn hillsides running up to naked rimrock . . . fluttering around the snowdrifts, flashing in the sun, were gaily coloured butterflies—sulphurs and the gaudy black-white-and-reds. I began to climb and at 4,000 feet I came over the rim of the valley and on to the plateau, the grazing lands of the wild white sheep. Miles and miles of close cropped alpine turf, still bright with flowers . . . streaked with beds of gravel in which quartz crystals flashed like diamonds, rent with creek canyons and deep valleys out of which came the noise of water and the boiling cloud vapours—God, there was no end to it and a man could go on for ever over the great, green upland country that lay before me with the sunlight and the cloud shadows and the wind sweeping over it.*

Even from down along the Liard River, I could see well into Patterson's South Nahanni paradise. I could feel the absolute free power of the place still intact even in this modern world, the energy drifting down from the high country and rolling through the forest and across the river. If we do indeed get the opportunity to come back to life again, to be reborn, to reincarnate, make my next trip up this way in the Far North as it was one hundred years ago. Some of those "sulphurs" that Patterson mentioned are grouped on the fringes of a moist track in the road, their bright yellow wings slowly opening and closing. The movement brings a small patch of dirt to vibrant life. I keep looking, then realize it's time for lunch, and then more driving. I've still got two hundred miles of rough road and one terrifying bridge to go before a motel room, a hot shower, a T-bone steak cooked rare, cable television, and a few belts of whiskey greet me in Fort Nelson. I'll have to sacrifice so much of this perceived modern luxury when next I come back to life one hundred years ago. Such is life, lives, living.

By now I'm heading almost dead south with the wide Liard on my right, to the west. The river's glass surface glistens largely silver with splashes of green, blue, and passing white of afternoon cumulous clouds. Fort Liard (*Echaot'je Kue*, or "people of the land of giants place") began as a trading post. Many of the buildings are constructed with thick logs cut from trees that grow to well over one hundred feet due largely to the warm Pacific air that holds in the valley. As I pull into town, by dropping down a hill off the highway, I pass through a canopy of trees, then along a residential street that swings up a brief rise to a gas station, general store, trading post, and a trailer turned restaurant. A similar structure nearby offers lodging for travelers and oil and gas exploration workers. (I remember having a cheeseburger and a warm milkshake in the place a couple of years ago before heading down the road.) I make a quick tour of the village to refresh my memory, then it's back to the main road, now turned greasy, muddy slop with the coming and quick going of a predictable rain storm. I slip and slide for about twenty-five miles to the British Columbia border. Now the road is hard and dusty. I pound down the empty stretch at fifty miles an hour. The wooden bridge that crosses the Nelson River is near. The forest is mainly birch with clean white bark marked with black rough areas. All of the trees are healthy and capped with large green leaves that form a towering canopy that filters the sunlight and adds a hint of green to the light.

Two huge trucks power by with blaring engine whine, air brake releases, exhaust rattling, and a gagging stream of dust that hangs over the road like a shroud for a couple of minutes. I pull over and wait. The bridge is less than two miles away. My stomach churns. The wooden sucker is one-lane without ostentatious amenities, such as guardrails or warning lights, that might possibly hint at approaching semis. It was built by our army during the Second World War, when the Alaska Highway was under construction. This is a bit of no-frills military handiwork that rivals any amusement park ride I've ever been on. There aren't any guarantees of safety or survival on this northern British Columbia drive. The damned thing hangs above the water more then one hundred feet high and a quarter-mile long. Even the people who live up here respect and fear the bridge. Whenever I mention it to someone, they look at me with wide, understanding eyes and shake their heads, often saying, "She's a bitch" or "That's a bad one." What the hell? I'm into my reincarnation delusion now. If I die, I'll be back here that much sooner in a time frame I want. Bring the wooden beast on! I wind around a couple of sweeping turns and drop down to the high-bank approach to the river. The first time across this thing was with Ginny some summers back. She hid on the floor and prayed. I fired up an unfiltered Camel, left the thing in my mouth like Robert Mitchum in the movie *Thunder Road,* and roared across the bridge as fast as I dared—thirty-five miles an hour—staring straight down the hood directly in front of me. I didn't breath the entire time, and I never even thought about glancing at the river so far below.

This time I stop on the side of the road about thirty feet from the bridge. I get out and look down at the green river, then across the bridge and into the trees scanning for telltale signs of road dust that would indicate approaching tankers and death (they don't, won't, and can't stop). No sign. Nor is there any sound of an approaching rig. I fire up a smoke, climb in the Suburban and gun across the bridge, wooden ties creaking and pinching beneath the tires, the eight-by-eight posts that pass for protection on the sides looking like twigs. A little more than halfway across, I look up and see clouds of dust rising up and through the trees at the approach turn on the far side.

"Shit!"

Flooring the Suburban, I careen across the bridge climbing above forty-five miles an hour, which feels like one hundred twenty, and whip to the dirt slope on the right as soon as the front tires leave the bridge. I clatter down to a flat area as a tanker as large as the Queen Elizabeth screams past, horns roaring, lights blazing, wheels churning, dust clouds boiling. Damn. I got me a north country trucker song staring me right in the eyes. Just missed winding up a mangled, crunched pile of flying debris destined for the turbid waters of the Nelson River. Dealing with big rigs is the main attraction, even more so than the weather, where driving is concerned up here. Truckers own the road. That's an accepted given.

"Never again," I say as I stagger out of the car and back to the cooler for a cold ale. The icy liquid and the accompanying cigarette taste intense, really good. I have one more of each and repeat, "Never again, Holt. Never again." Next time I'd drop back down the Mackenzie Highway through northern Alberta to Dawson Creek and up to Fort Nelson through Fort St. John, Toad River, and the rest of northeastern British Columbia. So I give up a few days in the detouring process. This bridge was a wilderness, man-made death trap waiting for fools like me.

The remaining forty-odd miles into Fort Nelson is a walk in the park. I hit Highway 97 in a cloud of dust, turn right, and zip into town at one hundred twenty kilometers an hour. I grab a room at a motel called the Bluebell or Huckleberry or something and haul a few things inside—cooler, knapsack, *Winter in the Blood,* a novel by James Welch. I shower, then gas up across the street at a Shell station, buy groceries nearby, and zip up a side road to a provincial liquor store for a bit of whiskey and wine for the journey to Dawson City. The town isn't big and everything is close in and easy to find, especially if you've been through the place a few times before. I park in front of a restaurant, walk in, and order the biggest steak they have. I nail the salad bar, have a couple of Canadians on ice (not as twisted as this may initially sound), pay, walk out, march back to the room, build a real drink, turn on the tube, and watch the Cubs blow an eight-to-one lead to the Giants in one inning. Three errors, a passed ball, a hit batter, and a grandslam are part of the festivities. The modern life and all its wonders. You gotta love it.

By nine the next clear-blue morning, I am at the summit of the first range of mountains I will cross today on my way to the Yukon. This part of the Alaska Highway—about forty miles west of Fort Nelson—is excellent, paved and wide with concrete guardrails. I pull over at a spot on the edge of the road. Mountains stretch for fifty to one hundred miles to the west and south. Behind me the foothills and broken country that lead to Alberta roll away in blue green drifting to purple haze. Rock and timbered peaks of this range cover the north. I drive on, dropping down into a forested valley that pinches in on the road. Aside from the highway, there is no sign of humans from this vantage point.

Log cabins are scattered along the narrowed, now broken-surfaced road. One of the structures, or rather a group of old buildings, is a commercial venture selling superb cinnamon rolls. I buy five and eat three, along with orange juice, for brunch, while sitting on an old table next to a small stream. The rolls are still warm, the dough dense but airy at the same time. All of them are covered in rich frosting. Clearly this is one more addiction I'm staring down the barrel of.

Rapidly soaring on a sugar rush, I motor on and the road soon climbs again toward Summit Lake in Stone Mountain Provincial Park. There is little traffic and the road is like any mountain road winding through forest and scree; that is, until I pass beyond the summit. Then the way clings to the side of an ochre cliff as it narrowly winds down into a broad alluvial valley. To my left, the south, enormous cuts in the mountains tear down to this rock- and boulder-jumbled floor. Spring runoff is over. I can only imagine the vast torrents that carved the openings that slice for miles into the hard rock of the mountains and finally twist out of view. A motor home with Alberta plates creeps up the highway on the outside. The driver is leaning in toward me as is the woman passenger, who is clearly terrified. Groups of wild mountain sheep are licking at salt deposits all along the road. They don't bother looking up or moving much at my approach. The Toad River is cloudy sapphire because the water is laced with large amounts of glacial flow. The road continues steeply and crookedly down to the river and into a dense forest of pine, birch, and alder choking the banks of tiny tributary creeks and streams. I spot isolated woodland caribou; their coats are gray, silver, brown going toward black; their snouts are jet-black. They stare at me with dark eyes, motionless. Enormous walls of granite distorted by forces beyond my imagination into frozen ripples, serrations, and waves tower thousands of feet above me. I come around a sharp bend, just missing a trio of motor homes going in the opposite direction and hogging the centerline. The emerald sapphire Toad River rushes over slate gray rock and gravel on my right, the force of the current—thick ribbons of water that slip by in serpentine groups of standing waves—has torn through the bedrock leaving timbered, narrow islands in midstream.

Soon I cross a steel girdered bridge over the river, which flows down over braided seams of stone that stretch far back into the

GINNY DIERS PHOTO

ALONG THE YUKON RIVERFRONT IN DAWSON CITY.

mountains guarding the southwest horizon. The ice- and snow-covered peaks slide in and out of rainstorms that appear as dark purple curtains that brighten to yellow silver where the sun hides, then fade back to deep dark with thick white streams of rain trailing beneath. The road immediately starts to climb back up into the mountains. Near the top I pull over for the view and a smoke. Blackflies are around and nearly invisible, but their burning bites are ample announcement of their presence.

I look back on the country I've just climbed through. Sheer rock walls drop down to tree lines of dense forest and overhangs draped in mats of moss. The river, side streams, and creeks splash and tumble quickly downhill in cloudy shades of blue. Sunlight spotlights a section of the highway far below, where a pickup-camper rig plods along looking like a toy seen from a jet's window. Narrow valleys carved through millions of years of rock arc sharply out of view. The sound of wind in several different pitches varied by topography reaches me. The air smells of pine, snow, and cold rock. The remaining miles to Muncho Lake wind through more of these mountains, then along vast washes of boulders, rocks, and gray gravels that pour out of gaps in the mountains and frequently spill over onto the pavement before continuing down to the large, deep lake that is flanked by timbered then barefaced mountains on the western shore. A series of motionless rivers of rock.

I stop briefly at a store and gas station and pick up a loaf of just-baked bread made by a guy who has been doing this special work ever since I've been passing this way. He's sitting outside on top of a picnic table, a handrolled cigarette held between two long fingers. He recognizes the Suburban, the Montana plates, then me. He waves. I wave. That says it all between us. I follow my nose along the growing scent of baking and pass through an old screen door into a kitchen/counter/table area awash in the aroma of new bread. A doughy woman smiles, then wraps a loaf I point to. I pay for bread and emerge carrying the wrapped-in-paper loaf in my hands. The baker smiles. I shrug and take off down the road. There is an expensive lodge here, but I blow off its obvious ostentation. About a mile farther on is an old, rustic, slightly battered joint that is both a restaurant and bar, and a motel. I can top off my gas tank here in the morning, too. I pull in and get the room I always get just down the hill; the one that leaks a little over the small bed in the main area; the one with the curtained windows overlooking the lake. It suits me fine. I bend down and twist a knob that fires the ancient propane heater that ignites in an easy "whoosh." The metal begins to tick as it expands in the heat. On the table is a paperback copy of Robert Ludlum's *The Osterman Weekend.* I unload, then walk up to the restaurant. There are a few local families—parents, kids of all ages, grandparents—and several older tourists hunched around a table by the counter. Two motor homes out front with Washington plates must be theirs. The air outside is cold with the passing of a storm, but the fire from a brick fireplace throws plenty of warm, dry air my way. A crazy, old, wrinkled Chinese woman comes up to take my order. She's always been up this way, too.

"Double cheeseburger and double fries and two double whiskeys," I say.

"I remember you," she says with crinkled eyes and a cackle. "Double on everything. Especially the whiskey. Welcome. Welcome."

I watch her shuffle down some steps, her black slippers making "shushing" sounds on the wood plank floor. She disappears through one door and then, seemingly in an instant, returns coming out another door with my drinks, one in each hand. She places them in front of me.

"Double on everything," and she's off to another table.

I like places like this. God! I haven't been here in nearly a year, but I'm remembered. This far from home, this far up north by myself, such casual recognition feels as welcome in my stomach as the cheap whiskey I'm sipping right now. I look out the window and watch large snowflakes tumble down. My food arrives. I take my time eating and finishing my drinks, before leaving enough pretty Canadian paper money for payment and a tip. My Chinese lady is back in the kitchen. I hear her laughing. I shove through the entrance door, and walk past my room down to the lake that is at once sparkling in the shafts of evening sunlight and glowering in white-capped bands of cloud. The air is cooler still. The waves wash loudly upon the sand and gravel shore. A dead trout, white from exposure, drifts back and forth in the eternal wave action. I'm alone here, and I look forward to the country I'll be getting into tomorrow. I go back to my room, shower, climb into bed, and continue reading James Welch's good book.

The morning is foggy. After a breakfast of ham, eggs, hash browns, orange juice, and coffee, it is still foggy—thick crud that strangles the air and drips from the roof of the café, car bumpers, gas pumps, and trees. I fill up and start down the road that I know is a good one as long as I don't stray too close to the edges and drop-offs. I can see perhaps three car lengths ahead. The trees on the road edges are ghosts with no color or definition. There are a few hairpin curves ahead that no one takes quickly even on good days, so I keep the Suburban at thirty miles an hour with my brights on, the wipers banging back and forth, the defrost fan humming away. I slip on some John Coltrane recorded over forty years ago in Stockholm; perfect music that keeps my head in the concentration game of moving through fog without becoming hypnotized. Magic movement by the jazzman up and down chromatic scales, shedding auditory spectrums of color throughout the monotone morning. Soft yellow glows gain intensity, then turn into headlights of semis, an old Chevy, a gaggle of ubiquitous motor homes, a pickup. They approach in silence, then pass in a wet hiss of tires before being swallowed by the fog as if they never existed. I come around a tight turn, then start uphill, and face still more tight curves before the road becomes a wide two-lane that has dreams of being four lanes. I know where I am now.

The Liard River Valley is off to my right, on the north, and down several hundred feet. The channel the river has cut over the eons is miles wide and hundreds of feet deep. If I could see them, the banks would be a mixture of pines, deciduous trees, rock outcrops, and exposed brown earth. The river would be slipping around midstream gravel bars now that runoff is, for the most part, over. Soon I'll be dropping down again into another valley, this time a wild, scary scenario in a state of constant change as the huge Liard churns down to the Mackenzie River at Fort Simpson, and a ratty, crumbling, narrow cement highway bumps and bucks toward Watson Lake.

I cross a large iron bridge. The Suburban's tires buzz on the metal surface, and then I'm at Liard Hot Springs, a dismal, slightly weird, anomalously tight-assed spot on the Far North map. The hotel here is new, modern, and uncomfortable. The help is standoffish.

When I check in they look at me as though I am beneath their lofty standards, which I may be, but money is money. The restaurant is "plasticville" with no bar, just greasy food and warm milkshakes. My room is large with a nice window. The beds are instruments of metal-spring torture, but the bathroom is clean. I put on a pair of cut-offs, drive over to the parking lot for the hot springs. A couple of Canadian tour busses and quite a few private vehicles are parked here. The first spring is filled with grandparents, beleaguered parents, teenaged malcontents, and little kids. There are stone benches. The water is blue and very clear. There is lots of noise. Oh boy! I follow a sign and a boardwalk over a swampy, steaming flat, then up into cedars for a quarter-mile, eventually coming to the upper spring. No people. No noise except for the brewing-coffee sounds of hot, bubbling gray water. The sulfur smell is quite strong. I walk around to the far end, take off my T-shirt and tennis shoes, and step down a slippery wood ladder into the turbid soup. The water is warm flirting with hot, and I ease myself down to a rung that allows my head to remain above the surface. I have the place to myself and am soon in a somnambulant state, like a mud turtle floating in a shallow pond beneath a hot sun.

The sound of footsteps, bare feet I notice, rally my senses. A young lad in his early twenties strolls across the far boardwalk, obviously quite pleased with his trim physique. He is carrying a pair of beach towels, which he spreads out with great care and ostentation. Then he steps back and stands with his arms crossed and his legs spread like a roman warrior. His gaze is fixed on the spot where the trail emerges from the trees. In a few seconds I hear more bare feet, then a stately princess appears wearing a colorful one-piece bathing suit. She has immaculate, short black hair and perfect alabaster skin. She walks toward her guardian as if she is a finalist in the Miss Universe Contest, though I suspect mortal doings of that nature are beneath her dignity. She comes to the lad. They embrace passionately, then artfully descend another ladder about thirty feet from me. I rise and quietly go to my pack and grab a Molson and a smoke, then oh so subtly slip and crash on the ladder's third rung, sending waves racing toward the mythic couple, who interrupt their soft-porn display long enough to flash me the coldest of dismissive glances. I resettle myself, beer and cigarette intact (one learns a few modest tricks over the course of an often misspent life). The pair's silent-movie love making continues. I work on my smoke and the beer.

"Blaaarrrp!" Oops! I commit a social faux pas of immense magnitude—"Molsonus belchis interruptus." The two separate, and stiffly climb the ladder. The young lad gently wraps his princess in a towel. She strides with rigid dignity off into the woods and down the boardwalk. The lad follows. I don't exist. I am less than loathsome scum. I finish my beer, go for another and a smoke. I have this percolating pool to myself again. I enjoy my vulgar, ill-bred solitude for a long time in the late-running day. By the time I clumsily stroll back down the boardwalk, the sun is closing in on the horizon, the lower-pool crowds are long gone, and the parking lot is empty.

This evening I dine in my room on bread, sausage, cheese, orange juice, Almond Joys, and Chips Ahoy. I finish Welch's book, fight the surly bedspring for four hours, then pile into the Suburban for a 5 A.M start on the four hundred fifty miles, give or take, to near Whitehorse.

The stretch of road that runs along the north bank of the Liard River scares the hell out of me. It is narrow, pinched in, and dangerous. The road's concrete sections are separated, and the pavement is chipped and cracked. The truckers give no quarter to the small people such as myself. They pile drive up on my ass, massive chrome grills obliterating any rear view, then whip out in the oncoming lane with loud diesel wailings and much black exhaust. They then cut back so tightly, heavy loads swaying, that I frequently have to hit the brakes to avoid being sideswiped. Oncoming traffic must slow down and edge over. There is no shoulder, only a steep drop into the river. Why most of the truckers are murderously rude on this stretch eludes me, but they are, and I've learned to deal with it, to drive my mirrors, and to give them all the room I can when I see one of their kind bearing down on me.

The Liard River pushes through all of this, exposing its powerful personality when it surges in creamy jade torrents against midstream boulder obstructions as big as warehouses. Stopping at a pullover—one of the few—I walk down to the river and can feel its force, its strength. The river tugs at me, and I feel a perverse desire to jump in similar to the crazed need to leap off vertiginous places like dams or the exposed observation platform on the Sears Tower. I lean back and stumble my way to the Suburban.

Where the highway climbs far above the flow, the views to the forests and distant mountains of the west are staggering. These are the initial vistas that say that the land is shifting from north to Arctic north. The sky has a high, pale white sheen that radiates with an unreal frequency. The sense of new country fades with each dip down into the forest, but I know I'm closing in on the Yukon. Even from hundreds of feet above it, the Liard looks mighty impressive. All of the rivers up here send out a message of undisciplined power. The Liard is a combination of several serious rivers including the Dease running out of the Cassair Mountains in the west, the Kechika to the south, and the Frances and Hyland Rivers coming down from the Logan Mountains in the north. Each of them is larger than the Yellowstone River at Billings, Montana. Many of us, myself included initially, think of the Far North as a flat and barren—as a rock—snow- and ice-covered desert. Nothing could be further from reality. Mountain range after mountain range contribute snowmelt and also suck moisture from both Pacific and Arctic weather systems. Forests are lush. Undergrowth is thick. I could fish every day of my life for a thousand years and not touch more than 10 percent of the water up this way.

I battle through this bad stretch of highway and its chaotic traffic, all of it made even more difficult by a series of rainstorms. By the time I limp through the wayside towns of Coal River and Fireside, I am ready for a snack. The upcoming dirt and gravel section of under-construction highway will be a relief with its wide roadbed and much slower speeds. Semis roaring by at eighty miles an hour on the previous stretch make one appreciate the slower-paced aspects of life.

The road passes briefly into the Yukon, then makes a quick jog back down into British Columbia. It is either dusty or muddy, depending on how many minutes have gone by since the last shower. Heavy graders, big-time dump trucks, lots of workers, all them bustling to make as much progress on this nearly sixty-year-old road as the short warm season allows. The road was slammed through the forest, mountains, and swamps during World War II amid fears that the Japanese were soon to invade Alaska. In the 1940s, the road was a muddy quagmire or a skinny rock lane cut on the edge of tall cliffs. Lots of people died trying to drive along it over the early years. At one roadside stop, drinkers placed bets on whether truck drivers going downhill would survive. Going uphill was safer but an iffy proposition all the same. The Alaska Highway is now mostly paved, and the dirt stretches are in good shape. Gone are the days of ten tires blown to pieces on rough roads and no service stations or cafés for what seemed like forever.

From its beginning in 1942, the road took just eight months and twelve days to complete. Nearly one hundred men died during the construction, most from exposure, but a number of D-8 Caterpillar operators were killed by falling limbs and tree trunks. A fair amount of heavy machinery sank up to exhaust stacks in the muskeg after initial attempts to remove the muck failed. Some of the equipment could not be retrieved. Eventually, roads made of lengthwise and crosswise timbers covered with dirt solved the muskeg problem. Hot machinery left on the permafrost melted the ground and sank—the only way to deal with permafrost was to avoid crossing the frozen ground whenever possible. Deeply embedded ice made sinking posts along river banks for bridges difficult. Wrapping these posts in tarpaper solved this problem due to greatly increased friction from the wrapping. The Army's 97th Engineering Division was an all-black unit that received the dregs of the machinery and the worst country to hack through to make the road, but they accomplished nearly as much as any of the all-white engineering units. Members of the 97th would often run midnight raids on the whites' machinery, work like hell through the night, return the gear, and erect signs saying essentially "Think what we could do if we had the right equipment." The road was more than sixteen hundred miles long when completed in 1943, but constant improvements and straightening have dropped this figure to about fifteen hundred miles. An annual budget over $25 million is divided equally between maintenance and improvements. The number of tourists heading toward Whitehorse, then west and north to Alaska on the road originally called the Alcan, grows some each year. Herds of clumsy, sluggish camping rigs and motor homes bearing names like Prowler, Intruder, and Land Yacht clog the highway and account for most of the traffic from mid-June through mid-September. I'll lose all but a taste of this nonsense when I cut north at the territorial capital of Whitehorse alongside the Yukon River. Then I'll be on the Klondike Highway.

After a couple of hours of stops and starts necessitated by road equipment and blasting, I hit pavement again. I cross a much smaller section of the Liard River and within minutes enter the city limits of Watson Lake, though nothing resembling a town appears for five or six more miles. The road is now four lanes divided by an empty boulevard. Power poles, light posts, and business signs touting restaurants, motels, banks, and other roadside attractions are abundant—burgers, gas, food, booze, boating, tourist information, a modest ski hill, a rustic resort, a planetarium. Civilization approaches.

The thick forest is all around, though occasional glimpses of hills leading to rounded mountains peek through cuts in the trees. Rivers, streams, lakes, and ponds are everywhere, as are a few moose and black bears. Deer and elk, especially elk, are not as common up this way as they are in the Lower-48. There are far more Stone sheep—about 3,000—plus 19,000 Dall sheep. There are just 500 deer and 100 elk, 80 musk ox, 7,000 grizzlies, 280,000 caribou, 10,000 black bear, 55,000 moose, 4,500 wolves, 230 woodland bison, 2,000 mountain goats, and a mere 50 arctic fox. These are figures I gleaned from a Yukon tourist brochure. A number of people I spoke with, including a territorial biologist, said that the brochure figure for grizzlies is quite low, maybe by as much as half. This would translate into a grizzly for every two humans in the Yukon. With the population of humans slowly declining, there is the delightful possibility that one day there may be more griz than people.

On past trips, I've spent several nights at a couple of the motels in Watson Lake. The rooms were fine. The televisions work. I watched the third round of the British Open one year, and back-to-back episodes of *Dynasty* another. It was cold, with a thick, driving mixture of sleet and rain both nights. The food in the restaurants was fine. Good pizza. Pizza? The service workers were mostly pleasant. The show at the planetarium was vaguely diverting, though mediocre and a much too obvious area-tourist pitch. The people at the travel center were fine and helpful. And there were lots of brochures. The main claim to fame, the Sign Forest with more than fifty thousand license plates, mileage indicators, and street signs from all over the world—Vegas, Germany, South Korea, New Zealand, and Belle Plaine, Minnesota—was curious and interesting. It was started by a GI lonesome for home during the building of the highway and mushroomed from there. The modern bank is fine—its money spends and the ATM works.

But I would be remiss and most unfair if I failed to point out the vastly underappreciated highlight of Watson Lake—a very weird, surreal grocery store. Well, not the store itself but the mad soul who runs the place, who is always in the back hacking pieces of meat into smaller pieces with an enormous cleaver. Now I realize that this is what butchers do, but this individual plies his rough trade to very loud—I mean *LOUD*—music recordings smuggled into the country at, no doubt, great risk and expense. The stuff seems to be a hybrid mixture of Tibetan-Haitian-Zimbabwean temple music performed by musicians (and this seems to be a bit of a stretch) who are thoroughly wired on what is possibly a combination of mescaline, carbolic acid, and Ex-Lax. Grating, nerve-wracking, superbly annoying, even bone-chilling in a synaptic way. Yeah, all of the above. Filling a basket with bananas, milk, yogurt, cheese, and a candy bar takes on dimensions of some high-tech Central Intelligence Agency interrogation of Middle Eastern prisoners in Cuba. The meat locker is an avant-garde display of frenetic arrangement with chicken, beef, and cold cuts heaped, piled, and scattered in patterns beyond normal decency. And how he pulls off his main illusion from a blind vantage point in an isolated back room where he whacks away hour after hour, year after year is a mystery to me, but the guy is always at the counter ready to check me out. He never misses. He's always at the ready, standing there in a bloody white smock, thin, sandy Einstein-crazed hair, thick coke-bottle glasses, and wet smile. I bet I've paid $800 Canadian for $12 worth of goods, while madly repeating the mantra "Lord save my lame ass" over and over to myself. This store is part of the traveling-up-north Holtian road-show ritual these days. An act of ridiculous courage, and a vain challenge to the road gods' powers.

So I pull in the dirt parking lot, say a quick prayer to an appropriately arcane deity, pull back the door, and step in. The noise is a palpable wall this time around. Raucous. Racketing off the cement-block walls like a passing trio of F-16s flying just above the deck, all of it punctuated with the sound of the cleaver slicing through dead meat and striking a bloody wooden cutting board. (I see this through a gap in the partially open door to our hero's temple of savaged flesh.) I grab a basket, weave and totter down the isles snatching at the five previously mentioned items, and in a moment of madness, a can of Dinty Moore Beef Stew. All this is accomplished amid the lunatic cacophony of the "music." He's at the register waiting. The hard rubber produce conveyor belt spins dangerously. He waits for the basket to reach him. Time stands still. Then he enters each item after peering at it from assorted angles. He rings up a total. The lucky number is $17. I eagerly pay the guy $1,100.

"Hey, you really got it going now," I say.

"What?"

"The music. You can really hear all of it. Its richness and depth."

"What?"

"The music," I yell.

"New speakers," he says, and points to a pair of case-of-beer-sized speakers above the dairy cooler, then mutters something about "subwoofers" as he hotfoots it back to his sanctuary.

"Whack. Whack. Whack."

I stagger out to the car. Lord, what a place. Three minutes and its like I need to go to a detox center for the criminally insane.

I'm headed out of town. I'm done here. I know I'm not being fair to Watson Lake, but to me it's just another tourist trap way-up-north style. To be fair, a trap with a world-class bizarre grocery store, but still a trap. Maybe you would feel differently about the town. Could be. The plus to the place is that I know I'm close now to the good stuff. Amazing country, like the Dempster Highway, coming up in a couple of days.

Author's Note: While writing this I checked the word count for this chapter. More than nine thousand words with a few hundred miles to go. My books are all road reports in some way—views from all along the watch tower—this one more than most. I wanted at least one chapter of this book to wander down the narrative highway much as I did on my most recent trip to the North Country. This is only a slight informational aside to allow the reader a chance to assess the damage inflicted by the verbiage so far, similar in function to a commercial in the midst of the high drama of a late-night television movie.

One loop I plan to take the next time that I'm up here is the Robert Campell Highway that heads north, then west out of Watson Lake to Faro. The road is mainly unimproved dirt, and I heard from a soul at the Watson lake restaurant that it is something of a motoring experience à la semi-early Alaska Road conditions. To do this drive properly, I was told to plan on a week to ten days and to pray for good weather. (There are so many places to see up this way, for instance, the eight-hundred-mile loop from Whitehorse to Dawson City across the Yukon River into Alaska, down the Top-of-the-World Highway to Tetlin Juncton, farther south back into the Yukon and along the eastern slopes of the massive Saint Elias Mountains to Haines Junction, then back east to Whitehorse. Much of the enclosed mountainous country is extremely wild and still little explored.) Along the way there is also a turnoff onto the Canol Road, a World War II construction with plans to link up with the Northwest Territories to haul fuel and supplies, but the war ended before its completion. There is a trail of a few hundred miles along the corridor through some wild, beautiful country. This very rough and dicey jeep track heads along the Ross River into the Selwyn Mountains before petering out at the head of the Heritage hiking trail at the Northwest Territories border in the Keele River headwaters. Great fishing for northern pike and grayling is reported in the many streams up this way The small town of Faro is situated in the Tintina Trench that runs for hundreds of miles east and west and is visible from space. Moose, caribou, black and grizzly bears, wolf, lynx, and eagles are common, as are a small band of about one hundred Fannin Sheep. There may be only three thousand of these animals existent.

The valley is also a spring and fall migration corridor for sandhill cranes.

The road is fairly good between Watson Lake and Whitehorse as it travels through dense forest and along rivers like the Rancheria and Swift. I'd read in *The Fishing Encyclopedia* compiled by A. J. McClane about his adventures on the Rancheria, so I pull down a dusty two-track into the trees and next to the wide, clear, shallow river to try my luck. Wading is easy in the icy water and I see several grayling feeding along the streambed on what has to be small nymphs. I tie on a gray Hare's Ear and try my luck. The slightest splash too close to the fish sends them fleeing for cover. I look for broken water over deeper runs and cast well to the head of these. I connect with a number of grayling from thirteen to seventeen inches long, but I also notice many more running for their lives. Clearly, these fish are not the virginal opportunity McClane experienced decades before, and my decidedly delicate casting seems to have a deleterious effect on the action. A bit farther down the road, at a small, empty campground, I work an Elkhair Caddis in rapid pocket water and catch smaller fish on nearly every reasonably accurate cast to likely holding water. All in all, a pleasant bit of diversion

A few miles before Teslin Lake, where I plan to spend the night after an easy day's cruise, I come upon the wreckage of three semis. Debris is scattered all over the place at a bridge crossing. Royal Northwest Mounted Police squad cars and ambulances, lights flashing, are on each side of the wreck. Cabs, boxes, containers are blasted all over the place. A bloody sheet covers someone's remains. Others, obviously seriously injured, are being loaded into the rescue vehicles. While waiting to pass by the carnage, engine off and windows down, I hear an officer saying to a rescue worker that the disaster happened about ninety minutes ago. Apparently, a trucker had fallen asleep at the wheel, veered into the oncoming lane head-on with another truck that was itself slammed from behind by yet another rig. Traveling as much as I do, I see my fair share of grue-

GINNY DIERS PHOTO

THE TOMBSTONE MOUNTAINS ALONG THE DEMPSTER HIGHWAY.

AUTHOR PHOTO

A FLOAT PLANE IN BACK BAY OF YELLOWKNIFE.

AUTHOR PHOTO

ABOVE AND BELOW: THE HAY RIVER AND LOUISE FALLS IN THE SOUTHERN PART OF THE NORTHWEST TERRITORIES.

AUTHOR PHOTO

AUTHOR PHOTO

THE MACKENZIE HIGHWAY SOUTH OF WRIGLEY, WITH THE MACKENZIE RIVER ON RIGHT AND NAHANI BUTTE IN THE DISTANCE.

AUTHOR PHOTO

THE DISTINCTIVE POLAR BEAR LICENSE PLATE OF NORTHWEST TERRITORIES.

AUTHOR PHOTO

THE WILD CAT CAFÉ THE FIRST COMMERCIAL STRUCTURE IN YELLOWKNIFE SERVES GOOD FOOD TO THIS DAY.

AUTHOR PHOTO

THE FALLS ALONG THE LITTLE BUFFALO RIVER AT 11 P.M.

GINNY DIERS PHOTO

THE SIGNPOST FOREST IN WATSON LAKE, YUKON.

AUTHOR PHOTO

DOWNTOWN YELLOWKNIFE, THE OLD TOWN AND THE NEWER CITY IN THE DISTANCE, AS SEEN FROM PILOT'S MONUMENT.

GINNY DIERS PHOTO

AN ENORMOUS COAL MINE TAKING DOWN MOUNTAINS ON THE EASTERN EDGE OF JASPER PARK.

GINNY DIERS PHOTO

FISHING THE UPPER BLACKSTONE RIVER FOR GRAYLING.

AUTHOR PHOTO

RACHEL HOLT FISHING A SMALL RIVER ALONG THE LIARD HIGHWAY FOR GRAYLING AND NORTHERN PIKE IN THE NORTHWEST TERRITORIES.

AUTHOR PHOTO

AN OLD TRAPPER'S CABIN PRESERVED TO THIS DAY IN BACK BAY OF YELLOWKNIFE.

AUTHOR PHOTO

THE UPPER STRETCH OF CAMERON FALLS OUTSIDE OF YELLOWKNIFE.

GINNY DIERS PHOTO

AN ARCTIC GRAYLING TAKEN FROM BLACKSTONE RIVER ON A #14 ELKHAIR CADDIS.

GINNY DIERS PHOTO

AN INUKSHUK, OR THE INUIT METHOD OF MARKING TRAILS, ALONG THE DEMPSTER HIGHWAY FAR ABOVE THE RIVER VALLEYS.

GINNY DIERS PHOTO

THIS BLACK BEAR SMELLED OUR FISH ALONG THE OLGILVIE RIVER.

GINNY DIERS PHOTO

THE OLGILVIE RIVER COMING OUT OF THE OLGILVIE MOUNTAINS ABOVE ENGINEER CREEK.

GINNY DIERS PHOTO

A CLOUD FORMATION ABOVE THE MOUNTAINS ALONG THE DEMPSTER HIGHWAY.

GINNY DIERS PHOTO

AN ARCTIC GRAYLING SHOWING OFF ITS SURREAL COLORING AND DORSAL FIN.

GINNY DIERS PHOTO

A GIGANTIC COAL MINE SOUTH OF HINTON, ALBERTA ON THE EASTERN EDGE OF JASPER PARK.

AUTHOR PHOTO

THE BRIEF SUNSET ALONG THE MACKENZIE RIVER AT FORT SIMPSON AFTER MIDNIGHT IN LATE JUNE.

GINNY DIERS PHOTO

TUNDRA IN THE "DRUNKEN FOREST" ABOVE THE OLGILVIE RIVER ON THE DEMPSTER HIGHWAY.

some accidents. I always wonder if something I've done earlier in the day was responsible for delaying me so that I missed these appointments with death. Was the brief Rancheria River grayling foray just such a situation. Fate and timing are curious aspects of life, especially on the road.

I'd decided to spend the night at a lakeside cabin near Dawson Peaks on Teslin Lake. Owners Carolyn Allen and David Hett are great people who run an efficient, orderly place. The cabins are reasonable, and the daily special in their restaurant is always good. I check in, and they wonder how the past year has been, then ask where Ginny is. When I explain that we'd gone our separate ways there is some awkwardness, but I say, "Life rolls on. How 'bout I buy the three of us each a beer." We go outside and stand in the sun and flickering pine-tree-cast shade, look across Teslin Lake at the twin summits of Dawson Peaks, and talk of this and that. I tell them that I'll be back for dinner, then drive down the little trail to my cabin, the same place Ginny and I had stayed in the past. It has a front room and a sleeping area with a large bed and a modern bathroom. Home on the road once again.

I settle in, lay another book to read on the bedside table—*Blue Spruce* by David Long—take a long, hot shower, change into fresh clothes, build a Canadian whiskey and ice, walk out to the small front porch, and sit down to enjoy the view. The whiskey tastes cold and warm at the same time. The cigarette is one of those that makes me wonder if I'll ever quit (I did this winter), rich tasting and relaxing. A warm late afternoon breeze rustles the silvery birch leaves and kicks up a mild chop on Teslin Lake. During the heyday of the 1898 Klondike gold rush, steamers would cruise up this water bound for the Yukon River and the gold fields at Dawson City. The place still has the feeling of this adventure. It is not difficult to visualize the sternwheelers churning across the lake bound for the arctic El Dorado. Intriguing and beautiful but suddenly lonely and sad. I think of my former companion, Ginny. I don't miss her and don't want her back. Too much blood had spilled on the wide-ranging ground of our relationship over the years for that to happen. I miss and regret what might have been, but what I know realistically never had a chance. During our time together, she was a prisoner of her own demons—demons that she worshipped. I was a crazed but sharply focused writer who put strange verbal visions ahead of all else. A self-centered madman, who was difficult to live with. Ginny's talent as a photographer is immense and unique, but she took it for granted and treated her gift of visual alchemy like dirt. I couldn't handle that. We couldn't handle each other . . . and so it goes.

I drain my drink, make one more and the mood passes as I work on another golden cigarette. I walk up to the restaurant and have grilled salmon fresh from the Yukon River, wild rice, fresh peas, and some white wine. I say thanks and good evening to Carolyn and David, stroll down to the lake for a while, then retire to bed and David Long's curious, talented writings. It is early September and the day grows dark by 10 P.M The wind comes up and whistles through the trees. I read my book in peace.

A few miles west of David and Carolyn's place the next morning, I cross over the longest bridge on the Alaska Highway, the Nisutlin Bay Bridge, and enter the village of Teslin, population four hundred fifty. Members of the Teslin First Nation make up the majority of the residents. This area was originally a summer home for the coastal Tlingit, who finally settled here permanently in 1903 and make up the Teslin group.

A little farther north and west I roll through Johnson's Crossing over a very high bridge across the Teslin River as it cuts narrowly through a rock gorge. On the other side of the river is a gas station/motel/general store. I gas up with about one hundred forty liters of leaded plus; I was almost empty. This comes to around $70 Canadian, which at the time when the exchange rate was $1.50 to $1.00 in favor of the United States is about $47 Yankee greenbacks. (Over the past seven years I've seen the rate vary from $1.27 to

$1.00 to as high as $1.62 to $1.00. At any level, travel up here is something of a bargain. The most I ever paid for gas was the equivalent of $2.30 American a gallon and that was way up north above the Arctic Circle. As I write this in early February 2004, the rate is $1.34 to $1.00) I grab a bag of fresh-baked apple turnovers, a plastic container of orange juice, and a big Styrofoam cup of coffee. I am set for a rolling brunch.

The highway runs below enormous bluffs and cliffs of granite on its way to Jake's Corners. The road is wide open, relatively new, and in excellent shape. I cruise along at seventy-five miles an hour. Jake's Corners is a junction, where a traveler can cut south along enormous Atlin Lake or a few miles up at Carcross head south on another highway through British Columbia and into Skagway, Alaska, or continue on toward Whitehorse farther north. I opt for the latter route. From the junction to Whitehorse is perhaps thirty-five miles, but the road is always torn up in a state of road-delay, under-repair craziness. As I creep along the wet gravel construction zones, I stare out at Marsh Lake, the seagulls, and the beginnings of housing clusters that herald the approach of Whitehorse.

> Author's Note: This chapter is making a concerted attempt to run on forever, so in the interests of public reading decency, descriptions of the end-of-the-line madness that is Dawson City, then of my time back to the south in Whitehorse will be relegated to their very own chapter which follows this one.

Just north of Whitehorse, the Alaska Highway breaks to the left and west. I take the right fork, which winds uphill and is announced by a large sign as the beginning of the Klondike Highway. Soon the city of Whitehorse is well behind me as I roll along beneath rounded, bare-rock mountains that have limited tree cover except at their wide bases. I glimpse forested mountains through valley gaps rolling off far to the north and in some spots to the south. The Klondike does not have a large operating budget and it shows in some ways. The road is rough and narrow. Shoulders for emergency stops to avoid traffic are few and far between. Concentration and caution are the keys to safe passage on this road. Just ahead I see acres and acres of burned land devastated by wildfires of the late 1990s. The ground is black and brown but tinged with green and the brilliant oranges, reds, and yellows of the approaching autumn. Above all of this, stretching for miles on both sides of the highway and covering thousands of acres, is an intense coverlet of pink flowers that wave and flicker in the wind—fireweed. Driving through these normally barren hills and bluffs is like sailing on a glowing sea at sunset. Millions of these plants reflect the sunlight and lend a colorful soft-red cast to the entire countryside. Far in the distance, the dark green of the forest cloaking the lower slopes of bald mountains along the robin egg's blue of the sky provide pleasant contrast to this bright landscape.

In what seems like no time, I pass over the Yukon River at Carmacks Crossing on a narrow iron bridge. The river is already impressive, even this far upstream, flowing wide, deep, and dark green. The settlement was named after George Washington Carmack, one of the codiscovers of gold in the Klondike. Originally, this was a fueling station for riverboats. Located near the ancestral home of the Little Salmon Carmacks First Nation, the community is approximately midway between the Northern and Southern Tutchone First Nations. The aboriginal history dates back ten thousand years in the region.

On the other side of the Yukon River, the road climbs steeply along the edge of a towering embankment. Highway 4 cuts off to the east, completing the Faro loop begun in Watson Lake. Midway up the rise half of the road is gone, washed away into the river. Orange pylons mark the location. I edge by this with trepidation. My toes tingle. As I come around a bend, a magnificent view of the forested Yukon Valley stretches for many miles into the blue-sky west. The river rolls and sweeps through the timber, while the road switchbacks down to a campground at Tatchun Creek. Some years ago when Ginny and I first camped here, we had set up everything and were reclining around a fire when a pair of matching, and obviously rented, motor homes pulled into nearby spaces. After a flurry of extremely well-organized activity by the two couples, the four of them walked through our camp carefully checking everything. Blond hair, ruddy complexions, in their late fifties. German. Aryan for sure.

"Ya, good fire. Is warm," said one of the men. The other three nodded in agreement. "This camp is good, too. Laid out well." And with that they all bowed ever so slightly and returned to their encampment.

"We passed the Germans' inspection, John," said Ginny with a wink.

I'm German, too, so I understood. But this was a bit over the top even for the Yukon. I returned to reading the territorial fishing regulations that informed me that Tatchun Creek is closed to fishing from late August through September to protect spawning salmon up from the Pacific a thousand miles away. I looked over my shoulder. The stream was barren. That was then.

This year I pull in for a quick snack and to check the creek. It is two weeks later than the previous German-inspection time, so I approach the river with less than my usual angling cynicism. What I see blows me away—huge dark torpedo shapes moving up against the swift current. Salmon! Being an inland West, high plains guy I'd never seen this spectacle before. Dozens and dozens of salmon holding in calm areas or pushing up the deeper outside swings of undercut and overgrown banks. I watch for hours as the fish move on only to be replaced by others. They seem to run about ten pounds, and maybe much larger. I am enthralled. Hypnotized. So much so I decide to stay the night. I hastily set up camp, grab a beer, and snack from the cooler until dark as I sit in my folding chair on the bank above these magic fish. The thought of breaking the law and trying to catch just one (Just one? Right, Holt!) never occurs to me. When I wake in the morning the stream is empty, barren once again. I'd had my natural vision, a glimpse into the normally unseen here. I pack up and head for Dawson, now not all that far away.

Somewhere along the way this morning, my sense of time shifts from pondering the past—even what has just happened—to all that is now taking place; all that is current, timely, and immediate. This slight, but momentous, sensation always trips over me on the road west of Whitehorse. Perhaps my mind and internal timing mechanisms have absorbed enough of the Yukon by now to discard my traditional linear time approach to life. Whatever the reason, this redirected way of viewing the movement of life as it happens is intoxicating.

In less than an hour I cross the wide Pelly River at Pelly Crossing, the home of the Selkirk First Nation. In another thirty or forty miles I pass over the Stewert River and the junction with Highway 11, which leads to the out-of-the-way silver and lead mining district around Mayo and Keno. I'll get there some year, too. But I am closing in on the end of the highway for me at Dawson City, so I push on along the bumping, rolling, narrow thoroughfare as it crosses the McQuiston River and climbs onto a marshy plateau that sprawls with mile upon mile of muskeg swamp toward distant rolling mountains that are timbered, then bare silver gray rock along the summits. Moose graze on aquatic plants in the meandering streams and ponds and bogs. The mountains are not high by western United States standards, maybe five thousand to six thousand feet, but they are impressive all the same. I am in the middle of fiercely wild country now. I can feel it buzzing around and through me as I drive or when I stop to take in the view, the clear and cool air, the scent of the muskeg, the pines, and the arctic waiting only a few ridges beyond the northern horizon. The arctic sky is different in ineffable ways. Nothing looks dramatically changed from, say, southern Alberta or down in Montana. Clouds are clouds; blues seem to be similar blues; light resonates, reflects, and refracts in similar ways; but there must be sufficient minor variations to create an overall sensation of an otherworldly, wildly different environment. I feel like I always do, that I'm in the Far North, a land of tundra, musk ox, racing rivers, unexplored mountain valleys. The feeling beats the hell out of booze or drugs or anything else I've ever experienced. Pure, distilled, crystalline freedom. I take a deep breath of the cool, clean air. Paradise. As if to punctuate this impression, a large brown grizzly, with humped neck and muscular shoulders, ambles out of the forest on the opposite side of the highway on the far side of a creek about one hundred yards away. It winds me, stands and stares, then drops down and takes off with surprising ease, splashing and charging through the tangles of the muskeg.

I get in the Suburban and continue on, eventually coming down a hill to a spectacular pullover view of the Tintina Trench, the Tombstone Range, and the gateway to the arctic offered by the Dempster Highway running to my right and cutting north through a wedge in the mountains. The Klondike River flows in the distance as a ribbon of flashing silver and indigo, then disappears around a bend through the pines before showing itself once again as it rolls across and around braided gravel bars and islands. Dark purple, gray, and black clouds spin and roil over the far edge of the Tombstones. I can see lightning tearing at the jagged peaks, but the distance is too great for thunder to reach me. Wind comes and goes as does the sun with passing clouds. The air is warm, then cool, then cold, then bright hot, then cool once again. All is in flux, changing in the wandering rays of sunlight and the vagaries of arctic-inspired breezes.

Reluctantly, I get back in the Suburban and finish my drive to Dawson City that winds along the Klondike River, passing the turn to the Dempster Highway, then dredges through mile after mile of goldmine tailings that lie across the land like enormous stone graves. I cross the river on an old, rusting bridge, then round a sharp turn.

I'm in Dawson.

GINNY DIERS PHOTO

THE ARCTIC CIRCLE ALONG THE DEMPSTER. INUIT COUNTRY.

SIX /

BRIGHT LIGHTS, BIG CITIES

Some would call Dawson City a tourist trap, and they'd be right in a number of obvious ways. Dawson *was* the nexus for the Klondike gold rush that peaked in 1898. The town of about two thousand hardy souls has no qualms about catering to tourists who enjoy taking bus tours to places like Capital Hill or Disneyland or whatever that hideous country music dump in Missouri is called. Bunson Burner? Barnville? Branson? Old-time gold mining is big business in the twenty-first century. This bustling little place along the Yukon River is, at least on a superficial level, akin to the previously mentioned atrocities. Hustling the traveling road show of mooches out of their money is not a casual pursuit up here. People, both residents and visitors alike, wander around dressed in late-nineteenth-century garb, as though these superficial affectations lend some form of gold-rush veracity to the situation. This aspect of Dawson makes me at once queasy and disgusted. I don't have the patience for this type of silliness.

Stores named Klondike Nugget and Ivory Shop LTD., Gold Claim and Goldbottom Mine Tours offer real neat chances to purchase genuine gold nuggets or even pan for gold, and all at "bargain" prices reminiscent of the sky-high cost of everything from bread to gunpowder to oysters back in gold-fever days of more than a century ago when goods were commonly purchased with gold nuggets or dust. There's a Bonanza Esso gas station, Bonanza Meat Company (a pretty fair store), a Bonanza Gold Motel, the Gold Rush Campground RV Park, Bonanza Gold RV Park, Diamond Tooth Gerties Gambling Hall, the Gaslight Follies Sourdough Saloon, the Jack London Grill ("I'll have the Call of the Wild prime rib medium rare, please."), and the Gold City Travel Agency, to name a few. Busloads of bizarrely dressed visitors wearing coordinated outfits that may feature yellow Tyrolean felt hats with pink flamingo feathers, bright green and beer-belly stretched T-shirts with logos that announce unashamedly "Hell yes, I had a flat tire on the Alaska Highway," madras shorts, black silk kneesocks and white wicker sandals, motor homes full of gaily plumaged suckers from Georgia, Vancouver, Texas, carloads of fat, carsick kids and harried parents—all of them descend upon the community like a poorly imagined nightmare. The place is a madhouse-like Sell-out-ville, on par with West Yellowstone or perhaps Bozeman, not far from where I live in Montana.

Normally, I avoid these places like the proverbial plague of rat-like humanity they are, but there is something about Dawson in its board-walked and muddy streets; in the youthful, bright-eyed help at Klondike Kate's restaurant; in the surly anti-American drunk and sometimes strung out hardcore locals at The Pit; or the kids drinking in the pub at Bombay Peggy's, while Steely Dan plays in the background; and in the energy of the deep, dark Yukon River cutting by just off Front Street. For a couple of days at a shot, it appeals to my sense of the road and its varied adventure.

The river's kinetic energy drives the place, as it has for more than one hundred fifty years. From gold to tourism to the natural hum, the Yukon is quite the river. Even the derivation of the river's name is appropriate. "Yukon" was given by Hudson Bay Company trader John Bell, who in 1846 descended the Porcupine River from the Mackenzie Delta to its confluence with the Yukon. Bell named it the "Youcon," his version of the Loucheaux Indian word

Yuchoo, meaning "the Greatest River" or "Big River."

There are buzzing layers of the genuine article, the real thing, struggling through, beneath, and over the obvious venalities of tourism Yukon style. I catch occasional glimpses of this swirling in the miasma of phony period hustle. You can find this vibrant, often roughshod honesty scattered about the place much like at conglomerations of superficial travel indulgence in the American West—the Old Faithful Inn complex in Yellowstone Park, long-gone Jackson Hole, Kevin Costner-destroyed Deadwood, South Dakota, or gambling-crazed Las Vegas. You know what I'm aiming at here. The people who live in Dawson year-round or at least make an honest stab at doing so, along with some of the hard-core derelicts that often resemble my sedate yet sophisticated personage, seem to understand that there is an intrinsic, undeniable current of real power at work in Dawson City and throughout the Yukon. Something entirely different from the juice found in the Northwest Territories to the east, but clearly the two are related in a perfectly insane, electric way. Something strong enough to weather the blistering mediocrity of western touristaville at its most garish.

Dawson City is the northernmost community on the Klondike Highway. The city is located at the confluence of the Klondike and Yukon Rivers, just one hundred forty-four miles south of the Arctic Circle. The place was once known as the "Paris of the North," and one-hundred-year-old photos of wooden storefronts, quagmire mud streets replete with passed out drunks, along with tents used as makeshift salons, whorehouses, and stores certainly seem to bear out this appellation. By 1898 Dawson at forty thousand people, was the largest Canadian city west of Winnipeg. The city had running water and telephone service. More than one hundred thousand people started out for the gold fields from all over the world, many of them climbing the brutally steep mountain trail called Chilkoot Pass. Fewer than thirty thousand covered the entire distance to Dawson City and then on to places like Forty Mile, Eldorado, Bonanza, and

Hunker Creeks. Only a couple of hundred of these "Stampeders," as they were called, struck it rich. The odds were daunting. Most suffered extreme loneliness, hunger, financial depravation, or alcoholism. Many died from the weather, mining accidents, or by being murdered. Life for all but a few was anything but glamorous. By 1902 the gold rush was history and the population plummeted to five thousand. In 1953 the town lost its status as territorial capital to Whitehorse. Today as much money is generated by tourism as is from gold mining, even with the improvements in mineral extraction efficiency made over the past decade.

So do I really know what I'm trying to say here? Yes, but perhaps a casual and lightly debauched stay compressed from several frenetic arrivals in Dawson will serve to explain the arcane situation with more clarity.

There are two places I like to stay in town—Klondike Kate's and Bombay Peggy's. Both have their fair share of tourism plastic, but they possess good qualities as well. Kate's is easy and relatively inexpensive. Bombay Peggy's is a bit more upscale and pricey, so normally I crash at the former. There are two types of cabins at Kate's: the newer ones that are quite nice and modern, and the older ones that look like the somewhat dilapidated structures of my vacationing youth in northern Wisconsin. I prefer the lower-end cabins that are located next to the heated, screened (I've thought on occasion that razor wire would be more appropriate than screening as the evenings progress over there) dining and drinking area off the main restaurant.

I pull into the gravel lot behind Klondike Kate's main building and walk up an old wooden incline to the main office that reminds me of a bus station ticket office where all destinations are bound for nowhere. I tell them I'm here, want a room, and will settle up when I leave. I am handed a key, then I drive around for a few minutes assessing and finally deciding on the best approach to backing into my narrow slot. Some of the help on break watch my skilled maneuverings from their perch atop an outside picnic table. They are clearly impressed with my efforts and somewhat disappointed when I narrowly miss an expensive sport-utility vehicle parked at one end of the lot.

The cabins and rooms in the older part of the establishment are wedged together. My little cabin has a large bedroom with twin beds, plenty of framed windows, a narrow walkway to a small bathroom with a shower. For $35 American it's a deal. I toss my gear on the empty bed, make myself comfortable, then head down to the river and Front Street to Maximilian's Gold Rush Emporium to peruse their excellent regional book selection. I buy several books, along with a couple of packs of Canadian smokes. One title I grab is *The Death of Albert Johnson—Mad Trapper of Rat River*. I like twisted tales of mayhem and robbery and murder, so this book should fill the bill. I walk over and stare at the river for a while, watching the ferry move back and forth across the river in the evening sunlight. Below me, down beneath the thirty-foot-high riverbank, there is a muddy, brushy area about twenty feet wide running along the Yukon. Collapsed in a heap and partially hidden inside a grungy sleeping bag is a long-haired youth taking an early siesta. A couple of Indians, possibly Inuit, are sitting on rocks drinking wine and smashing old boards against other rocks. Maybe I should have saved my money and set up shop down there. I look around; at the river as it winds around a distant turn headed for Alaska, the rich, fecund smell of its waters drifting up from the mud banks and shoreline; at the heavily timbered hills that surround the townsite and hide the many ridges of mountains that roll off toward the north and the south; at the yellowish tan wash of dirt and rock that shows above the town like a landslide that ran out of gas; and at the lights coming on all over Dawson, some neon, some gaslight, mostly electric.

It's cocktail hour and I'm hungry, so I wander back to Kate's for the 9:30 P.M. seating. Or is it the 9:17? Or perhaps 10:02? At any rate the yellow board structure that is the main building of Kate's looms on the horizon at the corner of Third Avenue and King Street. The building was built in 1904 and retains much of the original construction.

There are at least seventeen recorded Klondike Kates listed in the record books, but Kathleen Eloisa Rockwell of Junction City, Kansas, is considered the original model. She was born in 1876 and began her career as a chorus girl in her midteens. While dancing and plying men with drinks in the halls of Spokane, Washington, Kate heard news of the gold rush and decided to head north. Following brief employment as a "buck-and-wing" tap dancer in Skagway and Whitehorse, she arrived in Dawson City in 1900 and began working at the Palace Grand. Red-haired Kate danced on until as late as 1904 before becoming involved with Alexander Pantages, owner of the Orpheum Theatre on Front Street. Eventually things fell apart, and she sued the man for breach of promise for $25,000. A Norwegian named Johnny Matson had been in love with Kate from afar for thirty years. He finally summoned up the courage to begin writing to her, and they were married two years later. Johnny died in 1946. Until her death in 1957 Kate actively promoted herself as Queen of the Yukon, Belle of Dawson, and Klondike Queen. One must imagine between these brief lines and wonder fully what Kate's life must have been like in Dawson City during the gold rush. A life catering to rough, often drunk and violent miners, grifters, and other hardcore criminals including murderers.

Life in Dawson ranged from the depths of alcoholism in the mud of the streets to true high-society extravagance of crystal chandeliers, imported champagne, exotic foods, opera singers from the East and Europe, and the like. The amount of money that flowed through Dawson was staggering. In 1900 a total of more than one million ounces—nearly 3.5 tons—of fine gold were produced and valued in the tens of millions by today's standards. Down-and-out roustabouts and societal outcasts from the Lower-48 became millionaires nearly overnight. It seems obvious that Kate managed to make a fair living from these suddenly wealthy men. Klondike Kate's maintains something of that legacy today, even now as I push through the door into the restaurant and head back to the screened porch and the loud music.

The place is about half full with a mixture of older individuals fresh off a tour bus and here for the obligatory salmon dinner and younger travelers dressed in jeans or the latest REI, Patagonia, Sierra outdoor wear. Many have long hair. Some of the young white men sport Rasta hair styles of mangy dreadlocks. Reggae legend Bob Marley would dig this level of "commitment and authenticity." I find a table isolated in a corner. Soon a young waitress appears and hands me a menu. I order a double Jim Beam and tell her to bring them on a regular basis, along with a large, rare rib-eye steak, baked potato, and vegetables with hollandaise. Their eggs Benedict are always excellent, so I knew they'd have the sauce on hand. She smiles and does as I ask. A drink arrives quickly and my meal about twenty minutes later. While I drink and eat, I watch one young couple get legitimately bombed on a variety of martinis offered by Kate's. The menu suggests that there may be a dozen or more. From what I can see from the two's collection of mostly empty glasses, some of the versions are blue, some feature everything but gin, some have fruit in them. I imagine what my late stepfather, Ken, would say about this heresy. I finish my meal, pay my bill, wander through the now rowdy, crowded place, and out the front door into the dusk of 9 P.M. People are waiting in line for tables.

I'm off to The Pit about three blocks away from Kate's. I'm looking forward to revisiting its charming collection of regulars with whom I have some years of pleasant history. I'm one of those foul Yanks from the "outside" and they're Canucks, and away we go in a cloud of profanity and mixed drinks. The bar is on the ground floor of the early-twentieth-century Westminster Hotel, an old wooden structure painted in a weird shade of tan mixed with pink. The place has some interesting murals in the populist tradition of crowds drinking and carousing in one-dimensional relief. The bar runs the length of the joint and the remaining 75 percent of the space is given over to tables, chairs, and a small stage for various musicians who make random appearances.

The first time I was here, the friendly bartender made me strong drinks while I was regaled with pointedly anti-American tunes played by an old drunk wearing a Chicago Cubs' jersey and strumming away on an acoustic guitar. I'd been speaking with a freakster at my elbow and within minutes he loudly announced to the assembled throng that I was from "Montana! In the USA!" The guitarist/songwriter continued to play but subtly shifted chromatic gears. Visions of the sophistication practiced by the likes of John Prine, Danny O'Keefe, and Harry Chapin came to mind. The wasted, strung-out patrons that were slouched, reclined, or collapsed at various tables looked like escapees from the movie *Salton Sea* starring Val Kilmer, but most of them rallied to some extent to slog through the dirges. They derived great delight in staring and pointing at me as they sang. I forget the words but they were something about some unknown battle in the early nineteenth century that the United States lost to Canada. I must have had that good old USA glow about me to be so clearly American in their bloodshot eyes. When they staggered to a discordant conclusion, I politely applauded their efforts, then proceeded to point back at them with what I felt was an appropriate finger. Clearly, we all were having a dandy evening that culminated several minutes later with me backing out the open front door and across the street amid a barrage of oaths, beer cans, and empty drink glasses. That old Holt magic plays well in Dawson City, too.

When I arrive at The Pit this time the same bartender is working. He looks up, recognizes me, says "Oh Shit!" and laughs. A double whiskey appears as if by magic. The old drunk in the Cubs' jersey, actually he is younger than me and a fair musician, is still playing. The regular crowd looks to be the same blasted crew—men with scruffy beards, ragged long hair, and black greatcoats; women with long hair, faded jeans, plaid shirts, and wool sweaters of Irish fisherman design—sort of a Dawson City version of *Mad Max Beyond the Thunderdome.* For several drinks, the bartender and I discuss this and that, including his dream of working in Las Vegas, but suddenly the strains of a familiar tune begin. The patrons' favorite war song. I'm busted. I look up and see a roomful of charming faces singing, staring, and pointing at me. Some things never change, but I try to moderate my Ugly American image by telling the bartender to buy a round for the house. This works for some of the serious drunks in their late thirties and forties who'd learned the hard way over the years that free is free no matter who's doing the buying, but a fair number of individuals pour their drinks on the floor and sing another chorus of our favorite song. I order two more drinks for myself, finish the first, and pour the second on the floor. When in Rome. . . . The bartender is laughing pretty good now, but suggests that I might want to leave. I do, employing my old backing-out-the-door shuffle once again, ducking and weaving like Ali amid a fusillade of imprecations, bottles, cans, and glasses. A Royal Northwest Mounted Police squad car rolls by, but seems unconcerned about this outburst and continues down the street. Several young couples, probably having an evening stroll, are stopped in their tracks on the littered walkway. They are speechless, some with mouths open in shock at this spectacle.

"Don't worry. We're all old friends," I say, as I continue to back across the muddy thoroughfare. A half-full glass of whiskey crashes at my feet. "I'm American. I stop in here every year to visit. To say hello to my friends" Several beer bottles clatter off the wooden boardwalk amid a spirited chorus of "Fuck you! Yank!" I smile and keep moving toward the far sidewalk. The couples remain motionless in the gathering night. I turn and head down Second Avenue toward Bombay Peggy's on Princess Street. Refuse rains down upon my wake.

Ginny and I first stayed at Peggy's one night four years ago, after we'd been run off the Blackstone River by a grizzly. He'd winded a meal of grilled grayling we were cooking alongside the stream. Instead of finding a safer camp, we decided to drive back down the Dempster Highway and get a room in Dawson City. A nice meal and drinks, a warm shower and a clean bed sounded great. Especially after several days battling the elements above the Arctic Circle. Unfortunately, Dawson City was packed with the last weekend's worth of bus-delivered tourists. After pleading our case at motels and hotels throughout town and along the outskirts, Ginny eventually discovered that Bombay Peggy's had one room left—their most expensive at about $140 American. We took it anyway. Designed in late-nineteenth-century high-class-bordello fashion on the second floor streetside corner of the perfectly and sumptuously renovated whorehouse, our room had silk sheets, expensive wallpaper, an ornate tile bathroom with a large tub perched on claw feet, antique chairs, dressers, tables, and mirrors. Plus hidden from view in an armoir was a high-tech television, video player, and stereo.

Ginny ran a hot bath, clouds of steam emanating from the crack in the bathroom doorway. Realizing that what she was experiencing was priceless in terms of domestic serenity, I left her paddling away like a happy springer spaniel. I went downstairs, out the hotel entrance, and around to the pub. The two are separated, as is customary due to a quaint and pleasant Canadian territorial law. I pulled up to the bar and passed a couple of hours talking and drinking with the owner, who was clearly a woman of means and fine taste. I ordered a drink to go, and when I entered the hotel side my drink was sitting in the middle of a walnut table on a silver platter. My kind of place. Ginny was ensconced in bed watching an old movie on television.

As I walk into the pub this time most of the tables are full and pushed close to the fireplace. The night is star-studded, cool, and cooling still more in the clear air. The fire throws welcome heat. I find my stool and order a drink. The owner is not in, but rather down the road three hundred twenty-five miles in Whitehorse attending to "business." I stay until well after 1 A.M. talking to travelers and locals who pass through the pleasant bar. Eventually, I totter off toward my cabin at Kate's. The Pit is now going full tilt as I walk past the entrance. Yelling, rock music, crashing glasses. I am tempted to go in for another belt, but decide to head to my room for a shower and lights out. Funny how running along in my fifties instills at least a modicum of restraint in my behavior.

I take my time getting back, wandering up and down the various streets. A three-quarter-full moon moves in and out of a few clouds, playing games with the rapidly moving scud. Shadows cast by the many original or restored buildings from the gold rush slide deepest indigo across the streets and stretch up the boarded fronts of buildings on the west and north sides of the thoroughfares. Northern Lights flash green shading toward turquoise, the luminescence folding and unfolding in a panorama of shifting sheets. I climb a rickety fire escape alongside a hotel to gain a better view. Now the aurora is shooting waves of light over my head to the south. Well-defined shafts of bright green light explode from this. The show gathers intensity, overriding the shadows. Within moments the lights shrink back down below the horizon, the only sign of their presence is the glow behind the timbered horizon. Returning to the street, I continue home.

The next morning after coffee and excellent eggs Benedict, I work my way down to the Dawson City Museum located in the Old Territorial Administration Building. They have a comprehensive collection of archival papers, and I want to spend several hours taking notes for this and future books before I head down the Klondike Highway to Whitehorse in the early afternoon. Every time I'm in this place time passes like it has no substance. In what seems like minutes, I fill fifteen pages with notes. My watch says 1:30 P.M. I'll be lucky to make Whitehorse by ten o'clock, so I say the hell with it and go back to the office at Kate's and re-up in the same cabin for another night. I'll get an early start tomorrow morning. The town feels empty on this Monday evening in late September. The tackily dressed, bus-driven hordes have vanished, blown away on an early winter's wind. The tourist season is finally over. As if to mark this event, a mass of thick clouds marches in bringing cold rain, then wet snow, then heavy flakes. By the time I head over for dinner there are four inches on the ground. Dawson is aiming toward winter. I order another medium-rare steak, pasta with garlic sauce, and a large salad with bleu cheese dressing, while plunked down by a large window at an inside table. The snow continues to fall, lights come on along King Street. A few pedestrians hustle to get to wherever they are headed. Vehicle traffic is nonexistent. This is a season of the Yukon that I am unfamiliar with. I like the solitude and sense of isolation. The drinks, the relative quiet, the food, and the warmth relax me. The waitress is an old friend by now and we chat about the weather, the lack of tourists, what book projects I am planning, her graduate work at the University of Alberta in Edmonton, and so on. I decide to pass on visiting my chums at The Pit for the evening, opting instead for a return to the cabin to take a scalding shower, then scan my notes and read in bed. The snow is over six inches deep as I climb the steps to my cabin. The drive to Whitehorse in the morning will be a sporting proposition. Maybe I'll call my kids in Livingston and tell them I am spending the winter here in Dawson, working on a confused novel about cold weather. Maybe. Probably not. At least not for a few more years.

When I wake around 6 A.M., it is still more dark than daybreak due in a large part to the thick mat of overcast that has settled over Dawson and the river valley. Nearly a foot of snow is on the ground and still coming down, though lightly. I am ahead of my time plan for this trip, so after learning from the woman at the office that the storm will move off later today and that tomorrow will be sunny and warm with temperatures in the fifties, I sign on for another twenty-four-hour tour. She smiles and says, "You're thinking of spending a winter here, eh?" I say, "Yes," then explain the situation back home. "You'll be back when they're off to the University. I see that much in you." We both smile, and I go next door for breakfast. I'll spend another day at the museum, then repack and gas up the Suburban, have a leisurely dinner and a couple of drinks at Bombay Peggy's before returning for some more reading. I am becoming far too comfortable with my newfound routine.

This trip to the Yukon is the first one I've taken in more than a dozen years without the chaining accoutrements of my work (I've been doing this for far too long to maintain the façade that what I did for a living was in any way associated with the concept of "profession"), or the responsibilities of traveling in strange country with a female companion. If I'd brought along my laptop and cameras, returning home would have been at serious issue; I could have photographed and written away the dark months up here. I am now a regular at several places, which translates into obvious warmth, lower prices on some items, and decidedly stronger drinks. No one in town knows much about me—my past, my writing, my madness. I am truly free during these wonderful but all too short days.

Yesterday passed all too quickly. The weather did indeed improve. By 8:00 this morning the air, while still crisp, is warming. High rafts of fluffy clouds hurry to the east and southeast, the general direction of my day's wanderings. The town's boardwalks are clearing in patches that quickly grow larger, the gray tan wood steaming in the hot light. I take my time over breakfast—cheese omelet, hash browns, blueberries with yogurt, whole-wheat toast, lots of unsalted butter and marmalade, and black coffee—then check out of Kate's and load the car. I intend to give the rising sun and the road crews space to clear Highway 2, the Klondike Highway. I am in no hurry, so there is plenty of time to improve the driving conditions. The second reason is that I don't want to leave. This entire trip by myself and my stay in Dawson makes me feel like I am in my twenties again. There is no one to worry about but my self-indulgent self. If I want to hit the road at 2 A.M. and drive under a star-filled sky, I can. If I want to stay out late and make a fool of myself, I can. If I want to harmlessly flirt with a waitress or a young lass at a bar, I can. An adult life riddled with blown marriages and relationships, as well as raising two children alone these past six years—all of this and more—has made me forget the joys of being by myself. I value my children, other family members, and friends, but I'm done with woman relationships (famous last words I realize). As the Sons of Champlin used to intone years ago, "Freedom!"

By midmorning, I hit the highway. The pavement still has some snow-packed stretches, but as I begin the climbing, twisting stretch up into the birch and pine just east of the Dempster Highway turnoff, the road is no more than wet in places. Water is dripping from the ends of countless pine needles and leaf tips. The forest is a cascade of moving diamonds and brilliant prisms of color. Streams, rivers, and ponds reflect this madcap light show that kaleidoscopes amid moving images of sky and cloud. I check the air temperature with my fishing thermometer. Not yet noon and closing in on sixty degrees, though two nights before it was winter. I cruise along at fifty-five to sixty miles an hour, the Suburban's engine making a satisfied hum at this pace, same as it does with only a slight mix of growl, at seventy-six to seventy-seven. It is three hundred thirty-three miles from Dawson City to Whitehorse. I'll be in town by 6 P.M., staying at a motel that I am familiar with that is comfortable, clean, and located near a good Chinese restaurant and a pair of pubs-and-music clubs my Alberta friend guitarist/singer/song writer Amos Garrett turned me on to. He'd apparently played both of them several times, and he said the crowds were hip and the drinks were honest. Good enough for me. For the rest of the drive I cruise along with the windows down as I retrace my steps back across the Stewart and Pelly Rivers and along both the Yukon and Nordenskiold Rivers.

I pull in at Tatchun Creek Campground for a lunch of croissants I'd picked up that morning at the Dawson City General Store's bakery along with some sausage, brie, and Swiss cheese from the deli. This, plus a bottle of cranberry juice and an apple, makes for an excellent meal as I sit on top of a picnic table above the creek. Pockets of virgin-white snow remain beneath clumps of underbrush and around the edges of open ground under large pines. The stream is perfectly clear. The salmon have moved on. A few small grayling slap and leap after midges hovering just above the water's surface. An eagle soars overhead loosing its high-pitched cry. Chickadees putter around the brush. A brown-furred animal that looks like a mink slinks along the far bank. I finish eating and move on. The day keeps growing better.

The sky turns bluer, a deeper, purer shade that cerulean or azure doesn't cover. The sun is brighter, blasting radiation down on the planet like it is determined to sear the memory of what it is capable of doing with an intensity that will survive the months of cold darkness. The air grows warmer, and the breeze softens. I pull over near a lookout that surveys an expanse of fireweed and burned land. The entire countryside shimmers in shades of pink, orange, purple, and crimson below the many greens of the forest rising in the distance. I stay for a long time, just drifting with the casually moving day.

By the time I arrive at the outskirts of Whitehorse it is past 7 P.M. Finding the Stratford Motel is easy. I drop down the ancient river bank, now a mile removed from the Yukon flowing dark blue green on the northern edge of the city, between its new banks carved over the centuries. Instead of following the city loop, I take a right on Fourth Street and there I am at the Stratford. Each time I've stayed here, the person behind the desk has given me the same room, Number 226. This time is no different. Why argue for change? Prices are reasonable, especially when compared against the well over $100 American at the "upscale" establishments. I park beneath

my lodgings and take a few things upstairs. When I come back down for one last load I notice several Harley's with Tennessee plates parked one car over. The doors to two adjoining rooms are open, and I can see a couple of husky gray-haired, pony-tailed, bearded men and their female companions. They are laughing and working on drinks. One of them spots me, waves, sees my license plate, and yells, "Montana. Come on in and have a drink." Why not? The Chinese place is open until 1 A.M. and the music goes on until two o'clock or later.

As soon as I walk in the room, I know the evening of fashionable dining and fine music is over. The boys are in a recreational mode. I am introduced to a can of Molson's and a mixed drink, then to Bob, LeRoy, and LaVerne (I could be in trouble with this), and Bonnie. What scares me is both these guys are former commercial airline pilots who'd retired several years back. Their wives are former flight attendants. Retirement funds and custom bike work back in Chattanooga keeps the four living in high style. They'd worked their way up to Sturgis for the annual motorcycle blowout, then decided to keep heading north for the Yukon and Alaska. Now they are on their way back down but resting up for a few days in "town," as they refer to Whitehorse. Of all the accents in the South, with the possible exception of the soft, lilting dialect practiced around Baton Rouge, Louisiana, the sound of those born and raised in Tennessee is my favorite. The sound is rich, warm, easy on the ears, and genuine.

We talk about nearly everything. The two pilots tell me about a new Cessna they'd recently purchased together and all of the improvements concerning instrumentation, horsepower, structural strength, and something about a wafer-thin deicing mesh. They ask what I do to make a buck. I tell them and unleash a barrage of questions that enthusiastically kills an hour. Things like "Yes, New York is out of it when it comes to serious writers," and "Agents are part of the problem not the solution. Finding one of these prima donnas to

take you on is like interviewing for a cabinet-level position in some insane and arcane government in East Africa," and so on. I go to the Suburban and grab several books, inscribing one each to the four travelers. This seems to mean a lot to them; they toast me and say I am all right for a northerner. We all become fast friends, exchanging addresses—e-mail and otherwise—and phone numbers.

Things gradually drift beyond my control, but I do have my Chinese meal—we order what seems to be three thousand dollars of take-out from Tung Lock a few blocks away. The "girls" power off on their bikes, then return shortly with bags and bags of some of the best Chinese food I've ever had. Ribs, shrimp, varieties of rice, chow mein, king pow, won tons, egg rolls, and a bunch of other stuff. I'm not sure this feast was prepared at the restaurant Amos Garrett mentioned. Because of the influx of coolie labor one hundred years ago, there are a number of Asian restaurants in town. We eat until we are all stuffed and glassy-eyed. I have one more drink to be sociable, hug my new friends goodnight, and walk off to bed. On the walkway in front of my room, I pause to take in the town.

Lights are on everywhere, setting off a glow that, unlike Dawson City, is fueled by the artificially intense colors of neon signs and storefront illuminations. There is just enough glow from the natural light of a dying day to show that, like Dawson, Whitehorse is surrounded by rolling, timbered hills. The Yukon curls away in the west heading for the town I'd left this morning. Again, like Dawson, the mountains can be felt but not seen. Mixed in with fumes of auto exhaust and vented commercial kitchens is the sweet tang of pine and the slightest taste of the river, its cold water suggesting aroma more than anything. In the clear sky, the northern lights are putting on another show, similar to the one recently in Dawson, but not quite as intense. I watch the magic until it too fades behind the horizon. I turn away.

The television in my room is still on. The weather forecast calls for another storm with sleet and snow to begin moving in the day after tomorrow. I decide to rise early, run some errands, push over six hundred miles to Fort Nelson in British Columbia, then at least as far as Grand Cache, possibly Hinton, Alberta the following day. I want to beat what my instincts are telling me is going to be one hell of a storm. If winter shows up early, making it back down south will be tough, particularly over the many mountain ranges in northern British Columbia. I drink a quart of orange juice to wash down the handful of aspirin I'd prescribed for myself and turn in after setting the alarm for 6:30 A.M. Lately, the days have all been full, worthwhile, and fun. I am grateful but also sorry not to have the chance to spend several days learning more about Whitehorse. Next summer I will make a point of this.

Whitehorse is named after the rapids nearby on the Yukon River that years earlier resembled the billowing manes of hard-charging white horses. These rapids, along with the deadly chutes of Miles Canyon, forced the Stampeders to make an arduous portage until a pair of sharp operators built tramways on either side of the river. For a fee, their horse-drawn tram cars carried goods and small boats around the rapids on log rails. A tent town called Canyon City sprang up on the east side of the river. A roadhouse and saloon offered rooms and refreshments for the thousands of would-be miners. Before the gold rush, the area was a First Nation campsite. The rapids disappeared on a wave of progress with the 1958 completion of the Whitehorse hydroelectric dam that formed Schwatka Reservoir.

In 1900 the construction of the White Pass & Yukon Route Railway from Skagway, Alaska, to a point beyond the whitewater was finished. The town of Whitehorse formed at this railhead. In 1920 the first airplane landed. The construction of the Alaska Highway in 1942 caused another boom in the city's fortunes, which evaporated at the end of World War II. Whitehorse incorporated as a city in 1950 and officially became the capital in 1953. Since that time, the bustling, compressed downtown—you can walk from one end to another in a few minutes—features many banks, expensive hotels, shops of all kinds, automotive services, restaurants of all descriptions, and as Amos Garrett said, "A hell of a nightlife if you're willing to look."

The alarm on my travel clock wakes me with its annoying electronic beeping. The poor instrument does a few feet of air time as I toss it in the direction of the sink near the bathroom. The device goes silent. I hop out of bed. Getting up in the morning no matter what shape I'm in has always been easy for me. A blessing, I guess. I dress and quickly load the Suburban. The day is clear and cold, maybe in the low twenties. The air smells of not-so-far-off snow.

I walk several blocks to Internet Yukon—Cyber Café, grab a terminal and a large mug of very strong, black Ethiopian Harrar, my favorite coffee. I plug into the new electronic age that follows me wherever I go. I've even connected through a phoneline at Eagle Plains, not far below the Arctic Circle on the Dempster Highway, and in Inuvik well above the Circle. Cyber cafés are located all over Canada and the rest of the world. I've filled magazine articles with digital photos from them. I write the pieces, select the pictures, put all of it in a folder, and when I connect I attach the folder to my e-mail and off the stuff goes. Making money while I play on the road. I check my e-mails. Mainly spam, but there are a couple of messages from friends, who wonder if I am still alive, and a few from editors who wonder the same thing. I answer these quickly, saying that I'll be back in Livingston within a week, most likely five days. I fire off notes to my children, Jack and Rachel, expounding on my arrival and a phone call I'd made the night before I left Dawson City. I miss them and look forward to seeing them in a little bit. Then I check the Chicago Cubs' Web site in time to discover that they appear to have clinched their division. I'll be home for the playoffs, which gives life new meaning along with the sweet promise of horrific disappointment. I pay for the coffee, along with a cup to go, and the computer time, before strolling down to Mac's Fireweed Books to buy a few more Yukon titles. (These titles are mentioned in the Further Reading section at the end of this book.)

The streets are already filled with traffic. People hustle toward their jobs, most of them dressed in suits or expensive casual wear. Mac's opens at eight o'clock, and I time things perfectly—an employee is unlocking the door as I approach. I could have spent hours at Mac's browsing the store's extensive selection, which includes rare out-of-print titles and nautical and topographic maps, but I quickly select five books, pay for them, and head for the car. Many miles over narrow, rough roads and dicey mountain passes lie waiting. A banzai expedition looming on the near horizon.

I fire up the rig. The biker crew is still asleep at the ungodly hour of 8:41 A.M. I bang on the door, which produces a few oaths, and yell "So long." They yell the same. I climb behind the wheel, adjust the mirrors, back out, and pull away from Whitehorse for another year. I can feel in my stomach that it is time to head home to Montana. The sun is well above the eastern horizon.

GINNY DIERS PHOTO

ALONG THE DEMPSTER HIGHWAY ON THE NORTH EDGE OF THE BLACKSTONE PLATEAU.

SEVEN /

PIERCING THE HEART OF THE YUKON

This is the Yukon. The heart of the Far North. Immense. Wild beyond anything I've experienced. Ridge after ridge of gray, jagged mountains roll off to the east. A river, the Olgilvie, pushes, twists, and slides through a dense forest of spruce as the cold water slashes and cascades across long gravel and rock bars, tapering downstream, the jumbles of stone littered with large skeletal trees piled like enormous mounds of corpses. Behind me, sailing off to the west toward Alaska and to the north toward the Beaufort Sea, are miles upon miles of dwarfed, wind-hammered fir leaning at odd angles like storm-damaged drunks, their black green shapes capturing in extreme slow motion the harshness of existence here just south of the Arctic Circle.

This is the Yukon. The heart of the Far North. Mountains and rivers and forests, all of it exploding beneath a sun-hardened sky that shimmers an alien blue. There is so much power sizzling through the air—this place is so damn strong—that for the first time in my life good country scares me. This is a land that expects a constant show of respect. Yet I sense a familiarity in it too, like seeing the friendly face of a person who I have never met but still recognize in ways vaguely understood.

Recognition. That's it. Seeing something for the first time, but knowing in my soul I've been here before.

The Yukon. Hundreds of millions of acres and only this crazy dirt, rock, mud road slicing through the middle of it.

•

Of the numerous trips I've made to the Yukon and the Northwest Territories, my former companion, photographer Ginny Diers, was along for the ride for several of them during the initial work on this book. For me not to include her in the narrative would be impossible. Good or bad, Ginny was part of the trip that is *Arctic Aurora.* To exclude her would be dishonest and certainly not faithful to the narrative. We spent many exciting and pleasant days traveling the Dempster Highway, hence her strong presence in this chapter.

•

This rough, often narrow track bounces and weaves like a slightly punch-drunk fighter, running as it does right next to thrashing rivers, clinging to the edge of moonscape mountains or wandering through silent hours of forest—calling this dangerous madness a "highway" is either extreme optimism on the part of those who built the road many years ago or attempted deception by the provincial tourism ministry. Four hundred sixty miles of roads were hacked out of this country and finally finished in 1979. Before then, the people that lived here received their goods and mail by foot, dogsled, or floatplane. Mineral survey seismic lines were laid out by hearty souls wearing snowshoes or work boots. The road is a primitive connection with the modern world, a luxury that often resembles a burden or, perhaps, a death sentence. Driving the Dempster Highway is dangerous work for trucker and road bum alike. The Yukon didn't even have any roads until World War II, when the U.S. Army built the Alaska Highway. Until then the means had never justified the end. Road building in this country is serious business. Machinery sinks through the permafrost and is abandoned. Insects drive men nuts.

The isolation of all of this untouched land makes men go still crazier with loneliness, and the cold can kill them.

Heavily laden semis roar past us in both directions carrying food, fuel, and other necessities to scattered outposts like Eagle Plains, Fort McPherson, and Inuvik that are sunk in the muddy gravel of the Mackenzie River Delta in the Northwest Territories. Traveling this road is tough, really not for the faint of heart. Driving at thirty-five miles an hour or five, whatever is possible, dodging holes and rocks, constantly scanning side mirrors and rearview mirrors for approaching trucks. When the trucks come, they come right down the middle of the road. I pull over to the edge, hoping the Suburban hangs on and doesn't slip down the cliff. Ginny holds her breath as they blast past us, the air the rigs churn up buffeting our car. When the dust clears I move on up the Dempster, eyes wide open. Here and there the remains, often charred, of campers, pickups, and some fool's Chevy sedan lie mangled and crushed in the trees or half-submerged in the tundra, with an arctic tern perched on a crumpled bumper.

The road drops down to another huge river, the Eagle. The grade is steep and its sides give way to vertiginous drops into a dwarf forest broken by patches of shrubland marked by *palsas,* irregularly shaped permafrost-cored mounds formed of segregated layers of ice and peat or mineral soil. Then the road climbs straight back up through dust turned deep mud from a sudden downpour. The way rises in wide swoops and curves until the view opens on all of the wilderness again, red pink wild flowers line the way, ravens that appear to be the size of turkeys peck away at something dead in the middle of the road. A caribou? The rack looks like a caribou's. The carcass is too small for a moose, though there are plenty around here. The ravens, unafraid, don't move. Their black heads turn and follow our passing, hunks of flesh hanging from long, rough beaks.

A few more miles down the Dempster and the moss and grasses of the subarctic tundra, rough fields littered with boulders discarded by some long-ago glacier, spread out ahead us before vanishing into the space of still more drop-offs. Now the road is one hundred feet wide, and a sign says "Emergency landing strip. Watch for aircraft." The landing area is perhaps one-quarter mile long, riddled with chuck holes as if from some crazed northland mortar attack. It slopes several degrees and lists at an even more severe angle towards the abyss. But hey, what the hell? When your airplane breaks and you're a million miles away from home, this ravaged little piece of sort-of-smooth openness probably looks like heaven on earth as your motor sputters, coughs, then dies, and the wind starts wailing over your wings as you go down.

The interior of Iceland, The Grand Erg Occidental on the western edge of the Sahara Desert, the bottom of the Grand Canyon—all of these are truly fantastic, but the Yukon is in its own league. This place is a natural drug that buries the manmade concoctions. Ginny and I are dizzy from all of it, wired from the visceral fear that all of this untouched country brings to the mind-game that is seeing new country, high on the freedom of a place that makes Yellowstone Park seem like a venue for a Sunday slow-pitch softball league.

The fog lifts. The rain quits. The thick cloud cover that dropped down on us in minutes vanishes. The late July sun shines with an intensity that turns forty degrees to seventy degrees in an instant. We stop, pour coffee, and look in all directions. The wind is puffing and gusting, so the billions of bloodthirsty mosquitoes and blackflies are down. The air carries the scent of the pine, the barren rock and a subtle taste of the sea lying one hundred miles north. Green hills roll off to purplish slate gray, treeless mountains. Small aquamarine creeks pour and tumble from narrow gaps in the high country. Snowbanks hide in shadowy creases of the tundra. A golden eagle soars overhead without sound. The Yukon is paradise in the most unforgiving of ways. You can't screw up. If you do, you are likely to wind up dead. Even when you're doing things right, the bugs savage you or a grizzly terrifies you, while the sound of Dall Sheep clattering across a narrow ledge hundreds of feet above bounces down to you. And in the winter it's just plain cold. Snow, wind, and the eternal darkness humming with the Northern Lights flashing riotous shades of ruby, emerald, sapphire, ghostly diamond white. Yeah, I could die here easily if I don't pay attention. The more I think about that, the more I ride the primal fear of the Yukon.

•

It has been a long day, and we've driven less than one hundred miles up from the Klondike Highway that leads to Dawson City. To get on the Dempster Highway, you hang north off the pavement, cross a one-lane bridge that spans the Klondike River, then navigate along a road that starts out with the best of intentions, but before long it degenerates into its true character of serious busted-up-road mayhem. The initial half of the Dempster traverses the south-central region of the Tombstone and Blackstone Uplands area in the North Yukon Plateau ecoregion. Forested valleys, brawling rivers, and ragged mountain ranges dominate this area. The Tintina Trench, a very wide, flat-bottomed valley formed by a large fault in the earth's crust slices from southeast to northwest for four hundred fifty miles.

From an overlook on the Klondike Highway yesterday, the land looked forbidding, ominous, mysterious as the light shifted and played natural tricks with the landscape. Thick bands of dark purple clouds, driven by Pacific wind, zipped across the panorama, slammed into foothills guarding the entrance to the plateau, broke up in small clusters of mad, swirling sheets of rain driving down from their ragged spinning bases, then reformed and swept on eastward. The Klondike River was a cerulean ribbon sulking its way through the dark green of the forest that looked forbidding in the gloomy light. Farther north, several peaks of the Tombstone Range, including the namesake mountain, flicked in and out of vision, hiding behind the clouds, then flashing a wicked, broken-toothed grin before fading behind rain squalls.

This is clearly serious country we are headed for, and it is hard for me to believe that hidden from sight somewhere in those trees and mountains is a giant gold mine that has already torn up and scarred thousands of acres. A sign at yesterday's highway overlook, thirty-five miles east of Dawson City, proudly proclaimed the operation's industrious nature and included photographs of earthmoving on a massive scale taking place at the mine. But we need the metal so we can flash some cuff and show off our gold Rolex's, don't we? No matter where I travel in the Yukon, this extractive tune is playing all too loudly. Lead, zinc, and uranium also appear in the sedimentary rock which was cooked millions of years ago by igneous intrusions that welled up from deep beneath the planet's crust.

This is old land with an ancient history, the floor of a sea two billion years back. Recently—that is, between ninety and forty-five million years ago—countless earthquakes caused two tectonic plates to slide horizontally in different directions, tearing the landscape apart and creating the Tintina Trench. Some of the land has been displaced by nearly three hundred miles, sliding one way or the other on a scale I can't imagine. The Tintina Trench is a transcurrent or strike-slip fault like the San Andreas in California. The geology around here is as tough as the countryside and the climate. Cataclysmic shifts are just around the geologic corner.

The ice ages here weren't slackers either. During the Pre-Reid glacial interval, between 2.6 and 2.9 million years ago, the Cordilleran ice sheet blocked the Yukon River to the south and east, sending it on its merry way cutting a new channel northwest to the Bering Sea. The Yukon used to empty into the Pacific Ocean. Where it flows past Dawson City it is a half-mile wide and perhaps fifty feet deep. No big deal up here in country where gigantic happenings are just the way it goes down.

About twenty thousand years ago the most recent ice age was at its peak. The Wisconsin Glaciation had gone on for the previous fifty to sixty thousand years and would continue for another ten thou-

GINNY DIERS PHOTO

THE TOMBSTONE MOUNTAINS ALONG THE DEMPSTER HIGHWAY.

sand. Ice sheets thousands of feet thick covered much of the land except for most of the Yukon and Alaska, which were cut off from the rest of unglaciated North America (the Lower-48 states today) by the continental ice sheets. Both the Yukon and Alaska survived as one of the few refugia (ice-free regions) during this ice age. The ice sheets sucked up much of the oceans' water resulting in a land bridge across the narrow Bering Strait between Siberia and North America. That area is now known as Beringia. During this period, Alaska and the Yukon were ecologically a part of Asia. Exchanges of species in both directions occurred, explaining the circumpolar distribution of species living today at these high latitudes. There is increasing evidence that humans also crossed this land bridge nearly fifty thousand years ago. The climate was very dry and cold, aided in part by prevailing winds blowing over the towering ice fields. Based on the number of grazing animals that roamed this vast area back then, the landscape may have been a combination of tundra and grassland. Fossil records indicate that herds of mastodon and western camel roamed here. Ivory carvings and jewelry are made for sale from tusks unearthed these days. Because the animals are extinct, this ivory is considered a possible alternative source that may reduce elephant poaching in Africa and India. The price for mastodon ivory has varied between $1.25 and $1,000 a pound. It is a legal item internationally and can be carried and sold anywhere without penalty. (However, based on the past few unpleasant experiences I've had with our delightful United States customs officials at the Alberta-Montana border, I suspect that trying to bring in anything more exotic than a paperback book might be one hell of a risk.) Musk ox and Dall sheep are two still extant species from that time. While the age of Beringia was relatively brief in terms of geologic time span, the effects of this curious age can still be seen today in the arctic.

The musk ox is the sole surviving member of a large group of ice-age oxen that is now extinct. Its name derives from the scent given off by the animals. Because of their thick, shaggy coats and underlying dense wool, musk oxen are the only mammals of the far north that don't seek shelter during winter blizzards. They conserve body heat by crowding together in slow-moving herds or, when the weather is unusually severe, they stop and huddle in groups, sometimes in outfacing circles. They also do this, with their calves wedged in between the adults, when threatened by predators like wolves. The animals sport impressive horns that span their foreheads and extend on both sides in a downward then upward curve, tapering to sharp, lethal points. Adult musk ox weigh between four hundred and six hundred pounds.

The Tombstone area, part of the seabed buried under many feet of saltwater eons ago, is at the edge of the enormous Beringa that, as I mentioned earlier, extended from eastern Siberia across Alaska and the northern Yukon to the Mackenzie River in the Northwest Territories. During the last ice age, Beringa provided a refuge for numerous plants and animals, among them now extinct megafauna like the woolly mammoth, steppe bison, lions, and scimitar (better known as saber-toothed) cats. The notion of wading a stream casting to arctic grayling while being stalked by a scimitar cat padding through the mosses and lichen on a course parallel to mine, large tooth-filled jaws drooling at my scent, is an intriguing variation on the Montana grizzly two-step fly-fishing dance. Remains of mammoths and other Ice Age animals are often unearthed today, many found in the northern Yukon in Old Crow Flats and at Bluefish Caves. Placer miners working gold in the Klondike drainage sometimes uncover mammoth bones and other Beringian fossils.

•

The first cast in this deep blue glide of the North Fork of the Klondike and I am hooked to a fish that I first thought was a mountain whitefish, but they don't live way up here. Instead, I realize I am connected to a three-pound grayling, which is large for this species. The Montana state record is barely over two pounds. As I pull the fish to me, its distinctive sail-like, turquoise-colored dorsal fin slicing the water, the sound of a sport-utility vehicle making a panic stop on the black gravel above ratchets through the still air.

"What the hell?" I say aloud. I drop my rod with the grayling still attached to the fly and leader and quick step up the steep bank to see if Ginny needs my assistance.

This country gets weirder and weirder, and we are only a few hours up the Dempster Highway. Three very animated men are speaking a language I am not familiar with. They are hopping up and down, laughing and gesticulating toward the back of their vehicle. One of them is in his early thirties, slight of build with wire-rimmed glasses, buzz-cut hair, fatigue pants, and a T-shirt depicting a woman performing fellatio on a man. The universal red circle with a slash through it covers the tender scene. Another man is the same age, balding and dressed in wool shirt and jeans. The oldest, maybe the father, has a beard, longish brown hair, and looks to be the sanest of the trio.

"Oh God!" I mutter. I really should drop the booze and drugs. This shit never stops. Follows me everywhere. I walk up and Ginny is laughing, perhaps a healthy sign. The three men are now opening the back of their little four-wheel drive and pulling out chunks of red flesh hermetically sealed in thick, clear plastic. The back of the rig is jam packed with camping and fishing gear along with cases of beer. The three of them are obviously proud and excited about the plastic-wrapped items. They are filled with manic energy, perhaps juiced on all of the freedom that is the Yukon. No rules. No time schedule to follow. They chatter in bursts of a language that apparently had its origins in some eastern European locale, no doubt a much more restrictive society and environment than they find themselves in now. Perhaps they come from the dark mountains near the Transylvanian homeland of Vlad the Impaler.

"Salmon. See? We rented boat in Valdez and caught all this. Many fish," says the one with the safe-sex shirt. His wide grin is electric. Infectious. I start to laugh and nod my head, for what reason I have no idea. "Our arms very tired. So many fish. What you do?" he asks, and points at my fly rod that is now slowly being drawn into the river by the impatient grayling I've hooked. "What you do?" he asks again. The other two, who obviously are from the same absurd road show, shout almost in unison, "Zbdgt arugula norsht?"

All right. I know when it's time to say, "The hell with it. This is interesting."

"Grayling. First cast. Three pounds. Great fishing here," I offer.

"Grzzhgting. Sfzrzt czst. Zthhgr pgknhgds. Zgtrt nglngzr," relays the one with the informative shirt to his friends.

"Dshzhtdt. Dshzhtdt," they exclaim between swigs from cans of Molson's ale. "Dshzhtdt. Good goddamn."

Fisherman. Fisherman everywhere. We all know what the play is.

"Damn straight," I say, "Dshzhtdt."

We are all laughing now, Ginny is taking photographs between grins, and I think, "My people have found me, here in the Yukon, on the Dempster, right beside a world-class grayling river." We learn that they are from Czechoslovakia and on their way to Inuvit to scuba dive in the Arctic Ocean. "When in Rome. . . ." had nothing on these guys. I look to the river and see that the grayling now has three feet of my rod in the water.

We talk some more, then with a hearty "Dshzhtdt" and in a cloud of Molson empties, they blast their way north up the Dempster. Great guys. We never see them again.

"Dshzhtdt" it is. I go down to my rod, now seven feet in the water, lift it up, pull in the fat fish, unhook the Elkhair Caddis from its tough, rubbery lip, return the grayling to the water, walk back to the Suburban, and off we go.

•

We planned to get as far as Engineer Creek that first day, close to two hundred miles. Here the Dempster Highway winds along beside the North Fork of the Klondike River as it cuts its way beneath the Olgilvie Mountains. Once up on the plateau, the road glides through the tundra with its rich growth of brush, scrub willow, moss, rough grass, and lichen; twenty-odd miles of relatively smooth sailing. Water is everywhere in the form of the Blackstone River (so named because of the numerous coal seams the native people observed), as well as creeks, rivulets, ponds, lakes, and small seeps percolating from the ground. Even though it is early August, temperatures are in the sixties during the day, which lasts nearly twenty-four hours as the sun barely sets below the northwest horizon sometime around 2 A.M., only to return less than an hour later in the northeast. Aufeis, or overflow ice, lines long stretches of the Blackstone. Aufeis is a German term for sheets of ice formed when overflow water accumulates and freezes during winter. Yellow caution signs along the road announce the presence of horses grazing on the grass near the ice. The animals belong to a local outfitter who leads hunters far into the backcountry—hell, it's all backcountry. Yukon paintbrush, crowberry, arctic lupine, blackish crazyweed, and countless other plants fire up the greens with their mad shades of red, blue, pink, yellow, orange, and white.

We see *pingos,* conical ice-covered hills formed in the permafrost that range from one hundred to seven thousand years old, rising above the tundra, looking like beaver lodges. Most of the pingos, an Inuktitut word the native people have for these odd shapes, are open-system features that form next to foothill slopes. When groundwater flowing down the slope is impeded by permafrost near the surface, or by some other frost feature, it begins pushing upward. As the permafrost freezes downward it puts pressure on the water trapped below. The water is forced up, pushing the permafrost into a dome that freezes to form the ice core of the hill. The pingos on this plateau rarely reach more than a few feet in height, but the ones up on the Mackenzie Delta are well over one hundred feet high.

We stop beside the Blackstone to fish. I take seven grayling in twenty minutes, missing several fish that look to be larger than my first one a few hours back. This country is alive with fish and game. Moose, wolf, caribou, grizzly, arctic fox, and on and on. Every stream seems to be teeming with grayling that are considered rare and exotic in the Lower-48. Up this way, First Nation People, such as the Inuktitut, net thousands of pounds of them in the spring, drying the meat for future hard times. The harvest does not seem to be affecting the grayling numbers. I know I can catch a couple of hundred in a day's fishing. No matter what I use—Elkhair Caddis, Royal Wulffs, Hare's Ear nymphs, Adams—the grayling leap and slash at the patterns. Some of the fish arc out of the water and crash down on the fly. Riffles, runs, pools, beneath pine-tree sweepers, or in slight seams of current along shore right next to the road, the fish are everywhere; all of them are from one to four pounds with silver, silvery purples, black spotting, turquoise spotting, carmine, or yellow fluorescing thin wavy lines on their fins. Remarkable fish. Strong, wild, and eager to take a fly. After a few hours of this I quit, sated and happy. I've kept a few for a roadside dinner later. The native people up here truly don't understand catch-and-release and would prefer that fish be kept for food, a more respectful treatment in their eyes. The fishing regulations explain this and encourage keeping some grayling (or northerns or char) for a meal. Recipes are even included in the regulations. Stores in many of the towns sell canned char, musk ox, and caribou. The land is still intact to the extent that this, done in moderation as it is up here, has a marginal effect on game populations. I feel that I'm playing the part of the good visitor by having sautéed grayling later tonight.

Farther on, the Dempster Highway dips down to the river, then climbs back into the Olgilvies, now treeless. Vast, wide valleys sweep down from the rounded, bare mountains. Huge alluvial fans of rocks, gravel, and boulders wash out and across the road. The entire landscape is shaded gray, light pink, and purple with subtle highlights of olive, lemon-green, bright emerald, and dark green of the scattered patches of pine and fir along the road. We stop at a wide spot near the summit of the pass through here. Only the wind and the rough screech of an eagle breaks a silence so complete that my ears ring.

This country goes on forever. The Tintina Trench. The Klondike River. The Tombstone Range. Tundra. The Blackstone River. The Olgilvies. Way up and over the crest of mountains to the east are still more ranges—the Nadaleens, the Knorrs, the Bonnet Plums, the Wernecke s. And farther east in the Northwest Territories there are the Backbones and the Canyons. And rivers called the Peel (full of sea-run Arctic Char, I hope), Hart, Wind, Vittrekwa, and Caribou. And there is the Richardson Range to the north running to the Beaufort Sea.

Then coming up a rise, the sound of a truck laboring and the clank, rip, screech of a wheel bearing long gone assaults us. An old Ford F-150 pickup, blue, battered, and rusted, lurches up the pass pulling a white camper trailer that zigs and zags like a lunatic boat in the pickup's wake of exhaust and dust. The noise of the rig grows to a roar and I see that on the left side of the trailer there is no tire, only a flattened, worn-to-shining rim that spews a steady stream of sparks as it drags across the hard surface of the Dempster. The truck's driver never notices us as he works hard at keeping the whole mess on the road. His hands grip the wheel as the truck shifts abruptly with the weight of the foundering trailer. His wife waves at us as if she doesn't have a care in the world. Ten minutes later we can still hear the sounds of that wheel and mufflerless engine as it grinds its way through the mountains and forest. I am beginning to realize that all kinds of us trip the Dempster fantastic.

Around 9 P.M. we pull into the Engineer Creek campground and find the last open campsite out of only thirteen, a narrow swath carved out of the birch and willow far from the creek. The ground is muddy black coal. Millions of mosquitoes descend upon us. We build a fire, cook and eat quickly, and are about to turn in for the evening when we notice a man ride in on a bicycle pulling a small carriage behind him. He is wearing black lycra shorts, yellow shirt, black helmet and gloves, blacker sunglasses, and, to put this gently, he looks beat, dead beat. He's well-tanned, but the welts from the bites of black flies and mosquitoes glow painful red through his sun-darkened color. He dismounts, drops his bike on the ground, asks the man who has the campsite next to us if he can sleep off in the far corner, receives a "Yes," then sets about putting up his tent, stowing gear, and going down to Engineer Creek to clean up.

Ginny and I, being curious at heart, wait a few minutes, then follow him. On his way back, he almost walks into and through us; he is that tired. "Oh, Hi," he says. He is in his midforties, muscular and fit, with long black hair going gray.

We ask where he is coming from. Where he's headed.

"Down from Inuvik, over two hundred fifty miles. To Dawson City. Seven days already," he says, with exhaustion we can feel, and introduces himself as Bill and adds that his companion will be in camp shortly. "The road just pounds you. No escape and same for the bugs." He tells us that he has biked all over the world, but says this is the hardest trip he's ever been on. He is near tears.

"In time you'll look back on this with good memories," Ginny tries to encourage him. Mosquitoes fill the air with an all-present hum. The three of us speak between swats.

"I don't think so."

"I admire your courage and stamina," I say.

"Be careful of what you admire," he laughs. "Good luck to you two. I've got to go lie down now," and he trudges off.

We look at each other and shrug. We hope he and his friend (and we hope after a trip like this they would still be friends) make it safely down off the Dempster and into Dawson City. We return to camp and go to bed at 1 A.M. in near daylight.

In the morning we see that Bill and his friend have broken camp.

They are already on the road. Long gone. The mosquitoes aren't. And neither is an elderly couple in a Dodge Van with Iowa plates. They ask Ginny which way is north. Her reply is that they should go back south to the relative safety of Dawson City, but the man wants to go for it despite his wife's abject terror. Off they drive. Godspeed.

•

The next day finds us at the Arctic Circle, where we take the obligatory photos next to the sign that marks the location. I stand in a constantly changing mixture of wind, rain, snow, sun, and fog waggling a golf club for the shot. Why not. Makes as much sense as anything after all this difficult driving. The land is now low mountains and soft hills edging vast tracts of tundra. We have gone above the arctic circle. Something we've always wanted to do, but, in truth, nothing looks all that much different than it did a few hours south. Still, we made it and are glad we did. The road is turning dangerously slippery in the rain. A couple of hours later, I ease the Suburban into the Rock River campground three hours north of the circle. We are the only ones here. I go off to fill in a registration form (they have this silliness even way up north) and to find some wood for a fire. Our friends the mosquitoes are here along with a couple of huge black ravens.

Back from accomplishing these duties, I tell Ginny that I met our only other company, a man from Austria who is going to camp at the other end of this place. She doesn't hear me.

"I saw a ghost John," she says. "Out of the corner of my eye I thought I saw you coming back, but this man was wearing a red shirt and had a beard. I looked at him, turned away, and then turned back to say 'Hello,' only he was gone."

Ghosts? The Yukon is filled with them. Tales of mysterious miners, trappers, native people, thieves, all of them flickering in and out of our awareness. Why not a spook here? I try to calm Ginny, then suggest we go fishing. We find Rock River, more of a creek here, to be barren, with no aquatic insect life and no fish—the first stream like this I've come across in the Yukon. We trudge back to camp, cook a dinner of bacon and eggs and toast, then turn in for a long night of so-called rest.

In the morning the rain returns, and we decide to turn back south. I learned from the Austrian that the road is truly horrible farther north, the mosquitoes worse, the blackflies are coming out now with a vengeance, and the Arctic Char are late this year and have not moved into the Peel River from the ocean. I'm burned-out from the drive; my nerves are shot, so Ginny takes over. We decide to pass on Inuvik just over the Yukon border less than eighty miles into the Northwest Territories from where we are now. We wanted to see the immense MacKenzie River Delta again (the delta is larger than several eastern states combined), a place of braided river channels, forest, scrub-covered flats, vast quantities of avian wildlife, a focus of First Nation Peoples culture, and much more.

I am a person who lives for unspoiled country, and Inuvik, with its name-brand hotel/motels/restaurants and tourists who only come here to say they've been to the end of the road and can now check off the town of nearly three thousand from their list of things to see and do, holds little fascination or even interest for me. Not because of the native people or the land, but because Inuvik is being hustled in a fashion—admittedly low-key by most standards—like Yellowstone Park or Banff or any of a bunch of other glorious locations that have already fallen victim to the hustle for a tourista buck. I prefer places that are still rough around the edges and untamed in their hearts—places like Fort Simpson or Faro or Wrigley. So we decide to head back down to Dawson City, a tourist town that admits to its weaknesses and still has an honest sense of adventure to it. Maybe I'm too hard on Inuvik, or maybe this is a function of too much to see and too little time and money, but that's how I see this.

Perhaps the next time up to Inuvik, I'll fly the eighty-five miles to Tuktoyaktuk, meaning "resembling caribou," north of Inuvik in Kugmallit Bay in the Beaufort Sea, east of the Mackenzie Delta.

Legend says that when caribou were abundant in this area, a woman looked at them as they waded in the water and the caribou petrified. (I have a feeling that there's a good deal more to this tale than the Inuits are telling.) Reefs resembling this image may be seen at low tide. Traditionally, villages in the this area were the home of whale-hunting Inuvialuit. Beginning in the early 1800s, European whalers established their operations, but they also brought epidemics of smallpox and syphilis that decimated native populations. Eventually Tuk was chosen from villages in the region as the best port. The first Hudson's Bay Store was built in 1937. There has been a fair amount of development, especially during the oil boom-and-bust cycle of the 1970s. Today Tuktoyaktuk remains the base for Beaufort Sea resource development and is within the grounds of the Reindeer Grazing Herd area. These smaller cousins of the caribou were imported several decades ago as an experiment in domestic animal farming. The herd is privately owned. There are also approximately 5,000 Beluga whales that live in the shallow waters of the Beaufort Sea. The mammals run up to 17 feet and 1,500 pounds. Bowhead whales are a much rarer site, though there are about 2,000 to 3,000 in the Western Arctic region. Up to 65 feet long and 110,000 pounds, bowheads are one of the largest mammals on the planet. The official bird of the Northwest Territories, the gyrfalcon, is also seen in this northern region.

Bird life in the high arctic is incredible. At various times of the year, particularly from May through September, you can see Canada geese, tundra swans, sandhill cranes, Lapland longspurs, common, arctic, yellow-billed and red-throated loons, red-necked phalaropes, gray-headed chickadees, golden and bald eagles, rough-legged hawks, harriers, peregrine falcons, merlins, and short-eared owls to name a few. A total of two hundred seventy-two species have been documented in the Yukon.

Another village I plan to visit is Aklavik, or "place of the barren land grizzly bear" in Inuvialuktan. This involves a thirty-seven-mile flight west across the Mackenzie Delta from Inuvik. In the winter an ice road reaches the community; in the summer boats make the trip. Situated on the Peel Channel of the Mackenzie Delta, not far from where the Mackenzie River flows into the Beaufort Sea, Aklavik was the place where the Inuvialuit and the Gwich'in (one of five Dene main bands) traditionally met and sometimes battled in the desperate search for often scarce food and fur. A small trading post was established across the river, and by 1918 a permanent settlement was located on the present site. The community quickly became the chief trapping, trading, and transportation center for the muskrat-rich delta. In the 1950s, flooding and erosion problems caused the federal government to relocate the town where Inuvik now stands. Although everything was moved to the new location, many Aklavik residents refused to leave. The village's motto, "Never say die," above a picture of a beaver came into being. Today the hamlet, with a population of over seven hundred, is home to Dene and Inuvialuit who follow a mainly traditional lifestyle of trapping, hunting, and fishing.

Ginny and I begin the drive back down the Dempster Highway to Dawson City several hundred miles distant. Competent, skilled, and cautious, Ginny eases us up a long, steep, muddy, greasy grade in four-wheel low. Rounding a bend we spot a pickup and camper twenty feet below us, upside down in the tundra, wheels still spinning, lights on. Clothes, maps, and food are scattered all over the place. A man who looks to be from the Middle East is pacing around the wreck and yelling to himself. He sees us and climbs the bank.

"I went too fast for the road and started skidding," he says, and points to several hundred yards of sloppy tire marks that fishtail about the Dempster. "Then over the edge. I have friends in Inuvik I work for. They can help me, I think," he stammered in a nervous, frightened voice, his dark eyes darting from the wreck that was his truck, to the ground, up to us, and back again to the truck.

Ginny gives him her coat, walks him to our car where she turns up the heat and gives him some water to drink.

We make plans to drive him back to the service-station truck stop five hours south at Eagle Plains and are about to leave when a road crew truck appears out of nowhere. More ghosts? They survey the scene, speak with the driver of the wreck, and call a wrecker from Eagle Plains. We continue to reassure Ahmad, who is badly shaken but uninjured except for a sprained wrist, as we transfer him to the road crew's truck. They thank us sincerely for stopping to help, and off we go into the rain, fog, and mud. Where did those guys come from? Thin air?

Ginny goes ever so slowly down a long, steep hill. The road drops away on both sides. Going off would be death, but she makes it without a slip, lights a cigarette, and keeps plowing along for seven hours all the way back down to Engineer Creek where we spend the night once more. Incredible driving. I think of my road-bum friends Bob Jones and John Talia. They would have been impressed with her work. Not a mistake or bad decision. Just sure-handed driving minute after minute on the toughest road I've ever been on. Yeah, they would have been in awe.

•

The next day is sunny, outrageous in its splendor. We roll down the now dry road at forty-five miles an hour, really living it up, stopping every now and then to catch grayling. At North Fork Pass, less than two hours from the perceived bliss of the Klondike Highway, we stop. The peaks of the Tombstone Range tower in the distance. Ginny wanders off with her tripod and camera fitted with a 600 mm lens. I glass the landscape with my grandfather's old 10 x 50 Tasco binoculars.

Up the long, brilliant green valley that climbs to the mountains, I visually follow one of the headwater tributaries of the North Fork of the Klondike River. (The name Klondike is a bastardization of the Indian *Thron-Duick* or *Tron-Deg*, which seems to have meant "hammer-water." Early miners had trouble pronouncing these words, so they evolved into "Clunedik," "Clundyke," or "Clondyke." A mining inspector with the Royal Northwest Mounted Police made the name "Klondyke," and over the years Americans in the region replaced the letter *y* with *i*.) What looks like relatively smooth, grassy terrain to my naked eyes is actually steep, brush-choked, nearly impassable country. Waterfalls that I thought were only ten feet high are really fifty to one hundred feet high. I know that there are grizzlies lurking in that bush. I work the lenses farther up-country until I reach the mountains. The view, through the binoculars, staggers me. Mountains that appeared awesome before are so damn far beyond that. Thousand-foot hunks of rust red, ochre, and purple rock sheer away from Tombstone Peak and shove into each other. Enormous faults tear through them. Frozen waterfalls of ice cling to the faces of the peaks. Huge masses of cloud stack up behind the mountains, then squeeze through the narrow gaps between the chaotic monoliths before exploding into rapidly expanding, billowing clouds once again. Rain drives down from the clouds at the point where they shoot through these granite creases. I follow the mountain walls up and down their entire lengths. This is an alpine still life that rocks with gigantic motion.

The rivers, the mountains, the road, the weather, the immense size of this land, all of it rips through me in a simultaneous flash. In a brief few days I've been hammered, knocked over, awed by the country. Nothing anywhere touches it. A thousand lifetimes could never cover this place.

I'll be back, but even if I were never to travel this road again, I'll always be here. This place has nailed me.

GINNY DIERS PHOTO

HAD FITZGERALD AND THE LOST PATROL MADE THE CORRECT TURNS, THEY WOULD HAVE TRAVELED THROUGH THIS COUNTRY ON THE HOME STRETCH OF THEIR DOGSLED TRIP ALONG WHAT IS NOW THE DEMPSTER HIGHWAY. THE BLACKSTONE RIVER AND FOOTHILLS OF THE TOMBSTONE MOUNTAINS ARE SHOWN.

EIGHT /

A NORTH COUNTRY LEGEND

There are many legends, along with disasters that have evolved into legends over time, riotous tales of lost gold or even emerald mines and haunted bordellos, and the ubiquitous accounts of crazed killers such as Albert Johnson, The Mad Trapper of Rat River. Because of the fierce nature of the North Country, these incidents are often eerie and unexplainable. Men die or just plain disappear in the harsh environment that is the Yukon and the Territories. Vast mineral riches are discovered by some slightly-crazed prospector who dies from cheap whiskey or old age taking his wealthy secret with him to his grave. Such is the story of The Lost Patrol. Everything about this tragedy strikes a rhythm that represents how I feel about the North. What follows is an account of this cold situation based on a fair amount of research I've done on the subject. I may even do a full-blown book on these men some day.

•

"All money in dispatch bag and bank, clothes, etc., I leave to my dearly beloved mother, Mrs. John Fitzgerald, Halifax. God bless all."

F. J. Fitzgerald, R.N.W.P Mar 24, 1911

Life is anything but cold or barren on this sunny, early-September afternoon in the 21st century. I'm standing in a shallow riffle of the Blackstone River not far from the Dempster Highway, a rough dirt and rock road that slices through the heart of the Yukon as it winds its way from east of Dawson City hundreds of miles north to Inuvik in the Northwest Territories well above the Arctic Circle. The road is a wild ride through paradise, through some of the last truly fine country anywhere. The tundra, brush, birch and pine trees, and mosses are glowing with an intense autumn radiance that flares briefly before the onset of the long, dark winter. Purples, oranges, crimsons, yellows, every color imaginable, shimmer beneath an intense sun and a clear blue sky. The air smells of approaching cold, the moving water and the trees, Moose stand shoulder deep in lakes and ponds munching aquatic plants, huge masses of green vegetation hanging from their jaws, water streaming down. Grizzly bears forage on nearby slopes in a late-season frenzy, the large animals crashing through the willow and alder. The bears devour berries, leaves, and stems. They aren't discriminate. There is no time for such luxuries. Grayling evolved over hundreds of thousands of years swimming in the truly ice-cold waters that tumbled and crashed at the bases of the mile-high or more ice sheets that covered much of North America periodically until about 10,000 years ago. The ice will return, and humans will be forced to move south into more and more cramped quarters, but the grayling will survive in this fierce, fluctuation boundary between ice and green land. The fish's large, sail-like dorsal fin is no doubt an adaptation that helped them maneuver in the harsh currents of the snow and ice melt of the glaciers. This fin serves the grayling well today in this river that flows with speed and power, sapphire elegance. I cast a small dry fly to a seam of current less than 40 feet away and a large grayling arcs above the surface, distinctive dorsal fin extended fully with turquoise spots fluorescing clearly, then pounces on the pattern. I reach back with the rod and the fish zips and zings in the river, jumps once, then gives up the fight. I bring it to me. Twenty inches and over three-pounds of perfection. Silver purple flanks, turquoise spots, white-tipped fins, all of this intensified as the colors fluoresce driven by the fish's anger and fear. I drop down in the water, twist the hook free, and point the grayling toward deeper water. It's power returns quickly and it disappears in seconds.

I stand up and follow the course of the Blackstone with my eyes as it rushes and glides beneath overhanging pines and along its bed of colorful rock and gravel. Then I look up at the mountains rising to the east. Dark pines cover the lower slopes, but a thousand feet above the valley floor the ridges and cirques are treeless, covered only with shrubs, and mosses that flicker in wavering intensities as a light band of clouds plays with the sun. I stare at the purple-gray rock of those mountains and then at the Blackstone and I wonder what it must have been like for Fitzgerald and his men over 90 years ago when no one was around to help and it was so very cold and eerily dark as only the perpetual night of an arctic winter can be. And I remembered a poem by Robert W. Service, the most honest and real voice of this country, a man who lived and wrote of the Yukon at the time of The Lost Patrol. This one is called *The Land God Forgot:*

The lonely sunsets flare forlorn
Down valleys dreadly desolate;
The lordly mountains soar in scorn
As still as death, as stern as fate.

The lonely sunsets flame and die;
The giant valleys gulp the night;
The monster mountains scrape the sky
Where eager stars are diamond bright.

So gaunt against the gibbous moon,
Piercing the silence velvet-piled,
A lone wolf howls his ancient rune—
The fell arch-spirit of the wild

O outcast land! O leper land!
Let the lone wolf-cry all express
The hate insensate of thy hand,
Thy heart's abysmal loneliness.

Service is truly one of the clarion voices of the North Country and this poem rings starkly real to me as I stand here in the middle of a vast wilderness that dwarfs anything I have ever experienced in Montana. This is like being on another planet with all my conceptions of how reality operates not just suspended but shattered. Anything is possible in this land. I don't think this. I know it. Perhaps Fitzgerald and his men were plagued by something as simple and destructive as voodoo. Not the weird stuff with snakes, candles, manic drumming, and crazed zombies raising hell at midnight in some third world jungle, but rather those inexplicable, seemingly-connected, series of events that lead to often unfathomable outcomes. That's the species of voodoo I'm talking about. There have been many instances of this difficult to quantify force in my more than 30 years on the road, both good and bad.

Last year on one of our drives to the north country to work on a book, my companion and I were rolling down a back road in northern Alberta on our way to the Yukon when our 1983 Suburban's engine suddenly quit running. I edge the car over to the side of the road fighting the now defunct power steering. When we stop I look over to my friend and say "Now what?" or something less delicate along those lines. At her suggestion I go out and raise the hood in the universal signal of abject defeat with no hope of rescue and little hope of redemption. I trudge back to the car and sit down, thinking that we will be here for a bit. In less than two minutes orange flashing light ricochets off the rearview mirror. Looking behind we see a tow truck. A what? And out here?

The driver hops down from the cab and says "Good morning. Looks like you two need help. I was on my way into the station when I saw you raise the hood."

Hell, it seems like we always need some kind of help. And by the way "What station?" I look around and see nothing but miles and miles of pine trees, swamp, and bugs.

Our savior tries to start the Suburban. No luck. He fiddles under the hood and says the fuel pump is probably shot. Within 15 minutes he's towed us to the station that is a couple of miles down the road hiding in the trees. The mechanic, a cheerful, grease-covered guy, comes out and fiddles his own tune with the Suburban's engine, looks up at us and says, "Fuel pump's shot," and smiles. "Nice thing about these old Suburban's [ours was an '83] is that parts are easy to locate, eh. You'll have to wait a bit though, maybe an hour, so go next door and have a cup of coffee. I'll ring over when it's ready, eh."

Forty-five minutes later we are running down the road bound for Grand Prairie. The entire incident took less than 90 minutes and one hundred dollars out of our lives. What were the chances of our breaking down under such fortuitous circumstances? Slim and none more than 500 miles above the Canadian-U.S. border. And to have the repair done so quickly. Even in our hometown of Livingston the whole deal would have consumed at least a couple of days and much more money.

That's good voodoo.

Bad voodoo is when we're driving to an isolated camp we have on the southern flanks of the Bears Paw Mountains in north central Montana and a sharp rock slices the sidewall with a nasty eight-inch gash of our left rear tire, and then a few miles later running and praying our way into Havre, the nearest town, to buy a replacement, a cousin of the first rock does in our spare in a similarly ugly fashion and no one comes by for two days, the nearest ranch being 40 miles away across broken, parched country filled with rattlesnakes and surly arachnids. In all the years of coming here I'd never had a single flat before. The tires we were running on are called Toyo. Rancher friends of mine recommended them because of their toughness and thick sidewalls that all but eliminate sidewall gashes, in theory anyway. So, two flat tires on rancher-endorsed Toyos was unexpected. So we camp in the middle of a mosquito-ridden sage flat in 110 degree heat and try not to go crazy, until long, very long, hours later a cowboy hauling a trailer holding a brace of quarter horses pulls up around 6 A.M. The truck is banged up and the engine rattles and coughs loudly without the aid of a muffler. Sweet music from our perspective in the early morning, dry heat. He asks with a good-natured wise-ass smile "You two havin' a good time over there?" and takes us to salvation, which in this case is a tire dealer, motel room, and some delivered pizza.

That's bad voodoo.

So I'm in the middle of the Blackstone River catching grayling and wondering if The Lost Patrol was nailed by that old black magic or did Fitzgerald and his men make a series of minor and not-so-minor mistakes that added up to failure of the most dire variety. I've experienced, read, and heard about so many instances of this voodoo—the word "luck" doesn't quite get the essence of the phenomenon for me—that I believe the power exists. Why voodoo happens in a certain place at a certain time is beyond my comprehension. Maybe as Spalding Gray says in his video *Swimming to Cambodia* who knows why evil happens where it does. Perhaps it's just swirling around our planet and drops down on a whim or at will. Good enough for me. And possibly this is what doomed The Lost Patrol.

The thing is, ever since I first learned of The Lost Patrol some years ago, Fitzgerald, his men and their horrible fate I've wondered about this. And fishing for these grayling in this remarkably beautiful

GINNY DIERS PHOTO

KLONDIKE KATE'S IS A SOURCE OF GOOD LODGING AND FOOD IN DAWSON CITY, YUKON.

river at a spot where Fitzgerald and his men would have traveled more than 90 years ago had they made their way across the mountains I'm looking at makes me consider this question. I find it difficult to believe that a man as experienced as Fitzgerald could have screwed up so badly. He was a respected, competent Mountie with many years of trekking through the harsh wilderness of what is now The Yukon and Northwest Territories. A number of his exploits were so difficult that it is beyond me how he accomplished them. He was an excellent officer of exceptional discipline and possessing abundant organizational skills, great stamina, and high principles. How would, how could, such a man lead such a disastrous mission, one that lesser men had made six times previously? And the word "lesser" is a relative term in this rough country. Mere survival translates easily to tough and resourceful.

Consider Fitzgerald's first posting in the far north, Herschell

Island in the Arctic Ocean, about 80 miles northwest of the mouth of the Mackenzie River. This post was to be an example of the importance of law and order even in one of the most remote regions on earth. Fitzgerald and the Mounties were up there to show that no matter what the cost , the laws of Canada would be enforced and the native population protected, in this case from the crews of the whaling ships that made Herschell their northernmost homeport. The men on these ships were rough, hard-drinking types who introduced the highly-susceptible Inuits to alcohol that ravaged the Indians as did the venereal disease and smallpox the crew members carried.

There is something appealing to my imagination when I consider then Sergeant Fitzgerald along with Constable Sutherland and Interpreter Thompson establishing law on this desolate, mossy-covered, rocky island that was constantly awash with gale-driven waves and battered by storms of the fiercest magnitude. It was the least inviting post in the entire Canadian Dominion. In these latitudes for two entire months the sun never rises above the horizon. The closest this island comes to daylight from the middle of November through the middle of January is an eerie twilight where the stars still shine and the northern lights flicker weirdly across the sky. There is no fresh water on the island, so blocks of ice were cut from a small lake in October to supply drinking water. In the summer this lake is unfit for use because it is clouded with sediment and choked with aquatic weeds. The barracks consisted of rude structures constructed of scavenged timber from the whaling ships and driftwood. This frame was covered with sod and the walls lined with canvas. Ventilation was made by punching holes in the roof. Imagine being confined in these huts in the middle of a raging blizzard that continued for long dark days with the temperature more than 40 below zero with only a smoky wood fire for heat and a crude oil lamp for light to read and fill out journals by. Yet within a year Fitzgerald and his tiny contingent had restored order to the island concerning the whaling crews and the natives. He had improved his quarters to the extent that the post now boasted a log headquarters complete with billiard room.

The point of this example is that Fitzgerald was a strong, determined and obviously self-sufficient individual. For a man of this caliber to disappear and eventually perish on a dogsled mail run sent shock waves through the land that are felt even in modern times.

So considering all of this, was The Lost Patrol victimized by bad judgment or by voodoo or by both?

•

The story of The Lost Patrol goes far beyond myth and legend in the Yukon and Northwest Territories. What happened to these four men could happen to anyone who lives in this country. Trappers, semi-truck drivers making the haul up the Dempster Highway in the middle of winter, gold miners, loggers, or just someone driving from Dawson City to visit family or friends in the Territorial Capital of Whitehorse 300 miles to the east. Even a small mistake in this place can translate into death. For that matter, no mistakes is no guarantee of survival. As Service says in his poem "As still as death, as stern as fate."

And the Royal Northwest Mounted Police were figures that commanded the utmost respect from men who lived hard, rough, brutal lives. Many of them were outlaws or murderers of the cruelest sort. Robbery and death over huge fortunes in gold nuggets and dust were common before the Mounties asserted themselves. A handful of these men in their red tunics could and did restore order to a gold-boom town like Dawson City filled with 10,000 rowdy, drunken miners, saloon operators, hustlers, and whores. Less than two dozen Mounties established relative calm and lawfulness from Dawson City all the way north above the Arctic Circle at the whaling port on windswept, barren Herschel Island. To cross a member of the RNWMP meant imprisonment or often death. They were the law of the land and all who lived in this region clearly understood this fact.

Sam Steele, a Mountie during a time more than 125 years ago summed up the absolute and supreme powers of the Corps in his book *Forty Years In Canada:*

> *"We had the detestable prohibitory liquor law to enforce, an insult to free people. Our powers under it were so great, in fact, so outrageous, that no self-respecting member of the corps, unless directly ordered, cared to exert them to the full extent. We were expected, on the slightest grounds of suspicion, to enter any habitation without a warrant, at any hour of the day or night, and search for intoxicants; no privacy need be respected."*

With essentially carte blanche concerning law enforcement granted as a result of parliament's fanatic concern about liquor consumption, the Mounties were able to tame—and this is a relative term even today—this frontier, a land that is still a wild outpost far from modern civilization.

So, when four men led by Inspector Ftizgerald vanished without a trace the news of this stunned the residents of the Yukon and Northwest Territories in 1911. And even today the mention of The Lost Patrol resonates with those who live up here. What happened to those men nearly a century ago, could happen to anyone in the North Country in an instant today. Death is a natural and accepted companion in the North. The tale of Fitzgerald and his men is not looked upon as romantic or even cautionary. The impact on contemporary residents of the dire fate of that long ago patrol is as real now as it was so many years past.

•

Fitzgerald had no way of knowing how many miles it is to Fort McPherson from far out here in the middle of the brutal weather that is the anthem of winter above the Arctic Circle. (Much of what follows I discovered through several days of research at the wonderful Dawson City Museum. The rest is informed conjecture based on a lifetime of poor decisions, bad judgment, and my own peculiar brand of voodoo.) I've never been as disoriented or so hopelessly lost as he and his men must have been during that winter march over 90 years ago. There have been times when I was unsure of where I was for several hours and found myself, for example, on a high, vertiginous ridge looking down at a mountain cirque lake where I had planned to camp. But situations such as this occurred for me in the relatively halcyon weather of summer or early autumn and not in the heart of a savage arctic winter. The Lost Patrol's condition must have been at once terrifying and maddening. Is the shelter and warmth of the fort just a few miles distant, perhaps around that sweeping bend to the north? Inspector Francis "Frank" J. Fitzgerald of the Royal Northwest Mounted Police was likely beyond the point of being concerned about the bitter cold. After a withering battle against minus 64 degree temperatures, blizzards, fierce winds, starvation, desperation that comes from being totally lost in country so untamed—so unexplored as to seem alien—he and his men had trudged through these last days beneath dense stands of trees, through dead brush and across snow-encrusted sweeps of shattered rock more than likely as men who understood that they were doomed to this ice-bound hell for eternity. His mind was no doubt numbed, staggered. His hands and feet were frozen stumps, the skin turned a ragged red and black from extreme frostbite. The wind howled down the steep slopes of the mountains above him. Barren peaks flashed in and out of dark gray-silver clouds, plumes of ice crystals streamed from the summits like ghosts for hundreds of yards as the gale screamed both above him in an almost subliminal wail and into his chest as the wind cut through the trees in an unwashed roar. There have been times when I've been working vast wheat fields reduced to rough stubble in late November, trudging these wide-open tracts on the northern high plains looking for late-season sharp-tailed grouse when a sudden winter storm roars down from the arctic, blasts across the nearby Alberta border and cuts through my wax-cotton coat, wool sweater, flannel shirt, and silk long-underwear like a knife blade of the purest ice. From nearly sweaty-warm to frozen hypothermic in mere minutes out in this exposed situation is brutal, but I have the warmth of my Suburban, visible less than a mile away, to count on, and beyond that a warm meal and motel room in a nearby town. Even with all of this modern opulence, imagining how Fitzgerald and his men must have felt when they were trapped in the middle of a serious Yukon winter is no big stretch for me. I've been there a little more than once. The air of the North Country surely smelled of polar cold and nothing else. Waves of snow swirled through the forest and across the ice-bound Peel River, or formed tight spirals that tore into the trees scattering pine needles and branches. Again, I've experienced this at times when cross-country skiing along the eastern edge of Glacier National Park as winter storms broke down from the Canadian north country with unrestrained and unbelievably cold ferocity. Trees snapped in the icy wind and diminutive tornados whipped between gaps in the forest and along sheer rock faces. Caribou, moose, wolverine, eagle, all of them are probably vanished from sight for The Lost Patrol like they never lived in the arctic, ever. There are less than four hours daylight at this time of year, and that is only a dull illumination like that of dusk edged by a soft silver glow to the south. Billions of stars, a planet or two and the northern lights burned above him in the always-night sky. The aurora spun and whipped in the solar wind, pinks, oranges, greens, and delicate blues lit the landscape in the subtlest of shades. The stars shone as they had for billions of years through all of this with an intensity that was bright enough to cast shadows from the trees. The dark shapes thrown by the pines danced grimly about him driven by the wind. They moved as the tree limbs outside my window move now in the windy winter darkness here in Livingston, Montana. He probably tried to rise from his hands and knees but was too weak from starvation to do so. His pain was constant and extreme. I've read enough accounts on dying by cold and hunger to know this. Those two are his awful companions now. He may have crawled across the ground to the body of Chief Constable Sam Carter. Carter's responsibility was to guide Inspector Francis Fitzgerald and his men through the ragged mountains and barren winter tundra of The Yukon and Northwest Territories. He had failed. He was dead as are two others: Constables George Francis Kinney and Richard O'Hara Taylor. The sled dogs have all been killed and eaten in a futile attempt at survival. Even the sled's leather harnesses have been gnawed for sustenance. Now only the Inspector remained.

Fitzgerald probably hooked his arms beneath Carter's armpits and dragged the corpse inches at a time away from the riverbank and the long-dead fire. After what seems hours he gave up, exhausted, out of breath and dizzy from hunger, loneliness, and the surety of his impending death. He arranged Carter's body lengthwise at the base of a large fir tree, feet pointing to the Peel, arms crossed upon his chest. He tore the remaining blanket in half and covered the man with this. He may have tried to push down Carter's eyelids but the body was already frozen solid in the intense cold. The dead man's eyes stared up at him. Perhaps he retrieved a ragged, scorched handkerchief from a pocket and draped it carefully over Carter's face in a small act of dignity and respect for the dead man. If he was anything like most of us, Fitzgerald sobbed in the gale, the emotion sending ripping pain through his frost-burned lungs. And I bet he looked back upstream along the wide banks of the Peel and wondered 'How far? How far?' then turned back to Carter and whispered through cracked and blackened lips, "Ye go with God. Along and farewell." Imagining still further, I see Fitzgerald pulling himself back to the blackened fire ring now largely covered over with gale-swept snow, righting himself into a sitting position, knees pulled to his chest. Fitzgerald then stretched what remained of his bare hands, long emaciated fingers extended out, over what had once been a modest blaze. He rubbed those hands together over imagined flames and felt the almost sacred warmth that comes from a life beyond desperation, a place where the body barely lives in this world and perhaps the soul is already moving to another.

His was a trip other men had made before him, six times between 1904-1910. The others had set out in winter like he had bound for Dawson City nearly 500 miles to the south to deliver reports, dispatches, and mail. They'd all made the arduous trek successfully, sometimes cold, hungry, and frostbitten, but they'd made the run. Those patrols completed their missions and then those men were able to enjoy the warmth, food, and nightlife that the gold-rush city of Dawson had to offer. But Fitzgerald's patrol was different. Everything seemed to go from wrong to bad to worse and the Inspector, who was a skilled far north campaigner, was no doubt unable to understand the nature of his failure nor was he likely capable of accepting his end. His expedition, he and his men and their final fate would be known forever as The Lost Patrol. I see him leaning closer to the fire now sparkling in his mind and saying to those dancing flames "Where did I go wrong? How did I fail? How did I fail?"

•

Much of human life is dictated by the surroundings we find ourselves in whether that is the dense tangle of people moving about in cities like New York and Cairo, or the agrarian lifestyle of an Iowa farmer or a small village in the Amazon jungle. Big cities equal fast pace. Farm life is slower and in tune with the rhythms of the land and planting cycles. Life in the jungle is subsistence orientated and the tribal members are closely united to share the work. Nowhere is this more evident than in the Yukon and Northwest Territories. I live in Montana, a vast land of mountain ranges, dense pine forests, wild rivers, enormous lakes and reservoirs, the wide open expanses of the northern high plains with its sage flats, coulees, and bluffs and always changing, frequently fierce weather. The people are friendly and open, but life tied to the land makes them shrewd judges of character. Honesty and straightforwardness count for much. There are times when I'm way out in this openness that the nature of our awesome aloneness hammers down with such an intensity that fear shows up. In the fall while I'm walking up a brush-choked draw hunting sharp-tailed grouse and I crest a rise and look out upon miles of rolling prairie and salmon-colored buttes topped with nothing but an enormous blue sky with maybe a trio of turkey vultures riding the thermals far above me, I am struck by the magnitude of how insignificant my life and the planet I live on really is—small planet, small solar system on the edge of a small galaxy whizzing through eternity. A frightening realization until after a few days away from all things civilized and electronic I gradually ease back into a more natural rhythm and subconsciously submit to the land. Then the immensity of Montana and the freedom it offers begins to make sense and I slide into a sense of peace and even wonder at the scale of the place. Sitting around a fire late at night listening to coyotes do their jazz-riff howlings among each other as a full-tilt moon rises above the land while miniature cyclones of sparks swirl above my small blaze, I look to the night sky and the billions of stars and galaxies. The numbers of them numbs my brain. They seem to drop down from the darkness and surround me. Meteors fizzle by overhead trailing a wake of silver-blue sparks. Northern lights glow instrument dash green on the northern horizon. The coyotes chatter away discussing the evening's activities. This is another world far from the manipulative, plastic television, computer, automobile-driven reality of the world we all know. The land out here above and surrounding my fire is a much grander, more powerful place. There's space to move, think, roam. I never thought anyplace would surpass this.

I was wrong.

The first time I went to the Northwest Territories I was unprepared for the boreal forest that began a few hours north of Grand

Prairie, Alberta. I figured this concentration of trees would be similar to that of the western U.S. Not even close. Hour after hour and hundreds of miles of birch and pine swept off in all directions. Cruising at 70 mph in the Suburban, Ginny and I would glide through the wide corridor of the Mackenzie Highway seeing only trees and an enclosed world of limited horizons. When we did top a rise the forest stretched forever in all directions. Never ending. Clouds drifted above the forest pulling shadows with them. Much of this country was located in swamp-like taiga similar to that found in Siberia. This is a place where streams and rivers barely moved, the current was undetectable as the water from snowmelt and rain collects in what amounts to a massive sponge. Slowly gravity asserts itself and all of this water works its way toward the Mackenzie River drainage, or other rivers, and finds its way to oceans such as the Pacific and Arctic. By the time this water escapes, the taiga rivers race and crash through carved rock corridors and plunge over towering falls. But not here in the heart of the boreal forest. Motion, what there is of it, is subtle in the extreme. And 50 feet from the road was a lost world of density and wildness. Biting insects the size of half-dollars and so-called moose flies roared at us from all directions. Their bites took chunks of flesh from our arms and faces. Fierce country. There was no wind. Only the sound of our car's cooling engine interrupted the total silence. By the time we reached the Territories the landscape seethed and flashed energy. The sky was a charged, glowing blue that vibrated and danced. When we reached Great Slave Lake, one of the largest and deepest in the world, we looked upon an inland sea that again rolled on forever. Waves crashed upon ragged reefs offshore before giving way to a dark freshwater wilderness that heaved and rolled to its own pace. The outlet of Great Slave was the Mackenzie River and the river was six miles wide. Immense country. Beyond anything I've experienced in Montana and this was only the beginning. The land stretched for a thousand miles north to the Arctic Ocean. Mountain ranges, uncharted rivers, lake trout weighing over 70 pounds and living more than 100 years, thousands of grizzlies and polar bears, woodland bison, waves of caribou whose numbers are measured in the hundreds of thousands and more and more. Now I'd thought I'd seen it all.

I was still wrong.

Driving along the Klondike Highway in the Yukon heading west from Watson Lake, bound for the gold-rush driven Dawson City we encountered the Liard and Yukon Rivers flowing with a swiftness and power that dwarfed anything I'd encountered in the West. Water powered over gigantic midstream boulders the size of condominiums. Standing waves rose eight, ten feet or more. The rivers flowed with such velocity and force that they created a wind that rustled the birch leaves in a downstream direction. The scale of the land was huge. Mountain ranges piled up upon one another in all directions. An enormous geological fault called The Tintina Trench ripped the land apart for hundreds of miles. Lesser rivers streamed down isolated valleys cloaked in virgin forest. The sky was right on top of us, the clouds scudding what seemed only a few feet above our heads. The land was immediate and possessing a scale beyond anything I'd experienced. The rivers were filled with grayling and in some cases salmon making their spawning runs up from the Pacific Ocean. Farther north Arctic Char colored blaze orange and deep purple swam upstream from the Beaufort Sea in autumn. Arctic terns zipped by. Others species we'd never seen perched in trees or hunted insects along the water. When we turned up the rock and gravel road known as The Dempster Highway all of this was amped up still another notch. Moose, grizzly, and caribou were everywhere grazing in the arctic tundra, wandering hillsides or standing near the road as we clattered by in either a cloud of dust or a sea of mud. The farther we went above the Arctic Circle the grander the scheme of the land. Vistas continued to expand taking our pedestrian conception of linear time with it. This was all new and crystal clear real. Along well-used game trails piles of rock left by native Dene First

Nation People hunters marked forks in the paths or possibly prime areas of game concentrations. Up on a long, wide ridge the trees were dwarfed in size and heaved at odd angles by the movements of the permafrost a few feet below the surface. These shiftings and heavings through the years had established a chaotic order in the forest, a varied but consistent rhythm. Farther north mountain ranges became treeless, rolling off both east and west as far as we could see, the distant peaks hidden by dark bands of boiling storm clouds. The wind came in from the north and smelled of the cold and faintly of the distant sea. The rivers powered through first timbered valley floors and then as they coursed more to the north the water pushed across gravel flats still partially covered in ice even in late August with the tundra lining these streams like a natural Persian carpet. And the sky glowed in blues, silvers, golds, and whites in hues that seemed otherworldly and alien. In the brief late-summer night when we camped just off The Dempster near rivers called Olgilvie or Peel we'd look up to see the northern lights blazing in unfamiliar colors. We imagined we could hear this aurora sizzle and snap in the brief dark. Sounds of large animals tracking through the forest fired our febrile imaginations. A wolf howled. In the morning we saw a timber wolf gliding on the mist not many yards from where we slept, the animal never giving us a glance but well aware of our presence.

And this story never ends. This wild, undisciplined often harsh country is many times the size of Montana. Much of it has not been explored or ever seen by human eyes. And this is the 21st century. Imagine what Fitzgerald and his men experienced almost a century ago and in the middle of an arctic winter. No roads. No people. Nothing but the land. This is the country that those men were forced to deal with and in many ways it was the genesis for the adventurous adult lives they lived. Maybe the natural wildness of this land was always the source of the voodoo.

•

Prior to the disaster that befell The Lost Patrol in the winter of 1910-11, The Royal Northwest Mounted Police had run six successful patrols either beginning in Dawson City in the Yukon Territory to the south and traveling north-northwest to the Hudson's Bay trading post at Fort McPherson in the Northwest Territories or in the reverse direction. All of these expeditions followed relatively the same route with minor variations that were dictated by the weather or the chance of finding a more expedient course of travel. In fact, Fitzgerald returned to his Herschel Island assignment, where his duty was to maintain order and decency at the whaling port between the sailors and the native Inuits, with the second patrol led by Constable Harry G. Mapley and guided by natives Sam Smith and Louis Cardinal. The group went by way of Mayo to the east of the accepted route so that they could follow the length of The Wind River. The patrol took 56 days to reach Fort McPherson, the longest of any in the 17-year history of the patrols. Temperatures dropped so fiercely that the men had to wait out the weather for up to four days at a time. Along the way the men shot five caribou and three moose. In addition they purchased 300 pounds of moose meat from Indians they encountered. It is quite possible that Fitzgerald's surviving the extreme cold and this group's hunting success—coupled with the meat purchased from the Inuits—influenced his planning for The Lost Patrol and directly led to the men's deaths. He may have figured that this second patrol handled weather that was as rough as it could get and may have also felt that being able to shoot and trade for game would see his men through the worst of times.

The first patrol encountered similar success, and was also led by Mapley. This initial patrol went northeast until it crossed the Blackstone River just south of where I caught grayling some 100 miles north up The Dempster Highway. From there the men turned east to reach trapper John Martin's cabin, a well-known source of shelter in a land of few dwellings, where they escaped from the cold for the night. Enough cannot be made of the extreme weather this far north in the winter. When temperatures reach minus 60 and the wind blows at over 40 mph the windchill reaches minus 150 and flesh can freeze in less than 30 seconds. Breathing through one's mouth can allow the icy air to crack teeth. Even the sled dogs with their thick, matted fur coats were not immune to the danger. Their paws would frequently become clogged with snow and ice that would wear through the skin creating raw wounds that rendered the animals useless. The only incident of note on this patrol was the injury to Inuit guide Little Pete who was replaced at the Blackstone Indian camp by Jacob Njootli. In his report, Mapley may have also contributed to The Lost Patrol's demise when he wrote that the Mounties would have been better off without civilians, meaning Inuit guides. Fitzgerald relied on Sam Carter instead of on men who had lived in the rugged mountains and valleys all their lives. Years of experience coupled with knowledge passed on by tribal elders is required to navigate the labyrinth of valleys and mountain ranges than can all begin to look the same when a man is lost and approaching panic in this country. Carter's inability to recognize crucial landmarks was instrumental in delaying The Lost Patrol, forcing the men to use up diminishing food supplies.

Carter made his only trip along the route in 1906-07 when he transferred duty stations from Dawson City to Herschel Island. Perhaps key here is that Carter went from south to north and not north to south as Fitzgerald's patrol would do three years later. Landmarks viewed from one direction can look entirely different when viewed from an angle reversed 180 degrees. The men on the Dawson City to Fort McPherson patrols also had the advantage of a horse and sled to break trail for the first 50 miles. Any time saved under winter conditions can mean the difference between life and death. Fitzgerald did not have this luxury. Based on his experience with this patrol, Carter was able to convince Fitzgerald of his abilities to guide the men to Dawson City. Carter's miscalculation concerning the location of Forrest Creek which gave way to the pass over the Wernecke Mountains and down into the Blackstone River drainage was critical. The third patrol's commander A. E. Forrest made these observations concerning this area of the trek in his diary:

> *"31st Dec. 1906, left camp at 8:30; traveled to head of creek and crossed over the divide into a creek (later named Forrest Creek) running into the Little Wind River; these divides are very low."*

> *"1st January, '07, left camp at 7:30; traveled down the creek to the Little Wind River, and down the river for about two miles and camped."*

> *"2nd, left camp at 8:00 a.m.; continued on down the Little Wind; had a hard time on the glaciers today, the ice being so smooth and the wind so high that it was almost impossible for men and dogs to travel."*

> *"3rd, left camp at 8:30; made mouth of Little Wind River, about 25 miles and camped."*

This is maybe one of the keys to The Lost Patrol's failure. Based on Forrest's diaries and examination of maps of the area, this third patrol traveled approximately 40 miles before turning down The Little Wind, then called Forrest Creek by the time of The Lost Patrol. Fitzgerald's log entries indicate that his men may have been at least eight miles above the all important turn up Forrest Creek (remember they were running in the opposite direction) before they began looking for it. In winter everything begins to look the same in the deep white covering of snow and the obscured vision caused by howling winds. Coupled with Forrest's endorsement of Carter as a guide and Fitzgerald's subsequently decision to use this individual instead of a native, The Lost Patrol was to have rough sledding. Very rough.

Diaries from the three other patrols seemed to indicate the value if not necessity of having a native guide. Whenever these groups of men ran low on food the native guide was able to head out in even the fiercest weather and shoot several caribou. Fitzgerald's men did not encounter any animals along the way. This is analogous to me working many square miles of the high plains in Montana hunting for my sharp-tailed grouse. Perhaps this is the first time in this part of the state and I am hunting without the aid of my springer spaniel. Tramping through the thigh-high native grasses that appear to offer excellent cover for the birds for three long, empty days I fail to flush a single bird. A few weeks later I return with a friend who has worked this country before and we both have our dogs with us. With my friend's experience, his knowing where small springs perk through the dry ground and where clumps of berries grow, coupled with the keen noses of our dogs we limit out each day and flush countless other grouse. Knowledge of the terrain is essential. Lifeless, barren land to Fitzgerald and his men may have actually contained sufficient caribou and moose to ensure their survival.

The rescue/recovery patrol headed by Corporal W.J.D. Dempster, the highway's namesake, encountered problems before eventually finding The Lost Patrol on March 24.

> *"We were now on the slope facing Trail River, and it was getting dusky and hazy, making the outline of the hills very indistinct . . . dropped down over a bad hill into a stream running in a general northeast direction, but very crooked. After traveling this stream for a couple hours we found that we were on Trail River, but had got on to it much higher than we should have."*

Even Dempster's patrol had problems and they were moving

through the country with the expanded daylight and warmer temperatures of approaching spring. Again, all of this country looks similar in a confusingly different sort of way. "That valley and river look familiar to me, but was that escarpment to the left there before?" Fitzgerald may have wondered. "Is this the right turn or is it the next stream ahead?" Mapmakers have consistently erred in locating Forrest Creek and the Little Wind River. Some maps show Forrest Creek as being part of the Little Wind River. Others have Forrest Creek coming into the Little Wind from the north when it actually enters from the west. Even small confusions in such a convoluted landscape can have extreme consequences.

Anthropologist Vilhjalmur Steffansson, who was camped along Coal Creek south of the Arctic Ocean, had this to say when he was informed of Fitzgerald's death:

> *"It is always easy to see when a tragedy has happened how it could have been avoided, but it has always seemed to me that so long as you are traveling in country supplied with game, you are safer to start with a rifle and resolution to find food (but without a pound of food on your sled) than you would be in starting with a sled heavily loaded with food and no provisions made for getting more when the sled load is used up."*

In other words, prepare for the worst in the North Country and plan on total self-reliance. To Steffansson the mindset of any expedition was of paramount importance. Without the determination to tough it out and rely on one's outdoor skills, any venture out into this country would be hazardous.

What is clear to me after my research and a good deal of reasonably coherent thought, is that Fitzgerald's fatal error was in choosing the inexperienced Carter as his guide instead of a native who was far more familiar with the country between McPherson and Dawson

City, and who also was better able to find and track game. Not taking more food than the bare minimum required for a trip that ran true to form on a tight schedule was another major error. Those fatal mistakes led to wrong turns, lost time, insufficient food supplies, hunger, and disorientation. Maybe all of this wasn't bad voodoo, just bad judgment. Or maybe the two are one in the same thing.

I think of all of this as I make one more cast along a bright riffle. A large grayling pounces on my fly then arcs above the water in a spray of silver, turquoise, and the faintest of indigo. The mountains that Fitzgerald never crossed so long ago provide a sternly beautiful background for the fleeing fish.

•

Staggering blind through the storm whirl,
Stumbling mad through the snow,
Frozen stiff in the ice-pack
Brittle and bent like a bow;
Featureless, formless, forsaken,
Scented by wolves in their flight
Left for the wind to make music
Through ribs that are glittering white;
Gnawing the black crust of failure,
Searching the pit of despair,
Crooking the toe in the trigger
Trying to patter a prayer;

Service could well have had The Lost Patrol in mind when he penned this stanza from *The Law of the Yukon.*

AUTHOR PHOTO

A VANISHING SITE IN NORTHERN ALBERTA PRISTINE WILDERNESS.

NINE /

WHAT THE HELL'S GOING ON UP HERE?

The drive home to Livingston, Montana, from either Dawson City or Yellowknife is a long one. In late September I head south from the Yukon following a blizzard of eight inches in a few hours. A brief taste of winter to come. Then a spell of warm, clear weather that is expected to last the entire time it takes me to cruise to Whitehorse, then Watson Lake, Fort Nelson, the Breland River, Fort McLeod, and home, all in one-day chunks that average about three hundred forty miles.

Prior to leaving on this trip to the Yukon, I worked things out with my son and daughter regarding places to stay, schoolwork, bail bonds, attorney phone numbers, the usual stuff. I rounded up a little money, and made the break for about three weeks. No camera, no note taking—just me, some fly rods, camping gear, and my always present mind of a child. It was my first extended road trip where I wasn't consciously working. I wanted to head up here just once for fun, for the hell of it, to grab some impressions for this book that were not completely driven by work. Pleasant work to be sure, but work nonetheless. The trip was rejuvenating to put a modest spin on the nearly sixty-five-hundred-mile jaunt. I'd missed doing the road alone.

So on my run back south to the "outside," as those select few fortunates who live up this way describe things, the northern lights are blasting with vehemence and intensity now, unlike anything I've ever seen elsewhere, in colors that the usual names fail to describe. Words like "electric," "other worldly," and "surreal" come up lame. The days are growing shorter by a dozen-odd minutes each twenty-four hour span. The nights are longer than the days. I can feel winter closing in, the process of shutting down for the cold, dark months accelerating. The north is alive with frantic, though eon-practiced, haste. Heavy weather is building above the ice cap at the pole. This is no time for lazy frivolities of green birch leaves fluttering in a sunny July breeze, grayling splashing and circling carelessly after emerging stoneflies, long days with no nights and a sun that is considering a quick dip behind a far-off ridge line of fir trees. All is compressed. Vivid. Time is palpable, lightly liquid, translucent. Gliding through all of this is smooth and easy when I'm aiming south.

This solo drive home is the first I've made from up here, and I have plenty of time to think about all I've seen not only on this trip but on all the others of the past few years. I eat, drive, fish, sleep, and think my way south on my own time. Sometimes I cruise down the road late at night or very early in the morning, when the only traffic is large trucks hauling dry goods and fuel north. The aurora flashes, sizzles, and explodes above me. Like many people up here—scientific analysis be damned—I hear the faint electric buzz of the lights whenever I stop the Suburban and get out for a smoke or to stretch my legs in the chill dark. A crazy, spaced-out noise. Nearly subliminal but real and all around. The stars in the very clean, cold night crackle with silver light as does a frozen-white slice of moon.

One afternoon I catch grayling on Rancheria River and cook a couple for dinner. Then I drink some whiskey, smoke a cigar, and rest until well into dark. And later I catch trout on Prairie Creek near Rocky Mountain House—large browns that weigh more than five or six pounds and are brightly colored as they approach spawning fervor. Browns can glow and simmer. These trout are proof. I spot one female over thirty inches motionlessly suspended over a large redd. An enormous, beautiful, stunning fish. And still later I cross the United States-Canada border at Coutts-Sweetgrass. The custom's official asks a few desultory questions, then waves me on. He's bored. The hell with an orange alert. And I'm too tired to look like a terrorist. All along the way I listen to music by Stevie Ray Vaughn, King Crimson, Joe Jackson, Nina Simone, The Allman Brothers, Them, the Grateful Dead, John Coltrane, Horace Silver, The Cowboy Junkies, Danny O'Keefe, Amos Garrett, Spirit, Chet Baker, Bobby Watson, and the Mission Mountain Wood Band. A good deal of the time I think about the freedom I experienced in the Yukon doing the road by myself for a change, with options to do whatever I wanted whenever I felt like it without consulting anyone. I've been living sans woman companion for two years now, and I like the solitude. Remember, I have all of those voices in my head to keep me company.

The last night in Dawson I had an excellent dinner of grilled king salmon at Klondike Kate's, out on the screened porch with the rest of the martini-swilling crazies. Jimmy Buffet was blaring his passé, but good-time, silliness from several speakers. On a television behind me, I noticed that ESPN—no escaping that monster—was airing a fly-fishing show featuring the emotionally stunted basketball coach from Texas Tech. A few minutes later, when I thought things couldn't get too much worse on the channel, another fishing show began its noisesome thirty-minute dirge. Fortunately, a young lass at a nearby table yelled, "Turn that shit off." This type of huckster crap is to be expected from a station that hired Rush Limbaugh as a football analyst. What is disturbing is that this type of bullshit, and almost all other shows related to fly fishing, is nothing more than product hustles, lame venues for even more lame practitioners of the worst aspects of what was once an arcane pursuit practiced by a small number of eccentrics, but is now big business. "Nice Fish!" "World-class trout!" "A real hawg!" Give me a fucking break. As jazz musician

Roland Kirk said so many years ago about society in general, "Clickety-clack. Somebody's mind went off the god-damned track." This puerile garbage needs to be jettisoned immediately. But I notice that once again I'm digressing with raging vehemence. The evening at Kate's lasted late into the night, and whoever I wound up talking with were the best friends I ever had, at least for that outing.

I spend long road-hours considering the fate of Canada's magnificent, unique North Country. Some of my thoughts are a bit contentious and angry. I live for good country and have never, will never, pull my punches when it comes to voicing my opinions about those who would destroy the land for any reason, especially to make a buck. Or against those that talk a good game but always have a lame excuse when it comes to putting their lazy asses on the line when it counts.

The widely held notion that Canada is taking excellent care of its wild, pristine lands far better than the gluttonous citizens in the United States is nothing more than a misperception approaching myth. Americans, or Yanks as they are often called up north, are frequently verbally assailed by Canadians with the misplaced, disingenuous, and perhaps naïve notion that all Americans are swine when it comes to caring for and preserving quality country. Canadians, in contrast, are valiant, conscientious souls who have no blood on their hands. This stance is at best spurious and possibly created to hide the obvious fact that the western provinces of Alberta and British Columbia, as well as the Yukon and Northwest Territories, are being plundered at an astonishing rate.

During my last trip to the Yukon, while having a couple of drinks in The Pit in Dawson City, a Canadian came up to me and asked where I was from. When I told him he said, "You damn Yanks don't give a damn about your own land. You log it and strip mine it all to hell. Then you come up here to enjoy our country." Over the years I've heard many comments along those lines.

True, there are individuals in Canada who have devoted their

GINNY DIERS PHOTO

PART OF A COAL-GENERATION OPERATION ALONG THE LITTLE SMOKEY RIVER IN NORTHERN ALBERTA.

lives to preserving the land and there are, as most of us know all too well, greedy bastards tearing apart the last remaining shreds of unspoiled country in the United States. But fair is fair, and the bottom line is that Canadians should take stock of their own environmental situation before gleefully casting aspersions America's way.

Forty years of being an inveterate road bum, traveling back roads on a skinny budget, fishing malarial bogs, inadvertently canoeing big-time white water, hiking nonexistent trails bound for nowhere, and unavoidably staying on top of environmental issues in Canada has provided me with an ongoing opportunity to see disturbing change in a land of incredible splendor and abundance—one peopled with some truly remarkable, generous, and creative individuals. In the last five years these destructive shifts in direction have been seismic, both metaphorically and literally.

From Fort Nelson in northern British Columbia to Rocky

Mountain House in central Alberta to the vast Tintina Trench region in the southern Yukon and over east to Yellowknife on Great Slave Lake in the Northwest Territories, the landscape is under siege. The extraction industries are running the show, tearing, blasting, sucking, and cutting every diamond, gold nugget, drop of oil, chunk of coal, and stick of timber they can access. If it's of value, these industries intend to have it. What's going down in western Canada puts the devastation being visited on states such as Montana, Wyoming, and West Virginia in a more balanced perspective. What are obviously horrendous clear-cuts or devastating open-pit coal mines in the American West are everyday situations in Canada, too. Both countries are mining their natural resources at an alarming rate.

"We want Earth to speed up, our forests don't grow fast enough for us," said David Suzuki several years ago in an interview in the *Hamilton Spectator*. Suzuki, a Canadian, has long been outspoken in his opposition to the Western world's enormous appetite for resources. "We have to realize," he wrote, "that humans are not the most important species on the planet."

Canadian provincial campgrounds are filled to the brim with late-model pickups tricked out with all the options and pulling expensive fifth-wheelers, pricey speedboats, all-terrain vehicles, or jet skis. The Cypress Hills along the Alberta-Saskatchewan border, the setting for Wallace Stegner's book *Wolf Willow*, are now so overrun that they resemble a scene from *National Lampoon's Vacation*. Housing developments in cities like Calgary and Edmonton stretch for miles with thousands of quarter-million-dollar homes. All of this wealth comes not only from the jobs provided by oil, gas, coal, and timber corporations but also from royalties paid by the industry based on the amount of a given mineral extracted from a province. In Alberta, this figure exceeds $6 billion annually just for coal. The money is flowing in direct proportion to the abundance of the oil coming from countless wells hammered into the Canadian countryside. The old phrase "a chicken in every pot" has been updated in the northland to "an oil pumpjack in every yard."

A good example—and there are many—is Rocky Mountain House, Alberta. This used to be a rather sedate town of a few thousand sometimes-impoverished souls, who enjoyed life on the bluffs above the North Fork of the Saskatchewan River. The residents could take part in all of the outdoor activities one would expect in an area that rests in the foothills along the east slope of the Canadian Rockies and is surrounded by dense, mature pine forest with countless rivers and streams pouring out onto the prairie. Lakes of the purest water abound, as do grizzlies, moose, eagles, deer, wolves, mountain lions, grayling, and various species of trout. For years, timber generated decent incomes for many residents, as did motels, restaurants, and service stations that supplied occasional tourists with basic needs. Most everyone knew everybody else, and crime rates were low.

The town, originally founded one hundred fifty years ago because of the fur trade and the natural highway provided by Saskatchewan, is now an insane riot of oil rigs, logging trucks, related workers, and the destructive craziness that comes from too much money deposited in a local economy far too quickly. Residents are now moving toward surliness, depression, and anger caused by these rapid changes to their lifestyle. During a recent trip up that way, I saw streets, even residential side streets, overrun with trucks of all sizes racing helter-skelter to the oil-and-gas business shuffle. Gas stations are constantly busy filling the tanks of industry vehicles. Beleaguered locals put on game but grim faces in the wake of this onslaught. A woman at a local bakery said, "I don't even remember what my town used to be. None of us knows anyone the way we used to. This place is frantic, like Calgary." Rocky Mountain House has more than tripled in population, and that doesn't include the countless oil and gas roustabouts, drilling maintenance crews, surveyors, and so on.

What is happening to longtime residents of Rocky Mountain

House and countless other towns scattered about the forests, mountains, and prairies of western Canada is to be expected wherever extractive industry moves in and shoves locals out of the way. What was once home is now a corporate compound replete with out-of-control drinking, drugs, prostitution, and the ubiquitous grifters plying a variety of hustles and cons—the ever-present tagalongs with this avaricious carnival. The townspeople don't know what's happening to them or their land. All that most of them see is the quick-money fix that blinds them to the negative and long-term changes of this way of life.

In an interview in the *Edmonton Sun*, David Suzuki said, "We're all in a great big car driving at a brick wall at 100 mph and everybody is arguing over where they want to sit. My point is it doesn't matter who's driving. Somebody has got to say, 'For God's sake, put the brakes on and turn the wheel.' "

"In terms of greenhouse gas emissions the U.S. is responsible for 25 percent and Canada two percent [of world emissions]," said Jim Fulton of the Vancouver-based David Suzuki Foundation. "But Canadians are the largest per capita users in the world. We use more energy on a daily basis than the entire continent of Africa.

"The impact from gas and oil exploration, especially in the boreal forest of Alberta, is catastrophic," said Fulton. "Exploratory roads are laid out in a grid pattern that runs for hundreds of miles east-and-west and north-and-south. The combined impact of seismic exploration, then bringing in heavy equipment and constructing storage facilities is enormous. Then these roads are used by people on ATVs. This affects wildlife including migratory birds, bears, and wolves. The terror experienced by caribou, deer, and moose from ATVs cannot be overstated. If these animals are forced to flee even short distances they frequently overheat or lose pregnancies. Often they die. In some areas moose populations have vanished leaving indigenous populations without sustenance.

"The oil reserves in our tar sands are the largest in the world, larger than those of Saudi Arabia," Fulton said. "And the oil and automotive industries are doing anything but encouraging fuel efficient vehicles and conservation. Members of the oil industry are criminals of the first order."

The continual boom-and-bust cycle of the American West is at play in Canada. Ten, maybe twenty, years of feast, then complete collapse, and all of the new homes and expensive toys go back to the banks, while the oil, coal, and timber companies are long gone, searching for the next valley to plunder. It's an old, ugly story that's been played out in Butte, Montana, in Deadwood, South Dakota, and in ghost towns with names like Garnet, Pony, and Como. Now the routine is playing in Canada.

Millions of acres of land in these western provinces are being surveyed, mapped, then exploited by these extraction industries. And production figures in oil and gas, coal and other minerals, along with timber, are climbing rapidly and in many cases equal or exceed production totals in the United States. Forest trunk roads that used to wind serenely through dense pine forest and alongside unspoiled rivers along the Rocky Mountain foothills are now bustling muddy or dusty corridors conveying a steady stream of enormous trucks hauling huge machinery.

A couple years ago, my companion Ginny Diers and I were traveling north from Rocky Mountain House on Forest trunk 743. We were working on a book about the northern high plains called *Coyote Nowhere—In Search of America's Last Frontier*. The late June weather was warm but rainy and the dirt roads were a muddy and treacherous quagmire. Even if there had been no other traffic the drive would have been a sporting proposition. We'd been warned by a forest employee the night before, at a campground along the Pembina River, to watch out for the steady stream of oil and coal rigs moving up and down these roads. "They don't stop or even move over for anyone. People are killed all of the time. Trucks, cars, campers—all of them sometimes crushed flat like empty beer cans. That's an extremely dangerous drive you're about to undertake." He wished us luck, then headed down the road to check on another campsite.

At the time I considered his warning a bit extreme, but I was to find out differently. The next morning as we drove north, a steady stream of enormous rigs roared past us; the tires on those machines were taller than our GMC Suburban. The noise of the engines was deafening as they belched thick black clouds of diesel exhaust. While climbing a sticky hill, a semi pulling drilling equipment moved well over to our side of the road, just missing us by inches and drenching the Suburban's windshield in a thick wash of slop. We barely made it to the top of the rise, driving blind, and just managing to skid over into a slight turnoff.

Getting out to collect ourselves and settle frayed nerves, I looked around. On both sides vast open-pit coal mines stretched deep into the ancient pine forest. Tall metal stacks that rose above the trees were crowned by flickering flames of natural gas being burned off at several pumping stations. Oil company signs said "No Trespassing" at the entrance to every side road. In the pits, large machinery was scooping up and hauling away coal. Dynamite blasting roared in the distance. Far in the west, the lofty crest of the Rockies flickered snow white between swirling openings in the cloud cover.

Fifteen years ago when I traveled this road on my way to the then-remote mountain town of Grand Cache (now overrun with the same madness as Rocky Mountain House), I felt like I was in the middle of a primeval forest, that a grizzly or moose could appear from the edge of the trees at any moment. When Ginny and I drove it a few years back, the atmosphere was more like a scene of some vast industrial park.

The rivers were running muddy along the road, and the only wildlife we saw was an occasional raven gliding high above what remained of the forest. This vision of desecration continued for sixty miles before we turned off onto another road, but that one soon led past a mammoth coal mine where mountains on the eastern edge of Jasper Park in the Gregg River drainage were being carved down to nothing. The air was filled with the noise of heavy machinery and choking with waves of black dust swirling in miniature tornadoes as the wind whipped down from the remaining mountains. We were more than eight hundred miles north of home, but felt like we were in Detroit.

Half of Canada is covered by either temperate forest (like that found in the American Northwest) or by boreal forest (similar to that found in Siberia). The boreal forest is a six-hundred-mile-wide band of timberland stretching from approximately three hundred miles north of the United States border to the tree line in the Arctic and spanning the breadth of the country. Approximately three hundred million acres of the country's forests are managed for timber production. This is an area more than one and one-half times the size of several Midwestern states. Two-thirds of Canada's estimated three hundred thousand wildlife species live in the forest.

The temperate and boreal forests, along with the arctic tundra, of these four provinces are extremely fragile. I spoke with a biologist at the Tombstone Campground Interpretive Center located on the Yukon's Dempster Highway. She pointed out that as few as twenty people walking the same line to a distant peak and back again would disturb the vegetation and soils of this boreal environment to the extent that it would take several decades to return to its natural state. Less than two dozen people treading lightly—not thousands of pieces of machinery the size of houses, thousands more workers, and thousands of tons of explosives, all ripping and digging away at some of the last wilderness left on the planet.

The following figures provide an idea of the magnitude of the extraction processes in Canada: The total timber harvest in Canada is near 8 billion board feet per year, up from 2.9 billion in 1950.

(In America this figure is around 4 billion board feet per year down from 6 billion in 1980.)

Canada's forests cover an area nearly three times the size of Europe. This is mainly boreal forest with some temperate forest, including temperate rain forest. This represents 10 percent of the world's forestry cover. Only 5.5 percent of this forest is under some form of legal protection or constraint related to logging. In terms of biomass, this is the most productive forest in the world. Approximately 10.8 million acres of logged forestlands in Canada (an area more than twice the size of Wales) remain denuded. If the present trend continues, all of Canada's suitable forest will be harvested within thirty to thirty-five years.

"Alberta is a very, very wealthy province compared to Montana, but that comes with its own baggage," said renowned Alberta guitarist Amos Garrett, who is also a devoted conservationist. "The provincial government is making millions in oil taxes and that just comes in the mail. Maybe there's $10 to $15 million coming in from sportsmen. That's paltry. So there are deaf ears in Edmonton [the provincial capital]. I don't think we have the programs that you have down there in the States. You do much more for the trout and upland birds than we do."

In British Columbia, ancient forests are vanishing at the rate of one acre every 70 seconds or 418,000 acres each year, an area the size of 190,000 football fields. In the time it takes to watch a thirty-minute sitcom on television, twenty-six acres of forest have been leveled. In the past decade, an area eight times the size of Connecticut has been clear-cut. Companies do not have to bid competitively to log public forests. Fees are typically set at one-fourth to one-third market value. The majority of logging in British Columbia is in old-growth forest, and the Canadian government estimates that the province is overcutting its forest by 20 percent. Clear-cutting makes up 80 percent of all logging. In British Columbia, it is legal to log smaller salmon streams down to the banks, destroying aquatic life and leaving no protections against fine sediment and high temperatures that are lethal to salmon eggs and fry. There is no endangered species legislation to protect wildlife from logging, despite the fact that the Committee on the Status of Endangered Wildlife in Canada now lists 387 species of plants and animals at risk of extinction (8 percent of these species are shared with the United States). This is an increase of 20 percent since 1992.

Coal production figures for Canada are similar. Alberta mines 27 million tons annually; British Columbia, 40 million tons. The Canadian oil and gas industry invested more than $20 billion in exploration and development in the year 2000, making it the largest capital investor in Canada. Oil production is not expected to peak for ten years. British Columbia government officials have asked leaders in Ottawa to lift a decades-old ban on offshore drilling along Canada's Pacific Coast. Geologists estimate that there could be up to 10 billion barrels of oil and 1.2 billion cubic meters of natural gas in the area.

"We risk enormous damage to British Columbia's environmental heritage, all for a short-term dollar," said David Hocking, communications director for the David Suzuki Foundation.

Much of America, from one coast to the other, has been devastated by coal mining. Canada's western provinces are experiencing a similar fate and the pace of the industries is accelerating. Within perhaps as little as two decades the ecosystem damage inflicted upon British Columbia, Alberta, the Yukon, and Northwest Territories will make what happened in this country pale in comparison. At the present rate, most natural resources will be exhausted in Canada within forty years. Even if Canada was exploiting its natural resources at only one half the rate of the United States, which it isn't, everything would be gone within a century.

Some of the reasons that the mineral extraction industries have engendered the ire of both U.S. and Canadian citizens is exemplified by comments from the Canadian Minister of Energy and Mines,

Richard Neufeld, in his opening address for the 44th Canadian Conference on Coal held in 2002 in British Columbia.

"We have eliminated corporate capital tax . . . reduced corporate income tax by 3 percent to 13.5 percent," said Neufeld. "Over 90 percent of our coal is exported, mainly to steel-making countries. . . . The philosophy behind our actions is simple—increase certainty. Streamline regulatory requirements and make BC a better place to do business. We've changed the Coal Act to accomplish this for coal exploration and mining. . . . As a result, coal exploration and development can proceed with fewer encumbrances.

"We will make dramatic cuts to prescriptive regulations under the Health, Safety, and Reclamation Code to give companies more flexibility to focus on results not process. We have amended the Mines Act and we are developing related regulations to allow most exploration activities to take place without the need for permits."

This "philosophy" sounds remarkably similar to that espoused by the current administration in Washington.

During a recent trip to the Yukon by myself, I pulled over at a wayside that offered a spectacular view of the Kondike River Valley and the seemingly endless sweep of mountains rolling north toward the Arctic Circle. The ragged, surreal peaks of the Tombstone Range ghosted in the distance. Looking to my left, I noticed a large display sign touting a gold mine that was hidden behind a near range of mountains. Pictures and words graphically showed the huge scope of the operation, and extolled it as providing jobs and money for Yukon residents. Certainly this is true, but what will the real cost to Canadians and all of us be when all is said, blasted, and done in the not-so-distant future?

So if everything is so grim in northern Canada, why bother to write this book in the first place?

"The real topic of nature writing, I think, is not nature but the evolving structure of communities from which nature has been removed, often as a consequence of modern economic development," wrote *Arctic Dreams* author, Barry Lopez, in an essay based in part on a presentation he gave at the Salamanca Writers Festival in Hobart, Tasmania, in March 1996. "It is writing concerned, further, with the biological and spiritual fate of those communities. It also assumes that the fate of humanity and nature are inseparable. . . . We keep each other alive with our stories. We need to share them as much as food. We also need good companions. One of the most extraordinary things about the land is that it knows this, and it compels language from some of us so that, as a community, we may actually speak of it."

There's a reason, actually many, why Lopez is considered one of the finest nature writers ever. In a little over one hundred words, he summed up what I've been doing with my life for over thirty years. Books like *Arctic Aurora* are written because some of us are compelled to write them. We have no choice, no say in the matter regardless of the outcome verbally, sales wise, personally, or financially. The various voices roaming the mental airwaves chose the appropriate writer to complete a given book, to tell their story with honest rhythms and pulses. I never consider any of the things I do in writing to be mine. I'm just the clown who puts down the story the way voices, or "the muse" as the Greeks refer to it, tell me to. These aren't my stories. They never have been. So if at times the stuff seems grim to the point of hopelessness, that's the way it goes—I'm just telling it how I hear it and see it. Though in the sometimes cautionary tale that is *Arctic Aurora* there is room for shreds of optimism, as in the following story filed by reporter Robert McClure of the *Seattle Post-Intelligencer* on the first of December 2003.

"One of the world's biggest forest-protection initiatives is being announced today in Canada—a pact involving environmentalists, First Nations peoples, and timber companies who want to keep logging and development out of an area seven times the size of Washington. The subject of the agreement is Canada's northern forest, stretching from Alaska to the Atlantic Ocean and covering just over half of Canada's land mass. Half the 1.3 billion acres would be put off-limits to logging and development. The rest would be open to only carefully planned, eco-friendly 'sustainable development.'

"The forest shelters more than a billion birds, many of them migratory species familiar to bird-watchers in Western Washington and elsewhere in the United States. It also provides a lot of the paper, wood, and other forest products consumed in this country. This northern, or 'boreal,' forest of Canada represents about one-tenth of the remaining forest on Earth—one-third of the globe's boreal forests and one of the largest intact or nearly intact ecosystems anywhere. About a third is covered by wetlands, and it includes some of Canada's largest rivers. Today's announcement involves timber and energy companies and tribal interests whose activities touch about one-sixth of Canada's boreal forest. They emphasize the importance of such a huge tract of greenery in slowing down global warming as well as providing clean air and water."

Cathy Wilkinson, director of the Canadian Boreal Initiative, said, "It's the first real national vision for the boreal that's ever been produced, and really it's the starting point for further conversations, "It's a very important first step just to have a national vision, because so often environmental conflicts are characterized by conflict over even what the goals are."

The initiative has its roots in the bitter fights over logging in the Pacific Northwest, including the 1990s civil disobedience challenging logging around Vancouver Island's Clayoquot Sound that sparked hundreds of arrests. "It's an unprecedented and unlikely group of partners," said Monte Hummel, president of World Wildlife Fund-Canada. "The idea was, could we for once head off the train wrecks and not just get involved in this when crises occur?"

The businesses involved in the new initiative are Suncor Energy Inc., a major oil and gas producer; Domtar Inc., one of Canada's biggest paper and lumber firms; Tembec Inc., a $3 billion-a-year timber company; and Alberta-Pacific Forest Industries Inc., a smaller paper and pulp company based in Alberta. Suncor and Domtar are counted among Canada's largest one hundred companies.

"It's a group of like-minded people who want to ensure there's a collaboration and a win-win for a sustainable environment and sustainable economy at the same time," said Bill Hunter, president and chief operating officer of Alberta-Pacific. "It's a very, very novel approach."

Joining with three First Nations bands and four environmental groups, the companies hope to persuade other firms, bands, and ultimately the federal and provincial governments to sign on. The initiative's sponsor is the Philadelphia-based Pew Charitable Trusts philanthropy, which has been closely allied with green groups in this country and provided $4.5 million to support the Canadian Boreal Initiative. In British Columbia, the head of a timber trade group said he had not yet heard about the initiative, but he has been following the debate over the boreal forest.

"It's the next place where the environmentalists want to see some different management issues," said John Allan, president and chief executive officer of the Council of Forest Industries. "They started in your part of the world and then moved to our coastal forest, and now they're moving inland."

What follows I gleaned from the rest of McClure's solid work, and from other stories I tracked down on the Net.

The initiative is seeking to influence a series of decisions about the boreal forest to be made over the next five to seven years by Canada's federal, provincial, and territorial governments. One of those is a land-use planning process affecting fifty thousand square miles just east of Lake Winnipeg in Manitoba, an area about the size of Louisiana. There, Ron Thiessen of the Western Canada Wilderness Committee hopes today's announcement moves the talks in the direction of conservation.

"It has a great potential to affect it," Thiessen said. He added that the initiative's environmental groups "have a lot of influence and a lot of strength. I hope it's going to have a lot of influence on the logging companies."

The initiative comes at a time when Canada's government is reexamining how its policies mesh with environmental and economic sustainability in an effort known as the National Roundtable on the Environment and the Economy. Aside from the World Wildlife Fund, the environmental groups involved are two mainstream organizations: the Canadian Parks and Wilderness Society and Ducks Unlimited Canada. Seattle is the home base for a related campaign, the Boreal Songbird Initiative, which points out that many of the birds seen in the state of Washington are dependent on the boreal forest.

The boreal forest "is right in our backyard, and we're so connected to it, not only through the resources we use, but also the birds that fly here," said Marilyn Heiman, director of the songbird campaign. "You have all these cumulative impacts, and that's what really affects birds. . . . It fragments the forests, and then they have no place to go. They lose the large patches, and they don't feel they have safe places to go."

The initiative advocates adherence to the "sustainable forestry" principles of the Forest Stewardship Council (FSC), which is backed by The Home Depot and Lowe's, among other businesses, and seeks to assure consumers who buy FSC-certified products that the wood, paper, and other products they buy are from responsibly managed forests. The initiative comes as Washington's Board of Natural Resources wrestles with whether to embrace FSC certification, or some other form of certification, as the state plans timber-harvest levels on state-owned forests over the next decade.

"We're no longer talking about clear-cutting like in the old days," said Peter Penashue, president of the Innu Nation in Labrador and Newfoundland, one of the First Nations involved in the Canadian initiative. "We're talking about sustainable development. We recognize that we all live on one planet and we all have to do our share."

Canadian environmentalists hope to influence American consumers through the boreal initiative because "we need to make sure that companies that are breaking ranks and stepping forward like this are getting ahead in the marketplace," said World Wildlife Fund-Canada's Monte Hummel.

So there's this to be optimistic about, if indeed it ever comes to pass, and after dealing with similar, though much smaller, proposals and initiatives in Montana for thirty years, I have my doubts. Talk is cheap, egos are fragile, and big money usually holds sway. So I'm a cynic about this one. I'll believe it, I'll get excited, when it happens.

What does give me cause for optimism is all of the committed, decent, honest, very alive people I've met over the years and the many thousands of miles in the North Country. Making a living in the arctic or near arctic is tough bordering on brutal for those who are permanent residents. The seventy thousand or so souls who call the Yukon or the Northwest Territories home live up here largely because they love the land and the way of life. Few of them ever get rich. Even fewer even give a damn about wealth. Their lives are compelled and directed much like the words writers put down, as Barry Lopez described earlier. Some of us have no choice in the flowing scheme of things. I've seen the insane, joyful acceptance of this fact and the freedom that comes from this simple, yet magnificent realization flashing from the eyes of the hundreds of people I spoke with up here. The land is in good hands. Corporate puppets like our current President and many of our representatives and senators—such as Conrad Burns, the corporately bought-and-paid-for Republican Senator from Montana—and big business chief executives are in for a hard-core, wicked fight if they believe that they are going to steamroll the people of this land in order to savage the place for a quick, rapacious buck.

I believe in this. It gives me a measure of optimism about our natural world's future.

AUTHOR PHOTO

THE MACKENZIE HIGHWAY HEADING NORTH TO WRIGLEY.

TEN /

DAYS OF FUTURES PAST

I suspect that men are going along this way for the last time, and I for one don't want to waste the trip. . . .

—Robert Traver, *Anatomy of a Fisherman*

What have I taken with me during all of these slightly crazed and curious travels through the Yukon and Northwest Territories? Have I learned or at least retained anything of value from all these weeks and miles of roaming this land?

One thing I know for sure is that I rediscovered what open country—land that is not gated or fenced—and personal freedom have to do with each other. You really can't have one without the other. Years ago when I first came West, Montana was like that. The possibilities, both personally and in terms of adventure, seemed limitless. But with soulless, avaricious developers buying up and overpricing much of the state, so that only the wealthy can afford to live here and pay the skyrocketing property taxes, those grand freedoms are vanishing into the greedy bastards' stock portfolios. Now with gated communities catering to the pathetically insecure well-moneyed hordes, with elected officials in Montana residing in the hip pockets of out-of-state interests, much of the good stuff is gone. Nothing symbolizes this more to me than fences, any kind of those structures. What immediately set the Far North apart from the American West, one I noticed the first day of my first trip to the Northwest Territories, was a lack of fences. That said a great deal to me.

My difficulties with fences began some years ago, a delicate transmutation arising from problems I had and still have with gates. Either my hands get scratched from trying to latch the ragged collections of weathered tree limbs and barbed wire that block passage to some exotic fishing water or I pinch my fingers in the workings of the newer hook-type mechanism or I become inextricably tangled in the wire while crossing through. And with the certainty of an eastern-horizon sunrise, I find myself on the wrong sides of these gates after closing them. Coming or going, it doesn't matter. The Suburban is always beyond the gate waiting for me to figure things out.

When I turned fifty, crossing fences became a struggle. I'm in fairly good shape and manage to totter around with a modest degree of authority, but now I cannot get over, under, or through a fence, particularly barbed-wire ones, without some sort of mishap. All of the shirts I wear fishing or bird hunting are torn along the shoulders and back. My sweaters have loops pulled from their tight knitting large enough to hold ice axes, and my waders leak, doing little more now than visually announce that I'm about to chase some fish.

One time along the Shields River in Montana, I became entangled while stooping and grunting through some wire that silently guarded a delightful stretch of prime water. Frustrated—I could hear trout splashing after caddis less than thirty feet away—I jerked free only to have the tip guide of my fly rod snag on a rusty barb. Jerking the rod sharply, I lost my footing and separated the rod at its midsection. I slid to the bottom of the embankment with line humming off the reel as though I'd hooked a five-pound brown. Nothing serious came of this calamity other than losing a few minutes of my life during regrouping. The tip guide was bent into a narrow oval and my torn shirt was now more torn. I was dusty and bedraggled, but that's how I wind up looking after fishing anyway. I went on to have a pleasant day catching a few browns, but that incident was the beginning of my firm dislike for fences and the beginning of an awareness concerning our obsession with closing land in, with delineating, with not so tacitly stating that a given piece of property that is owned is no longer a part of what's left of free range in the West.

We're all obsessed with possession. Relationships between the sexes are often defined by the scars of these emotional turf wars. That's to be expected. We're a flawed species. And purchasing a piece of land is overt possession, but controlling this land is absurd. Yeah, I understand that if someone pays the bucks they can do what they want with the acreage. Cattle must be managed. And riffraff, such as myself, need to be kept at bay. A dwindling few ranchers still allow access to their land if a person politely asks and remembers to thank them with a Christmas bottle of rye whiskey. But the whole ownership thing is out of control on the high plains. There are orange spray-painted fence posts by the millions, and "Keep Out," "No Hunting or Fishing," and "No Trespassing" signs swaying in the wind. How a person can do the former two without committing the latter is a mystery. This variation seems a case of restating the obvious. If you can't pass, you logically can't fish or hunt.

And I love the entrances to many of the newer ranches or ranchettes, the ones marked by a pair of enormous ponderosa pine trunks topped by an equally large trunk across the top. And dangling below the top brace in clear examples of human hauteur are signs that dance to the tune of "Smith's Ponderosa" or "Jones's Wild West Retreat," or, my personal favorite, "Wall Street Retreat." Thankfully the plains Indians never adopted this insecure form of territorialism. Visions of "Plenty Coups' Palace" or "Dull Knife's Estancia" come shakily to mind.

All of this makes sense to me. Yeh, damn right! Let's all hem in the land and its spirit with miles of barbed wire and announce to the world who exactly is responsible for this self-absorbed mayhem.

Like we own the good country in the long term. Recent wildfires in Montana and California say otherwise, as do drought, earthquake, and the inevitable ice age. I've never been a wannabe Indian. Not my style, and quite sensibly on the tribes' part, they don't want me. But whatever happened to respecting the land that can never be truly owned? What about honoring and submitting to the long-running buzz that is the electric spirit of the West?

On my numerous travels researching this book, I rarely saw a fence once I was outside of towns like Yellowknife, Carmacks, or Fort McPherson. And it seemed to me that many of those fences were placed around graveyards. I'm sure that eventually the free-spirited people who live in the Yukon and Northwest Territories will go over the top the way we have in the Lower-48 and in southern Canada with our hopeless obsession to possess any piece of land we possibly can. For now I'm enjoying the sense of acceptance and submission that not just First Nations People have for wild country, but nearly everyone I came in contact with up north. And this even includes several miners I spoke with, who seemed to express a reverence for the land they were so ruthlessly and permanently destroying all for the sake of diamonds. The land in the north is so vast and so few people live there that the rat-like sense of overcrowding and the mistaken perception that possession equates to freedom and power have not taken hold. I hope this remains the case for many more decades, but I have my doubts.

Sure fencing one's property ensures at least the illusion of privacy and security. We can all drive down our private lanes, sit on the front porch and arrogantly say, while sipping some expensive single malt, "I've got mine. You can't have it. I'm really living now." The mentality that made us great, hideously guts the essence of open space.

Up until a few years ago I couldn't imagine what Montana or the Dakotas would have been like one hundred fifty years ago. A land of no fences, few people, and a vastness filled with wild animals that

AUTHOR PHOTO

A WOLF PRINT IN NORTHERN ALBERTA WITH RACHEL HOLT'S HAND NEXT TO IT.

rivaled Africa's now-ravaged Serengeti. When I first drove through the hundreds of miles of the Far North's uncut boreal forest and crossed rivers like the Mackenzie that are more than a mile wide and forty feet deep, when I saw thousands of woodland bison grazing by the dirt roads that are called highways up there, I was blown away. To finally experience such an immense wealth of wilderness with so few signs of people was staggering. To catch countless grayling of several pounds from one small stretch of river was stunning.

One day as I cruised up to the First Nations Dene Deh Cho settlement of Pedzah Ki, I watched the Mackenzie power its way north to above the Arctic Circle and finally into the Beaufort Sea. The Canyon Range, then the Mackenzie Range, then other mountains rolled away to the west for hundreds of miles. Moose ghosted through stands of dwarf birch. Black bears were all over the place feeding on the rich green grasses of a short, intense summer.

Through binoculars I sighted grizzlies wandering the slopes of the McConnell Range. Fifty miles to the south, Nahanni Butte shimmered silvery blue. For days I saw only a few settlements of maybe one hundred people each. No phone or electric lines. No fences. The difference in the energy, in the feel, of this land was palpable. The countryside sizzled and seemed to flicker with a light that is not seen by the eyes. This must have been what the Big Sky country felt like a couple of centuries past. Montana is home in my heart, but the Far North in its—for now—untamed radiance owns my soul.

Experiencing all of this up north made me see that we don't improve things for ourselves or, more importantly, for the good country when we attempt to stamp our designs of control on the landscape. Instead, we cut out the heart of the place and in the process slice away chunks of ourselves. In a few years I'm going to move out of Livingston and back into the empty, open spaces. I'd like to believe that I'll tear down all of the fences on whatever place I find, but knowing myself, I doubt it. I want my piece of paradise just like anyone else.

One October, while returning from another day fishing on the Shields River, I crossed several fences on the way back to the Suburban. Angus cattle were casually grazing on the last of the year's good grass. As is normal these days, I fought with a fence near the highway. When I finally passed through, I looked up and saw a lone cow standing on the road side of the fence. Cattle do this. They always want what they see on the other side, then decide that they really need to return to their original side of the obstruction. The animal was pushing against the barbed wire trying to rejoin its herd. The cow bawled in its frustration. A large gash ran along its flank. Blood from the wound glistened in the sunlight. I turned away, unlocked the back doors of the rig, and started to put away my gear. I looked down at my right hand. A long scratch ran from the base of the little finger to the wrist. There was a good deal of blood that, too, glistened in the light.

AUTHOR'S NOTE: Another aspect of my life that became clearer from doing this book concerned my obsession with fishing. I've often wondered why this activity has such a powerful hold on me. Why I forget about writing, friends, or anything else when the urge to wade a river strikes. My wanderings have taken me to many remote places in Iceland, Morocco, tiny streams in the desert Southwest, and, with increasing frequency, the Yukon and Northwest Territories. Whenever I fish rivers like the Blackstone, Olgilvie, Trout, or Willow Lake, I realize how much the unpopulated, unspoiled waters of Canada's North Country remind me of home sweet Montana of thirty-five years ago. That is one of the strongest pulls the Yukon and Northwest Territories exert on me. The following is the result of many hours and miles of pondering the subject while rolling from Point A to Point B up north. This is the closest I've come to explaining the situation. Perhaps this makes some sense to a few of us. Perhaps not.

•

How in the hell did I get here? I've fished this stretch of the Shields River many times, but everything seems madly changed in the most unnoticeable of ways. I've been here spring and summer and, finest of all, autumn.

Early October is when large browns lose their secretive, shadowy behavior. The trout, now driven by the spawning urge, are roaming the shallow gravel runs where the females will build their redds in earnest in a week or so. In summer they are holding way back in the darkness of brushy, undercut banks. Most times browns are secretive loners. Even the chaotic splash of a suicidal grasshopper a few feet out in the open water rarely causes them to move. Nymphs, minnows, smaller trout, any of these that happen to wander in front of the large predators will be killed quickly, but otherwise they won't budge. I know. I've tried launching everything from

Woolly Buggers to hefty nymphs to saltwater patterns like Deceivers. Rarely will one of the browns take my offering, one made with the most honest of intentions. I want to connect, to feel a wild fish as it runs for cover at the bite of the hook or walks and crashes along the surface. The trout's fight for survival makes me feel alive. Perhaps a cruel way to get one's kicks, but I'm a predator, too; an emotional one above all else.

So after taking a half-dozen browns, a small brook trout, and a Yellowstone cutthroat, everything is pretty much as I've always remembered it over the years. I notice this as I sit down on a fallen tree trunk along the bank. The stream is low and clear. The streambed sparkles in gemlike colors beneath the golden copper light of the fall sun. The leaves on willows, birch, and cottonwoods are going brilliant yellow, manipulating light in carefree ways. The undergrowth is a mixture of colorful life and death—the buff browns of dying grasses swirled with riffs of crimson and purple from wild berries and rosehips. The freshly white peaks of the Crazies are visible over the ridge in the east and the Bridgers glow dark-blue, gray, and white. Shadows tinted in the same shades creep down the mountain cirques and valleys as the sun moves west. A pair of sandhill cranes clacks away in that dying grass. I see their heads and necks bobbing and lurching as they strut away from me. Strings of geese are moving south with their common cries. Pairs of mallards whistle through the air. Deer silently observe my movements from a distance, as do Angus cattle that pause from their loud munchings to check me out. The last dregs of this year's mayflies bounce above the river's surface. Ahead I see an oval depression of newly cleared stone. The first brown trout spawning bed. One of many that will be dotted along this isolated stretch of water before much longer.

Yeah, all of this seems the same, but just like the end of last season and the one before and so on, everything is different in ways that are visible, but not to the eyes. This valley and everywhere else I travel in Montana at this time of the year seems to have shifted to a slightly different slice of time than the one I'm buzzing in. There's just enough of this movement to make me feel as though I'm in the middle of the gentlest of earthquakes or passing through a mild moment of dizziness or in a room where the furniture has been subtly rearranged with such sophistication that I can't notice the changes.

I know I'm crazy. I have been so as long as I can remember. I once had some concern about this to the extent that I used to down large quantities of whiskey to try and feel sane. It didn't work. Drunk is drunk, and hungover is hell growing ever larger as I get older. The changes I'm experiencing aren't associated with being loony. They seem to be more involved with experience and the smallest of advancements in awareness. One would think that an individual as self-absorbed as I am would see any growth in perception as enormous, but it doesn't work that way. And I've noticed this for years in a number of places. Fishing's to blame. Hanging out in undisturbed nowhere is at fault. Casting to trout or bass or pike is strong stuff, much stronger than whiskey. The power has little to do with landing a large trout, though, like sex, following fly-fishing to its commonly accepted conclusion is of brief satisfaction.

I first drifted through this mild oddity in vision a dozen years ago down at Tongue River country, the Montana home of my heart. The coulees, eroding rock, native grasses, turkeys, coyotes, and the vast aloneness are sensible to me. One October I'd shot a pair of sharp-tailed grouse on a flat just off the red-dust two-track that winds to a dry camp I have near a stand of old ponderosa pine. There were lots of the birds feeding on fat crickets. When they took wing at my approach, their flight was labored and the shooting straightforward. Next I drove to a pond that used to hold rainbows, still does in a non-fishing way. An hour of relaxed casting netted me several trout. I killed one to go with my grouse, baked potato, and roasted onion dinner. As I was cleaning this fish I felt as though the landscape slipped sideways. I put the rainbow in the cooler on ice, opened a Pabst, lit a smoke, and looked around. The land was silent. Nothing but yellow sunlight shifting toward orange moving over the country dragging purple shadows with it. This was as alone as I'd ever felt—like I was the only person on the planet. In some ways I was terrified. Then giving in to the unnamed but obviously deep fear, a sense of power ripped through me. The rush faded. I have no concept of what is meant by serenity, but I felt at peace for the first time in I don't know how many damn years. What had I done to earn this respite from the day-to-day anxiety? Well, I'd walked a windy flat, killed a couple of birds, then fished for some trout. Nothing more or less. Not one for examining my psychological navel, I finished my beer and moved on.

Since that bit of mini-enlightenment, there have been many other moments of oh-so-modest revelation, such as when I fished the Yellowstone here in Livingston with a longtime friend. I hooked a brown, then slipped on a rock, fell in and gaily floated downstream with the angry fish pulling on my line as I tried to keep the rod above water and avoid drowning. I lost the fish, but I saved my life. I remember the sound of my companion laughing from his vantage point on a high cutbank and his yelling, "Holt, I can't understand why Orvis won't send you any more stuff. You're fly-fishing's poster child." And then that slight lateral shift of reality, of life, of whatever, materialized. A touch of fear, aloneness (not loneliness, that's something else), and then happy calm. I doubt I would have felt this way at a sports bar or a concert or a restaurant.

I've never been much for fishing with guides or doing the in-thing like traveling to the latest hot river or lodge. I'm a true loner, like brown trout, and simpler is better. It avoids confusion and eventual torment. This is how fly-fishing, bird hunting, any outdoor avocation, was shown me. Catching fish; yes, that's nice. Killing a few pheasants; not bad either. Owning quality gear that makes all of this easier and more enjoyable; nothing wrong here. But that's not really the point. Those who have patiently guided me along a life that centers on good country have all said in their own curious ways, "That's cool that you made that cast that caught that fish, but that's not what's important. What counts, kid, is that river you're standing in. Those mountains over there. That blood-red prairie we crossed at sunrise—how all of it makes you feel. That's the game you're really after."

And I finally grasped the natural concept. Basically, it's brain-dead simple—lose the ego and submit to the land. Connect with the feral buzz, then recognize my insignificant, yet worthwhile, place in the untamed, unfathomable scheme of things. None of the good stuff is related to fancy clothing, pricey fly rods, or high-end lodge gigs. Get wet and a little muddy. Then feel good enough to slide along in a strange dance for no good reason.

The light of October is special. It glows with an amber influence. I look up from my tree-trunk seat and spot a brown holding in a soft run about forty feet upstream. Only its fins and slight flicks of its tail reveal motion. Slowly, I work out line to cover the distance, make the cast, and start the retrieve. The fish hits the pattern with its head once, then again. It circles back and slams the streamer. The white of its mouth flashes. This fish thrashes across the surface, tires quickly, and comes easily to me as I kneel in a few inches of water. Reds, browns, blacks, pale greens, and bronze flanks. The lower jaw is formed into a hook or a kype—a male. I twist the hook free and watch as the trout swims slowly across stream to a deep hole beneath the tangled roots of an old cottonwood. And my fragile, lunatic world shifts casually out of kilter. I'm a bit afraid, then serene again, then laughing. "Completely nuts, Holt," I say out loud to no one, and I feel good about it all.

•

That's the best I can do. Substitute any references to Montana with those of the Far North and you'd have a fair discussion of how I feel about fishing up this way. Mainly this pursuit, this avocation, this love gives me some peace in a life that for many reasons—most of them my own doing—is often filled with pain, anger, and anxiety. I live for time in the country where wild gamefish swim, and I need the fix on occasion of the drug that shoots through the line into my hands and then the rest of me when I manage to connect with a large fish. That's pretty much the way of this. No more. No less.

•

Last and most important, spending so much time in the Yukon and the Northwest Territories has made one thing perfectly clear to me. I am a loner. I always will be a loner, and whenever I try to pretend that I'm anything different I get in one hell of a lot of trouble. I have some of the best friends anyone could ever have. Individuals who have stuck by me through good and horrible times. We've traveled into fantastic country and shared special times chasing rainbows and bass in small high plains reservoirs or shot sharptails in isolated coulees or stayed up talking about a little bit of nothing while sipping drinks around a late-night fire as a lonely wind blew through our camp. But the one thing I've discovered is that all of us—old friends—live many miles from each other. Hundreds, even thousands of miles. Seeing each other several times a year works out just fine. Any more than this and chaos would ensue. We are all independent, headstrong mavericks. A little of each of us goes a long way. The same is true of the members of my family. Even my children. If I don't make a break in one way or another from them I go crazy and often become angry for no good reason. As for relationships with women, forget it. I'm too focused on my own silly writing life to give someone the attention they deserve on this level. I value my lonesome freedom far too much to ever risk sacrificing this again.

Admittedly, most people come to some realizations in these arenas before they reach their fifties, but I'm a very slow learner in many important respects. I'm grateful to the eternal, wild madness of Canada's Far North for showing me these things along with some of the most out-of-this-world country I've ever wandered through.

Recently, I found a pilot in the Yukon who is willing to fly me into Peel River country and drop me off near where rescuers found the frozen bodies of The Lost Patrol in the late winter of 1911. I want to spend several days in the area dancing with these ghosts by myself with an eye toward both a factual account of what happened and a novel concerning some other aspects of living and what the Yukon and Northwest Territories have to offer.

It is mid-February as I conclude this and my thoughts are turning to spring. The geese down along the Yellowstone River are growing territorial. The days are lengthening. The sun is a bit higher and farther north in the sky. Already I'm planning various trips to my special, isolated places out on the windswept high plains of Montana. And now each year at this time I begin to plan for Canada's North Country.

One thing I truly learned from all of this is that there can never be too many good places. In this type of landscape lies my sanity. The Yukon and Northwest Territories are such places.

GINNY DIERS PHOTO

THIS PHOTO SHOWS THE SETTING FOR THE SHORT STORY THAT IS THE EPILOGUE.

EPILOGUE

PALE FIRE

Author's Note: I've had the idea for this story running around in my head for a couple of years. On my last trip to the Yukon, I spent an evening in my room at Klondike Kate's in Dawson City and roughed the thing out. The story says much about my feelings for the Far North and how this mighty landscape affects me.

The remains of my Suburban are down in the bottom of Engineer Creek gulch. The rig is lying upside down, smashed, flattened, ruined. I am lying in the middle of the greasy-turning-to-ice mess of a road, my face bloodied, right wrist sprained, jeans torn from the ragged escape. A storm is wailing down from the southern slopes of the moonlike Richardson Mountains; ice-hard snow is slamming into the ground and ripping across the gray-brown drab-green countryside in a quality Yukon whiteout. The light is a ghostly silvery blue in the dimming early October afternoon.

I'd been way back in this isolated bit of nowhere camping by myself along a small stream loaded with twelve-inch grayling. I caught dozens of them, keeping a few each evening for dinner. By now the grizzlies and black bears were either denned up or leaning in that direction, so I wasn't concerned about an ursine raid on my camp. I was cautious in a clean camp way, but not worried. Aside from the silver- and purple-shaded turquoise fish and an occasional moose wandering the swampy margins of the creek, most of the wildlife seemed to be long gone. Around noon today, from a vantage point on the crest of a rock ridge over fifteen hundred feet above camp, I saw a ragged, boiling line of spinning storm clouds beating down from the north. The weather had been crisp, autumn perfect. I'd even managed to catch a few grayling in several calm runs of the Olgilvie, a river that for some reason had been difficult for me to fish successfully in past years. Late-night fires, Honduran cigars, and what not. A peaceful time up to the point of winter's mad arrival.

Throwing everything into the back of the Suburban, I thought I could beat the front if I managed to slip through this three-hundred-foot-long slippery dip in the Dempster Highway, which eventually returned to a relatively decent road that heads to the Klondike Highway and Dawson City about two hundred miles away. A cabin at Klondike Kate's, a long, hot shower, some grilled salmon and pasta at the restaurant next door, some bourbon, and then a peaceful night reading of Exley's *Pages From a Cold Island* were calling. I was wrong. I didn't make it.

Even creeping along in four-wheel drive the rig begin to slip, gathering speed as soon it pointed its nose over the rise that gave way to a steep grade. In seconds the machine decided to see what was over the abrupt edge. I pushed open the door and rolled out, bouncing in the slop like a paint can tossed from a window of a fast-moving 1964 Chevy Impala. While sliding along, doing my own dysfunctional two-step, I could hear sounds of metal crunching and tearing and glass shattering. All I remember saying was, "Oh shit!" as the car went out of control. I should have stayed put at my camp and waited out the snow, but Edgar Allen Poe's *The Imp of the Perverse* got the better of me and I made a moron's decision. I've made many of these over the years. This one ranks right up there in the top five.

Now what? I step to the edge of the drop-off and look below.

I sit on my ass and begin to work my way to the bottom of the draw. The bank is loose gravel, mud, and rocks, with fir trees tilting at precarious angles in the thin soil, roots exposed. There is food, a tent, and matches down there. Eventually this blizzard will let up, though it is howling now through the dead ground cover, brush, and dormant trees. Some trucker hauling fuel or food farther up the road above the Arctic Circle to Inuvik will notice the wreck on his way up the road tomorrow or the next day.

Engineer Creek flows dirty orange from the dissolved mineral content, and my Suburban is tan and brown. Maybe the wreck won't be as easy to spot as I just thought. What the hell? Someone will eventually spot the mess and me. In time I'd have another foolish story to tell. And at least the Suburban hadn't exploded in a fireball of overpriced gas. As the weather continues to fall apart by the minute, I can just make out the rig's dark, battered shape. Eventually I reach the wreck, very cold, soaked, and frozen. The need to start a fire is obvious. There is plenty of wood in the form of gnarled limbs and sticks lying along the sides of the narrow streambed and now being covered in snow.

My waxed cotton coat and some shooting gloves are hanging out the remains of the passenger-side window opening. A wool hat is in one of the coat's pockets. Everything else I need is wedged in the pancaked wreck. I'd attend to the tent and sleeping bag later, but first a fire and some heat. I always carry a box of Ohio Blue Tip matches in one of the coat's many pockets. I clear a spot in the snow in the lee of a boulder, make a fire ring from nearby rocks, lay in a pile of twigs and sticks. I'm beginning to ease off the adrenaline rush of the motorized mayhem. The thought of freezing to death out here flashes briefly, then slips away with the swirling wind. I begin to think of family and friends as I prepare to strike the first match.

The flame is bright in the gloom, and I imagine that I see my mother sitting in front of the fireplace at her home in Whitefish sipping her customary evening old-fashioned. She turns to me in the flickering light of the match and says, "I always told you to get a cell phone. You never know when something like this will happen, and now it has. I hope you weren't drinking when this happened." I hadn't been, though based on past exploits this was a reasonable inquiry. Mom has always been on my side, right there with me through all of the chaos I manage to stagger into, but I find it odd that all of this was taking place within the bright confines of a match flame flickering in my cupped hands.

"Call me when you get home," she says, then turns to the fire and sips her drink. The match goes out. Nice thought about the cell phone, except that I'm way out of range this far up the Dempster Highway.

I find a couple of yellow receipts from the Livingston, Montana, Napa Auto Parts store in my pocket—brake pads and a headlight—and work them beneath the twigs. I strike a Blue Tip, but it fizzles, smokes, and dies. I rip another along the side of the box and it catches. Shoving it next to the paper, hunching over to protect it from the wind with my body, the beginnings of fire curl up to the wood. In the light, this time I see a woman I'd known briefly some years ago. I think to myself, "Holt, you're truly nuts this time around." But there she is, well-tanned, short brown hair, sitting in a chaise lounge on the front porch of her home along the Bitterroot River near Darby, Montana. I can see the thick green grass of her front yard, the crabapple trees, and across the gravel road, a farmer working a hayfield in the last of the day's sunlight. Her name is Ann Marie, and she says quite clearly, her voice sounding like there is no storm raging around me at all, "You know John, if you weren't such an outspoken loner you'd have more friends. As it is now, you either scare the hell out of us or piss us off with your hardcore pronouncements. Ease up on us, would you? And do yourself a favor and cut yourself some slack." She lights a cigarette with a silver Zippo lighter before concluding with, "And lay off the damned booze. You turn into a babbling idiot, repeating yourself over and over. Better yet, just go away for good and leave us in peace." Ann Marie draws on her Marlboro before blowing out a thick blue cloud of smoke. A puff of icy wind snuffs out the match and the paper. Well, perhaps this charming event will make me "just go away for good." That would be too bad. Ann Marie's a damn fine woman, though her Sicilian blood makes her a bit impatient and hot tempered at times. Has a bit of money, too. One must consider these things.

Nuts or not, I don't need this. I need a fire and a few drinks to make me an "idiot." Right now I'm a cold, wet idiot. I'd prefer being a warm, drying out idiot. I get up, already stiff from the wreck and the lovely weather, and lurch over to the Suburban to see if I can find more paper. I manage to pull pieces of a reasonably dry grocery bag out from beneath the twisted back seat. I return to my pile of sticks, which is somewhat sheltered by the boulder dropped off in this location thousands of years ago by an enormous blast of spring runoff. I pull the box of matches from my coat and try again. Man, just give me some serious flame and none of this concerned advice silliness, though I am curious to see who will show up next.

The match sizzles and bursts into flame, the paper ignites, and small sticks began to pop and crackle. I'm home or rather, because of the madness of the wavering flames, I'm sitting on the front steps of my old friend Myerson's home. He is rubbing the ears of his yellow Labrador Bart, or maybe it's Jake. I often confuse the two. He turns to me and starts to say something, and I say once again with original brilliance "Oh shit!"

"Don't interrupt me, dammit," Myerson said. "We've been friends for a long time. Been through hell and back more than once," and he reaches down for a stick that he tosses in some tall grass. Jake leaps to the chase. "You always run along the precipice of things looking for trouble. Your life isn't some twisted Nabokov novel like *Ada* or *Laughter in the Dark.* And I sure as hell hope it isn't *Lolita*. Ease up on yourself. Relax a little. I'd suggest finding a good woman, but we both damn well know how that would turn out. So, get the damn fire going and don't pay any attention to what Ann Marie just said. Make yourself a stiff drink and ride out the night. We've got those browns on the Marias to play with next fall." I start to say something, but a wicked downdraft of frigid air packed with snow mashes my fire into nothing. I smell damp smoke.

Even while I am courting hypothermia, I realize that I am having an episode of sorts. One that is odd even in my arcane experiences. Perhaps I really am nuts, or at least I'm making a game effort to go in that direction. I've always seen and heard things that either people didn't or wouldn't admit to experiencing or didn't want to believe existed. But with a certain amount of effort I've managed to keep the trip between the white lines to the extent that I've never been locked up in the state mental asylum at Warm Springs. I'm saving that one for when the going really turns rough, like when I finally make the money I feel I so richly deserve and become the intolerable bastard so many people already think I am. Then I'll need a white room, quality meds, and lots of solitude of an institutional variety.

"Screw it," I say, and return to getting the fire going.

I strike a lot of matches and hear from a lot of people during the next thirty minutes, but the gods eventually take pity on me and the wood finally burns. I build the sucker up into a blaze by diligently adding stick upon larger stick. Maybe the crash landing on the road up above has knocked me crazier than usual. Maybe I am having a brief interlude with mortality. Whatever. In the coals that glow in the darkness of early night, I see everything that is the North Country for me—my friends, the freedom of isolation, and the peaceful side of this vast, lonesome, and unbelievably powerful land. I begin to warm up and think of getting some more wood and making at least the illusion of shelter with my tent and sleeping bag. The whiteout has transmogrified into a straightforward snowfall. The wind is all but dead and large flakes drift down, many of them hissing before turning to vapor above the fire.

From down in this drainage, about two hundred feet below the Dempster Highway, there are no signs of the modern world other than the remains of my rig, which admittedly are substantial. Watching the flames, looking at the tent and the gear I've arranged into a cooking area near the fire circle, I imagine that I'm actually here in a time period one hundred years in the past. The Suburban is covered in snow. I visualize it as a large boulder. A few hundred yards downstream of where I'm standing, I see the Olgilvie River running wide and pewter along its streambed of stone and silent conifers. The water drifts in and out of view depending on the intensity of the falling snow. The only sounds are the creek slipping down to the river, the cracklings of the fire, and my breathing. I know that the road is only a couple of minutes away, but I feel completely isolated from the rest of the world. My existence is centered in this concentrated niche of wilderness. Whether I'm ever found or not means nothing to me at this point. I'm already dead, or maybe finally alive in the most basic of ways. The difference between those two states no longer exists for me. I place a couple of large pieces of wood across the orange coals that shimmer in waves of heat.

A flicker of movement out at the edges of vision catches my attention. Ann Marie taught me to never look these appearances straight on. Rather, let them fully materialize if that's their intent. This takes practice and will power. Slowly the image becomes concrete and moves into view. An enormous gray wolf. The fur along its back, at the edges of its ears, and along its muzzle are shaded toward charcoal. The eyes are black but glow with the light of being totally alive. We stare at each other through the snow and the growing darkness for I don't know how long. A limb makes a loud snap as it burns through in the fire. My attention is diverted. When I look back the wolf is gone. I walk over to where the animal stood. There are four foot prints where he was. None to mark his coming or going. What can I say? Nothing, so I laugh and return to my fire.

I'd decide that I'd had enough conversation, and most likely one vision too many for this evening. I walk over to the wreck, my boots pushing through a half-foot of Yukon snow, in search of a bottle of whiskey to build that stiff drink Myerson suggested.

FURTHER READING

The literature of the Far North is extensive. The following are reference titles that I found informative, entertaining, and helpful while researching this book.

Aboriginal Plant Use in Canada's Northwest Boreal Forest, by Robin J. Marles, et al., is an excellent book on the food, medicinal, and utilitarian uses of more than two hundred plants by First Nation Peoples in Canada. Concisely written, with quality color photographs and excellent appendices and index. (UPC Press, 2000.)

Alaska Stories, edited by John and Kirsten Miller, has selections on the North by, among others, Jack London, John Muir, Anne Morrow Lindbergh, and John McPhee. A nice collection of short fiction. (Chronicle Books, 1995.)

Alberta Fishing Guide, published by Barry Mitchell, contains solid information about fishing northern Alberta, and by the slightest of extensions, the Yukon and Northwest Territories. Indispensable for non-natives and first-time visitors. (Barry Mitchell Publications, 2004; tel. 403-347-5079.)

Alberta History Along the Highway, by Ted Stone, provides excellent mile-by-mile information about the major roads of Alberta, including the Mackenzie Highway, with plenty of brief explanations and anecdotal asides. Good list of further reading. (Red Deer College Press, 1996.)

Arctic Dreams: Imagination and Desire in a Northern Landscape, by Barry Lopez. There's a reason this won a National Book Award. Must Far North reading. An intellectual yet passionate look at things up north. (Scribner, 1986.)

A Naturalist's Guide to the Arctic, by E. C. Pielou, is probably the best done, most comprehensive natural history guide book for the arctic. I spent hours looking through this book while sitting around various campfires. Excellent illustrations. (The University of Chicago Press, 1994.)

Aurora: The Mysterious Northern Lights, by Candace Savage, is an excellent and easy to understand book about the northern lights—the science, history, and lore—with many quality photographs and illustrations. (Sierra Club Books, 1994.)

The Best of Robert Service, who, along with Jack London, is the voice of the Far North. Wonderful black-and-white archival photographs included with the poems. (Running Press, 1983.)

The Book of Dene, a delightful little book containing many native tales of myth and creation. Children will love the stories. (Programme Development Division, Dept. of Education, Yellowknife, N.W.T., 1976.)

The Buffalo Head, by R. M. Patterson is an account by one of the finest of all adventure writers about his homesteading days in Alberta's Highwood country. Patterson writes of a landscape that is only a day's drive from my home in Livingston, Montana, but that is now lost for all time. This book, along with his other titles, is written the way adventure books should be written. (William Sloane Associates, 1961.)

Call of the Wild, White Fang, by Jack London, are a pair of classic novels about the North Country. An excellent volume containing these two novels and several others was published by Amaranth Press in 1983.

Canada, by Mark Lightbody, et al., is a thorough guide to traveling in the North Country, with information on places to see, where to eat and stay, history, flora, and fauna, along with lots of maps. A nuts-and-bolts volume. (Lonely Planet, 1983.)

Coppermine Journey, by Farley Mowat, is an edited version of the journals of Samuel Hearn's 1769 exploration of the Northwest Territories from Hudson Bay to the Coppermine River above the Arctic Circle near the Mackenzie River Delta. (McClelland and Stewart Inc., 1958.)

Dangerous River, by R. M. Patterson, details the author's life in the South Nahani River drainage, the mountains, canyons, creeks, forests, all of it, of the Northwest Territories in the 1920s. This is a dangerous book for me. Just looking at it sitting on my shelf makes me want to say the hell with it all and move up north. (William Sloan Associates, 1954.)

Dead Silence, by John Geiger and Owen Beattie, chronicles the 1989 expedition that set out to discover the fate of James Knight and his two-ship outing to Hudson Bay in 1719. (Viking, 1993.)

The Death of Albert Johnson—Mad Trapper of Rat River, by F. W. Anderson and Art Downs, describes the manhunt in 1932 of a serious whacko even by Arctic standards. (Heritage House, 1986.)

Denedeh, with excellent photographs by Rene Fumoleau, gives a real glimpse into the lives of the Dene in the Northwest Territories. (The Dene Nation, 1984.)

Dene Nation: The Colony Within, edited by Mel Watkins, is a collection of papers that shows the determined mindset of the Dene concerning their land and lifestyle as they attempt to block an oil pipeline planned through the heart of their country, and, more importantly, deal with our mad modern age. (University of Toronto Press, 1977.)

Due North of Montana, by Chris Dawson, covers fishing in Alberta all the way to the Northwest Territories. Written in an anecdotal style with solid information and good photos. (Johnson Books, 1996.)

Far Pastures, by R. M. Patterson, is a collection of his writings covering his adventures from Alberta to the Northwest Territories from the 1920s into the 1950s. A tough, determined guy and a fine writer. (Evergreen Press Limited, 1963.)

Fly Fishing in the Northwest Territories of Canada, by Chris Hanks, who clearly loves to fish in the NWT. An excellent overview of the fishing with wonderful anecdotes about his travels in the country supported by a number of good black-and-white photographs. (Frank Amato Publications, 1996.)

Forty Years in Canada, by Sam Steele, chronicles "The Lion of the North's" experiences as a member of the Royal Northwest Mounted Police in the second half of the nineteenth century. (Prospero Books, 2000.)

Haunted Hotels, by Robin Mead, is a collection of tales of haunted facilities around North America. Some of them have interest. (Rutledge Hill Press, 1995.)

The Ice-Shirt, by William T. Vollmann, is part of his fictional Seven Dreams sequence of books that reinvents the mythology/history of the western world. This one is about Iceland, Greenland, and North America centuries ago. Vollmann lives hard and is a capable writer, but his ego has run riot. (Penguin Books, 1990.)

Kalbloona in the Yellow Kayak: One Woman's Journey Through the North West Passage, by Victoria Jason is an incredible account of one individual's kayaking journey along the northern shore of North America, her encounters with polar bears, the friendships she made with native peoples, her struggles with the weather and Arctic seas. Hers is a true tale of Far North adventure. (Turnstone Press, 1999.)

Law of the Yukon, by Helene Dobrowsky, is a pictorial history of the Mounted Police in the Yukon. An excellent effort that takes you back one hundred years with many candid photographs. (Lost Moose Publishing, 1995.)

Lost Moose Catalogue, is a contemporary version of the *Whole Earth Catalogue* Yukon style. Lots of curiosities in here. A good time-killer if you're ever stuck in a motel up north for whatever reason. (Lost Moose Publishing, 1997.)

The Lost Patrol, by Dick North, is a nuts and bolts examination of the ill-fated Lost Patrol of 1910 that met disaster along the way from Fort McPherson to Dawson City by dogsled. Concise. Well-done. (Raincoast Books, 1978.)

Magnetic North, by David Halsey, is an enchanting book about a trek across Canada from the Pacific to the Atlantic by foot, dogsled, and canoe. I read this one several times. (Sierra Club Books, 1990.)

Mammal Tracking in North America, by James Halfpenny. It's nice to know what those tracks—or that scat you're looking at—belong to, especially if you are the one being hunted. (Johnson Books, 1988.)

Native People, Native Lands, edited by Bruce Alden Cox, contains a number of essays and studies on the First Nation Peoples of Canada. A bit dry and technical, but worth the effort. (Carleton University Press, 1988.)

Northwest Epic: The Building of the Alaska Highway, by Heath Twichell. An excellent description of the construction of one of the toughest roads in the world, with interesting black-and-white photographs. (St. Martin's Press, 1992.)

On the Edge of Nowhere, by James Huntington, is a narrative that truly captures the immense mystery, hardship, and adventure of life in the Far North. A great book. (Crown Publishers, Inc., 1966.)

Paper Stays Put: A Collection of Inuit Writing, edited by Robin Gedalof, is a group of valuable oral histories of a vanishing way of native life. (Hurtig Publishers, 1980.)

Plants of the Western Boreal Forest and Aspen Parkland, by Derek Johnson, et al., is the best field guide I've run across on this subject for this region. Quality drawings and photographs. (Lone Pine Publishing, 1995.)

Polar Bears, by Ian Stirling and Dan Guravich, is an excellent account of the lives and behavior of these incredible, fearsome, and at times menacing animals of the high arctic. (University of Michigan Press, 1988.)

Report on an Exploration in the Yukon District and Adjacent Portion of Northern British Columbia—1887. The title explains this effort. (Reprinted by Yukon Historical and Museum's Association, Whitehorse, 1987.)

The Riders of the Plains, by A. L. Haydon, is a record of the Royal Northwest Mounted Police from 1873-1910. (Hurtig Publishers, 1971.)

The Rifles, by William T. Vollmann, is the best of the Seven Dreams books. This one covers the search for a Northwest Passage in the mid-1800s, all done in Vollmann's vaguely psychotic and unique style. (Penguin Books, 1994.)

Tour Book: Western Canada and Alaska, is solid, basic travel information for the region from hotels to restaurants to locations. A travel agent in book form. (AAA Publishing, 2002.)

Trekking Russia and Central Asia, by Frith Maier, expands ones knowledge of the North Country with Siberian overtones. (The Mountaineers, 1994.)

Trout, edited by Judith Stoltz and Judith Schnell, while some of the information in this book is dated or inaccurate, it, along with titles by Robert Behnke and Robert Smith, is still one of the best overviews on the subject. (Stackpole Books, 1991.)

Trout Streams of Alberta, by Jim McLennan, is another quality book about fishing Canada's western North Country. (Johnson Gorman Publishers, 1996.)

Two Old Women, by Velma Wallis, is a strong novel of survival along the Yukon River. A sleeper of a book, and a quick read. (Epicenter Press, 1993.)

Yukon: The Last Frontier, by Melody Webb, is an excellent and quite detailed overview of the history of the Yukon River drainage. Good selection of photos and maps. (University of Nebraska Press, 1985.)

Yukon Places and Names, by R. Coutts, is a fine reference for place names in the North Country and, indirectly, a good source of regional history.(Gray's Publishing Limited, 1980.)

Yukon's Tombstone Range and Blackstone Uplands, Sarah Locke, editor, is a well-done book on the geologic history, the flora, fauna, and hiking trails of some of the wildest country on the planet. Excellent photos and maps. (Yukon Chapter of the Canadian Parks and Wilderness Society, 2000.)